THE
PHYSICIAN

Nancy Veldman

D1444268

Nancy Veldman

ISBN: 1453842950
ISBN-13: 9781453842959

THE PHYSICIAN'S OATH

I solemnly pledge myself to consecrate my life to the service of humanity.
I will give to my teachers the respect and gratitude which is their due.
I will practice my profession with conscience and dignity.
The health of my patient will be my first consideration.

I will maintain by all the means in my power the honor
and the noble traditions of the medical profession.
My colleagues will be my brothers.

I will not permit considerations of religion, nationality, race, party politics
or social standing to intervene between my duty and my patient.
I will maintain the utmost respect for human life
from the time of conception even under threat.
I will not use my medical knowledge contrary to the laws of humanity.

I make these promises solemnly, freely, and upon my honor

PROLOGUE

All the years in medical school and the oath I took to become a doctor did not prepare me for what has happened in my life. I guess we are none of us prepared for what takes place in the future. That's the irony of life. Instead, I've taken a step off the cliff of uncertainty into a world of secrets and desperation. In fact, I've become a secret keeper. A listener. I wouldn't wish this upon any of my colleagues, for the courage it has taken to go in this direction has pushed me beyond limits I never dreamed of reaching. I realize we all need to enlarge our horizons, but it's crucial not to get so involved that we dig ourselves into a hole so deep we can't get out.

I'm learning as I go. The years that I've spent in practice have shown me that the real learning is in the field with the patients. Not in the books. No disease I've faced in my office is straight out of a textbook, for every individual is different in how they respond. Most diseases will make a liar out of you. And I've also humbly noticed that most diseases will clear up on their own given enough time. So I've tried to have an open mind when diagnosing my patients and at the same time pull from what I was taught in those long dreadful years in medical school. I love my work, but as I'm aging, I'm amazed at what I don't know and how difficult it is to keep up with technology. I'm shocked at what I didn't learn in school, and as I now stare at the large collection of medical books in my library, I shudder to think that even with all this information at the tips of my fingers, someone's life is in my hands the majority of my day, and I may not have the answers they need to get well.

I arise in the morning, watching the rays of a new sun coming through the window nestling themselves in the blanket across my legs. I go to the kitchen and make strong coffee and revel in the first bite of a chocolate-laden donut that I would tell my patients never to eat. Then I spend the first hour of my day studying new journals that hold within them new cures, new drugs to try, and a whole new direction that the medical world is being forced to take. I also have on my desk a new journal of natural medicine that I've promised my daughter I would delve into. My work is cut out for me, and I can feel overwhelmed before I even have my first patient for the day. But I remind myself of the oath I took and realize that I may find in my blindness to the truth that this difficult road I'm on is a holy place to be walking.

I feel alone, and I feel crowded at the same time.

CHAPTER 1

M y phone rang at 6:00 a.m. There'd been an accident on I-240, the highway that winds around the outer edges of the city. A bad accident. I was tired from a long week of seeing patients and listening to my partner in crime, Dr. Case McPhail, talking about his fishing trip that he'd planned for the last two weeks in July. I don't fish, but by gosh, he's going to turn me into a fisherman or die tryin'. He wants me to go but we both can't leave the office at the same time. So one more time I'd been saved from having to buy a reel, bait, and a license to sit on the water and sweat.

Quickly doing a mental assessment of the EMT's report, I jumped out of bed and hit the shower, wanting to be at the hospital as quickly as possible. I had no idea who the guy was that ran into a light pole and guardrail. Whoever it was it couldn't be good news.

"Dr. Lankford?" A young intern was calling my name as I was walking through the doors of the ER.

"Yep, that's me. What you got for me, James?"

"A twenty-two-year-old white male, MVA, with head lacerations, multiple fractures on the lower extremities. He's in the last room on the left."

I poked my head through the curtain and the first thing I saw was blood everywhere. The nurses were rushing around cleaning him up, trying to start a line, taking vitals, and applying pressure. I spotted the resident doctor on the floor and raced to catch him before he headed into the next room.

"Dr. Glover, Lankford here. I know one of my patients, Matthew Jones, came in just a second ago with multiple fractures and serious head injury. Can you send me copies of everything and I will make a note to myself to check back in with the hospital later today?"

"No problem, Lankford. Do you know this guy?"

"Looks like the Jones boy, Matthew. I've seen him a few times in my office. Don't really know the family at all."

"Okay. I'll send you all the info I get from the X-rays and blood work. Looks like we're going to be doing surgery on him to set the fractures, but I'll know more after the X-rays are done."

"I'll wait to hear from you. Thanks."

I stepped away and turned to go back to the room Matthew was in. I walked up to the bed and touched his head. He turned and moaned. He was going in and out of consciousness so there was no point in my trying to get anything out of him.

"Matthew? They're going to take real good care of you in here. Just relax. You're going to be okay, now. Don't worry. I'll be back to check on you later."

Matthew never responded. I didn't have a great feeling about him, but kept that tidbit of information to myself. His head wound was horrific, and that was just what I could see on the outside. His family was coming through the doors as I was walking out.

"Hello, Mr. and Mrs. Jones. I'm so sorry about Matthew. He's being taken care of right now and there will be X-rays taken to determine what his injuries are. He was in a car accident on I-240 and apparently hit the guardrail and a light pole. Here's my card. I want you to feel free to call me anytime. Dr. Glover is the attending physician here today and will be working with Matthew. He'll let you know his findings when the reports come in from all the tests. You can see Matthew for a second, but you don't need to stay in the room as there's a lot going on right now to get Matthew stable."

I could see the looks on their faces and knew that this news was a total shock to them. I had read on the report that alcohol was found in his blood. I left quickly and headed to the office. This day hadn't started so well, but hopefully things would improve. I said a prayer for Matthew.

I found out later in the day that Matthew never woke up. His life was short-ened by one mistake he made on a morning when the sun shone too brightly into the windshield, and the drinks he drank to help him cope with the abuse his father had done to his mother in the end clouded his vision.

୬୬

My life had been pretty textbook from the day I graduated from medical school. I did well in my internship and married Jill in the middle of all the bedlam that goes along with becoming a doctor. I met her at a friend's house on a summer evening in August. I was a proud bachelor and had no plans to marry. She was so beautiful that I couldn't even talk around her. I found myself slipping in my determination, and next thing you know we were married and I no longer belonged to the brotherhood of bachelors. I sound like I was dragged into marriage but that wasn't the case at all. I simply fell head over heels for a girl that could've married anyone in the world. Why she picked me, I'll never know. But I chose her because she was perfect for me. She "got" me. That was and is the most powerful thing in our relationship. We got each other. If it weren't for her, I wouldn't have made it through the rigorous training they put us through as interns. I had her to come home to at night.

Not too long into our marriage we had a daughter. We named her Anna Grace after our two mothers, and that ended a nine-month argument about what to name our child, which if it had continued, could have ruined our marriage. Thank God we only had one child. I don't think we could've taken arguing over another name.

୬୬

We've lived in St. Martins, Minnesota for thirty years and recently we've been discussing moving to Crosgrove, Michigan, where Anna Grace lives with her husband. I'm about ready for a change in my practice, but I'll miss Case terribly. He's been my best friend since childhood and I can't imagine living too far away from him. I haven't broken the news to him yet, as Jill and I are still working through some issues about the move. We have many friends in St. Martin's and I have an established practice here. It will take a monumental effort at my age to re-establish myself somewhere else and make enough money to support us. I've done fairly well in this partnership with Case, but alone, I don't know what to expect.

Case and I grew up together in Masontown. We both were raised on a farm and loved the outdoors. He loved to fish at an early age, and refused to take no for an answer every time he was heading to the lake to catch "the big one." We sneaked off many a night to smoke cigarettes behind our barn, knowing full well that my father would have our heads if he found out. Once we ran away and caught a train to Newtonville with only a five dollar bill in our pockets. I don't remember why we ran, but it was the most fun I had in my whole childhood, being on that train with Case. We pretended that we were cowboys and that the Indians were going to raid the train. We laughed and hid in a boxcar full of hay and litter that hobos had left. Our hearts were racing when we jumped off the train and rolled down a hill that landed us right next to a green pond full of scum. We walked the rest of the way to Newtonville, ate at a soda fountain, and then caught a ride back home on a truck headed to Masontown. We could've gotten into real trouble, but I was told by my parents later that God protects fools.

When we were fifteen, we shared a terrible experience that would seal our friendship and set it in stone. It was a warm December day, and the smell of snow was in the air. We were full of energy and wanted to go ice skating on the lake in the middle of the town square. My sister Mava begged to come with us. She was only nine years old, but I couldn't turn her down. We carried our skates on our shoulders and walked the three miles into town. We were so young and happy. We had no idea the horror we would face that afternoon. Hundreds of people were out that day, skating or watching all the skaters dance around the lake. By afternoon it began to get colder, and Case and I were about ready to head home. We had watched Mava closely, and when her little friends pulled her away from us to go skate with them, we nodded and off she went. Time flew by, and when we were ready to go, we suddenly realized we hadn't seen Mava in a while. I called out to her friends, but they didn't know where she was. We skated around the lake and came across a hole near a tree that had bent itself across the water. The ice was pretty thick in the middle of the lake but on this edge it was thinner. I called and called Mava's name out, but heard nothing. We got frantic and asked some adults for help that were standing around the lake. We took them over to the hole but we had no way to look into the water to see if she was there. I gazed off the shore and saw Mava's neck scarf stuck to a tree limb. My stomach knotted up—I feared we'd lost her. Someone called the police and a rescue team went out on the ice. Meanwhile, neighbors looked for her in the surrounding wooded area, but found nothing. No trace of her.

The rescue team cracked open the ice, and there, frozen in time, was my Mava. I couldn't move. I barely breathed. I think I was afraid my heart would stop, for I couldn't imagine life without her. She looked like a doll suspended in the cold water. How in the world would I tell my parents that I'd allowed Mava to slip away into the lake and drown? Just thinking about this brings it all back. The feeling of guilt and horror. Case stood by me the whole time, never leaving my side for one moment. We walked through the funeral and visitation like two wooden soldiers. I had no feelings left inside. My parents were strong in their faith and that helped us all through the loss. But even now I miss Mava. Case was my strength and my best friend. I owe him my life for being there during that time. All I have to do is look at Case, and if I'm thinking about her, he can sense it. He'll come over and put his hand on my arm. Our eyes will lock for a moment and we both travel back in time to that day on the lake.

Thinking about leaving Case is tough. Olivia, his wife, is Jill's best friend. We've become very close through the years, and this move will be hard on us all. But for some reason, I'm ready to slow down in my practice and spend more time with Anna Grace and her husband. They wanted to have a baby and this would be a great time to move closer. As I headed into to work, I knew this conversation was going to happen. I just had to get my head wrapped around how to get the words out of my mouth when I looked at Case.

"Hey, Michael! Good morning! Boy, what a day it's been already. I've seen three patients this morning with the flu. It must be going around."

"Well, I just left the hospital. Matthew Jones was in a terrible car accident and I just received a message that he didn't make it. Alcohol. I ran into his parents as I was leaving the hospital. They were shocked to hear that he was hurt so badly. I hated to have to give them the news. And now he's gone for good."

"That's terrible, Michael. And when is there not alcohol involved with these kids?"

"Yep, it's rampant. Won't these kids ever learn?"

"Well, we drank, buddy. Only we drank behind a barn, not on the road. There's a big difference today with kids. They think nothing of drinking and driving."

"I want to talk to you sometime today, Case. You got some extra time? Maybe at lunch?"

"Sounds good. I'll let Marge know and I'll buzz your pager when I'm ready to go. Marge can take care of the office while we're at lunch."

I called Jill and told her about the Jones boy and about the talk with Case I was planning to have at lunch.

"Don't worry, honey. Case will understand. Even though he doesn't have children of his own, he knows how much Anna Grace means to us. I know he won't want you to leave; you two are like brothers. But he can come to visit. I'm already thinking of when Olivia and I can go shopping."

"I know, I know. This is just not a good day for me, Jill. But I know it's time. It just feels like life is slipping by and I don't feel like I've made a difference at all. Don't pay any attention to me! I'll get through this. Have a good day, honey, and I'll call later."

The morning flew by and I looked at my watch. It was noon, so I asked Marge to buzz Case's pager. Marge Johnson was a piece of work. She'd gotten old on us lately, but man, she could put out the work. We just couldn't push her too far or she'd turn on us in a minute… Leaving her directions on a few patients, I cleaned up my desk, locked my door and headed out to the front office. Case met me at the doorway and we walked out to my car.

"It feels good to get out of the office today. For some reason, I just feel tired of it all."

"Well, let's go get a burger at Frank's Diner, Mike. Nothing like a hamburger and a shake to get your mind off the stress."

CHAPTER 2

I took a huge bite out of my hamburger and sat there chewing, looking down at my plate. I was trying my best to form the words that would tell Case I wanted to start over alone in Crosgrove. Without him. He wasn't stupid. I could tell he was trying to read my mind. Now that I was about to talk to him about it, I started doubting whether it was a good idea or not. I'd heard that some people moved late in life to be near their children and it was a friggin' nightmare. I sure didn't want to ruin our relationship with Anna Grace. *I might as well bite the bullet. If I sit here much longer he'll figure it out on his own.*

"How old are we, anyway, Case?"

"Last I checked we were about fifty-nine, buddy."

"Well, I've been thinking. Jill and I've talked about moving away. Maybe to Crosgrove to be near our daughter." I looked at his face to see if he was frowning. "I've been thinking about slowing down a little, Case. We've worked so hard, and done pretty good." He held up his hand to stop me but I kept on going, feeling pretty lame. "I know, I know. Why quit when things are going so well? But Case, aren't you ready to slow down? To enjoy life a little more? To find a way to make a difference in this world?"

"That's what I thought we were doing, my friend, in our own way, here at the clinic. We help people who have no money. We turn no one away. What else can we do?"

"I don't have any idea, Case. But I just know I'm gettin' restless and feelin' like there is something else out there for me. Some other way to use my medical knowledge. I don't know yet what that is. But it's been on my mind for quite a while, and I feel like I need to act on it pretty soon. Just wanted to shoot this by you."

Case put his head in his hands and sighed. "I knew this couldn't last forever. But I didn't think it would end just yet. Michael, we've been together for many years. It'd feel weird if you weren't here, but I won't stand in your way if you want to leave. You seem pretty bent on it. Are you dead sure? Is Jill sure? You have to sell your house, find a new one. That alone is quite an endeavor."

"I realize all of that, Case. But now is the time. I won't want to do it if I wait until I get older. Please back me up on this. I need to know you're behind me on it. You and I have always wanted what was best for each other. You're like my brother, Case. We go way back, ya know?"

"Oh, I know. We go back to my early fishin' days." He rolled his head back and laughed, and his laughter caught me off guard. *Have I lost my mind? Leaving now after all these years?*

"Well, I may wait until fall to do it, but I just wanted you to know how I was thinking is all. So don't go upsetting Olivia or nothing. Jill is talking to her on her own. I'll keep you up to date on when, Case. I guess we need to talk about how to split up this practice; all the legal and financial issues. We have plenty of time, plenty of time. But at least I've taken the first step in telling you."

"Aw, Michael. Nothing's going to ruin our friendship. I've known you all my life, and I would do anything for you. I'll miss you is all. It's always been you and me. Maybe Olivia and I'll do the same thing. Slow down, I mean. Try to enjoy life. I'll talk to you more about this. Let me know if you put your house up for sale." He stood up and walked over to pay the cashier for our meals. He had a cough that sounded rough. I watched him from a distance and shook my head. Case was a good-looking man. Tall, dark hair, strong in stature. He always did the right thing; always surefooted. Me, I took the risks. I dared to try new things. If it were up to him he would stay just like we are right now until we both either went blind or dropped dead. I love the man. I've never actually said that to him, but I do. This was going to be tough. But I did feel compelled to make the change, and I usually was right if I listened to my gut feelings. He came towards me with his hands in his pockets, whistling, smiling. And I sat there thinking that no one in their right mind would leave the situation Case and I have and step off into the unknown at our age. *Should I cut off my arm and leave Case? Or stay and be frustrated for the rest of my life that I didn't do this thing I'm compelled to do . . . I'm not gettin' any younger, and Anna would love for us to move near her. Not the easiest decision but I've got to get my act together and make this thing happen. I may never feel one hundred percent right about it, so I can't count on my feelings.*

We walked to the car and hurried back to the office. No need in upsetting Marge. She already seemed to be in a foul mood.

CHAPTER 3

Jill asked Case and Olivia over for a last dinner together. We'd shared a wonderful Christmas and a new year had come in with a roar. We were caught up in our own thoughts, and I could feel the sadness in the room. It was hanging over us all like a large thundercloud full of water. I felt inside that if that water came out it would drown us all, and I would never be able to leave this place. Good friends are hard to come by, and Case was a rare bird. I didn't relish looking for another buddy to hang out with. Another doctor to discuss new strategies with. Another friend to rag me about fishing.

"Hey, Case. Let's go for a walk down by the lake. The girls can clean up after us; I'm sure they have things they want to talk about." I nodded to Jill and turned and grabbed my jacket and headed out the back door with Case behind me. We didn't say much until we got to the water's edge.

"Michael, I didn't think it would be so tough for us to say goodbye. I know you'll be around off and on, but it won't ever be the same. That's hard for me to swallow." He coughed again, and finally cleared his throat.

"You don't have to tell me how hard it's going to be. I'm second guessing everything right now, knowing full well that it's a good decision for my retirement. And for being around our daughter more." I looked at Case and shook my head. "Finding another you is impossible. You know that."

Case sat down by the edge of a fallen tree and motioned for me to sit beside him. The night was cool and it was dusk. My favorite time was when the light of the moon came across the water and lit up everything in a milky glow. It was magical and brought me back to our childhood and the many times we sat right here talking about our dreams.

"Remember when we played baseball for Cooper High and beat Jesse's team? What a game that was. I thought Jesse was going to blow a gasket when you tagged him out at home!" I fell out laughing at the memory.

"Yeah, I loved being catcher when you were pitching. We had a ball, Michael. I laughed so hard because he was such a bully. Whatever became of him? You know?"

"I heard that he was killed in a car accident. Now that I think of it, I read that in the local paper. I lost track of him when I went to medical school. He wasn't exactly our best friend."

"No. We ran in different crowds even in college and medical school. I remember the time old George Houston taught me how to fly fish. It was the most extraordinary experience I've ever had in my life! Do you remember that, Mike?"

"How could I forget? You talked about it for years. He was amazing, I'll admit. But you never quite got the hang of it. That man was magical to watch; the line was flying through the air with a gracefulness but also a power. He knew exactly what he was doing all the time. I stood mesmerized when he began the rhythm that would soon almost become a dance. It was so hot that sweat was running down my back but I never felt it. All I could see was Old George, the line, and the water. That rhythm that has to be there..."

"Yeah, he had it down. I made some pretty good stabs at it, but I just couldn't get the rhythm of it. Maybe that's what I'll do in my retirement; take fly fishing lessons!"

I turned my head and watched a bird resting on the end of the old tree trunk. "Case, we're rambling. None of this matters. I'm just going to say it out loud. These years with you were the best years of my life. Our practice went from a few meager patients into half the town finding their way to our door. I learned so much from you, Case. If I'm honest, I'm a bit scared to step out on my own. It's been pretty handy having you right down the hall if I ran up on a complicated case. I could always count on you."

"Aw, come on, Michael. Don't get mushy on me now. It's hard enough telling you goodbye as it is. I know it's going to be tough, but you're ready to go out and do something different with your life. You said so yourself. I'm here if you ever need me, you know that. But you also know you're the best doctor around for miles so don't give me that stuff about needing me around. Your work stands on its own. I don't want to hear it!"

"You don't have to be so cheerful, Case. I don't think I can take it!"

Case laughed and then went off in a fit of coughing again. "You keep me posted on things, now, Mike. I'll come up first weekend I can to see you. I can't wait to see your new office and check out the fishing in Crosgrove!"

"Say, Case, is that cough serious? Sounds pretty rough; I've been noticin' it now for several days."

"It's nothin', don't worry about it. Just a nagging cough I can't seem to shake. I'll be fine."

I didn't know it at the time, but this would be the last time Case and I would have together. Had I been able to see the future, I wouldn't have made the decision to leave. But God doesn't share that with us. If He did, I suppose we wouldn't be able to cope with what we saw. Good or bad. I already felt like I was walking in quicksand.

CHAPTER 4

Sitting in the spare bedroom of my daughter's home, I felt a little less apprehensive about making the move. I had already stopped into the Chamber of Commerce to check the demographics of Crosgrove and see what the property values were. I was looking for that perfect spot to open up a practice, not too populated but not secluded, either. I was missing Case already. He would've already found us something, signed a lease, and hung his name plate on the door. I work slower and I'm more deliberate. I think my slow pace can be annoying, but usually I make the best decision in the end. I had my eye on a small office at the east end of Morgan Avenue, a side street adjacent to a main artery that takes traffic around the downtown area of the city. The old building was red brick covered with ivy that had slowly taken over the whole north side, even growing over some of the windows. The shutters were black and there were small white columns in the front of the building. It looked official but welcoming and that's exactly what I was looking for. I made a few phone calls and snagged a time in the early afternoon to check the building out. I had a gut feeling this was it.

Crosgrove was really a suburb of Spartanville, which was an industrial city that was growing by leaps and bounds. Some of the residents of Crosgrove seemed to be wealthy types who just don't want the hustle bustle of a big city. All the streets were lined with large oaks that towered over the cars rushing by, and large streetlights lined all major streets. There was music in the square every Friday night and all the major Broadway plays were booked to perform at the local theatre. Crime was next to none, even though Crosgrove was like every other suburb across America in that it had a seedier side of town where the poor lived. There were meetings periodically at the local town hall to discuss issues and ways to improve the town. It was sounding more and more like the perfect place for me to wind down and retire. I couldn't wait to show Jill the office building and get her read on Crosgrove. She'd been out all afternoon with Anna Grace shopping and eating lunch.

"Hey, honey!" Jill came waltzing in with packages piled high and a big smile on her face.

"Hey, woman. Looks like you girls have had a busy day. I know you're enjoying this time with Anna. Guess what I found today?"

"What? A new car?"

"I'm going to ignore that sarcasm. No. I found the perfect place for my office!" I was certain she didn't miss the huge smile on my face.

"Already? Are you that sure you want to be here that you've already put your name on an office? This is going to be quite a change for us, Mike."

"I know, I know. But I was driving around today checking things out. I just happened upon this neat little place that looked like it would be just the right location for a medical office. It's brick with ivy all over it. I know you'll love it! I didn't put a bid in, but I bet I can get it for a good price. I meet with the realtor this afternoon to check out the inside. You wanna go?"

"Yeah, I'll go, Mike. Let me change clothes and get into something comfortable. How long do we have?"

"We need to be there around 2:30. You've got an hour."

"Okay, honey. Now you have my curiosity piqued. I can't wait to see it."

⟋⟍

Anna and Thomas, her husband, came in the door at the same time. I knew by the look on his face that something was up. I was sucker-punched when he opened his mouth.

"Hey, guys! We have some good news! Anna just heard back from the doctor's office, and you're going to be grandparents! So how's that for a welcome?"

Jill was speechless and then jumped up screaming. "Oh, my gosh! Are you kidding me? You're going to have a baby?"

"Yes, Mother! Can you believe it? Could the timing be any better? You and Dad are thinking about moving here, and I'm going to have a baby. We couldn't have planned that if we tried."

I was shocked and then pulled myself together. It felt like a train was sitting on my chest. This was my little girl telling me she was having a baby. "Congratulations, you guys! I know you're so happy. So we're going to have a little one running around here, huh? Wow. What a surprise!"

"Yeah, Dad. We had no idea it would happen so fast. I'm elated. I just can't believe we're going to be parents. It's April and I'll be due in December if I'm right about my calculations! Are you ready, Thomas?"

"I was born ready, Anna. I wanted kids the day after we got married. Now I'm finally going to be a father. I can't wait!"

I looked at Jill and the expression on her face took away any doubts that I might have had about moving to Crosgrove. She was the happiest I'd seen her in years. Her one daughter was going to be a mom. You don't get any better than that as a parent. And we were going to get to watch this kid grow up, which would add to the list of things Jill would have to do after we got our house and office settled.

"Honey, are you about ready to go? I hate to run right after that news, but we're supposed to meet the realtor in about ten minutes." I swung my daughter around in circles and gave her a big hug.

"I'm ready. Anna, we'll be back in about an hour or so. Then I want to hear all about it!"

We walked out the door, knowing they would love this time alone together. The roads were busy so I paid attention to my driving, but my thoughts were racing. A new house, a new office, and a new grandchild. This was turning out differently than I'd planned. Actually, there was no plan. I wouldn't admit that to Case, ever. But I came here thinking that things would fall into place as they were meant to be. And that's exactly what was happening. I wouldn't be surprised at all if my bid on this building was taken at first glance. Something is moving me forward at the speed of light toward I don't know what, and I'm not going to put up much resistance to it. In fact, I'm trying to relish the journey. I've worked hard to get where I am in life, but I am being pulled forward into an unknown place where things happen that are unexplained. I can feel it in my bones. I'm not afraid to go this route, but there's an odd feeling I don't have a name for that causes me to pause and look at where I've been and where I am now. For some reason, I'm thinking that the future isn't going to look like the past.

∽

I pulled up to the building and parked the car. "Jill, here it is. What do you think?"

"I'm holding my opinion until I see the inside. Let's go see what the realtor says."

We walked in and met Roger Martin at the door. He was a bit of a character; he wore his pants too high, a bow tie, and white buck shoes. He was nice as he could be, but he was fidgety and had a slight stutter. He showed us through the office and then let Jill and I walk around on our own. I began to breathe freer and took more time in each room to think about how I would use the space. It took about fifteen minutes before I saw a clear answer on Jill's face. Each room we walked through, every window, office space, and storage room, just confirmed my gut feeling that this was my building. We made two passes through all the rooms and met back at the front door. "Roger, I'm sold on this place. It felt good even before I came in, but now it's a done deal. You feel the same way, Jill?"

"You know without asking. It's perfect for what you want right now."

"I can draw up an offer, Mike, and get an answer for you tomorrow from the seller. We need to talk about price." Roger headed towards his desk.

"You and Roger get the price nailed down and I'll wait in the car."

Okay. Be right with you."

∽

I looked back in the rear view mirror at the building as I turned the corner to head back to Anna's. "Jill, you feel good about this now?"

"It all seems to be happening so fast. We just got here and find out we're going to be grandparents and you've signed an offer to purchase a building. There's no turning back now, I guess."

"It's going to be a different life here, Jill. I'm unsure about a lot of things, too. But it'll all fall into place. I have a feeling about Crosgrove. Can't put my finger on it, but something's different about this place. It feels good."

Jill gave me a questioning look. "What in the world are you talking about, Mike? What do you mean 'different?'"

"I don't know exactly. It's tough to explain. But somehow I feel we're supposed to be here. Like this is what God's planned for our lives. You know? We don't talk about it much, but something stronger than me is pushing me in a direction. I don't feel like I have much a choice right now. Does that make any sense?"

"It must be pretty powerful, honey. I've always trusted your decisions. I guess this time is no different. But just make sure that this is what you want, Mike. There's no rope tied around your neck pulling you in a direction you don't want to go. We're too old to take big risks with your career."

"I totally get what you're saying. But I don't feel like I'm taking a risk yet. Let's give it some time and see how things go. If it doesn't work out, I'm more than willing to move back to St. Martin. Case would take me back in a New York minute."

"I'm thrilled to be near Anna Grace and Thomas. Nothing would please me more than to be active in their lives and in the lives of their children. I just hope this isn't a whim of yours; an impulse. You seem so calm about it all. I guess that surprises me, Mike."

"It surprises me, too. That's why I think this is the right move. I promise you I'll be open with you about everything. And I want you to tell me if you can't make this place a home. Is that fair?"

"It's a deal. I've always supported you in every part of your career as a doctor. I'm not about to quit now. Just let me know if anymore great ideas come into your head before you act on them, okay?"

We both laughed but I could tell she was wondering if I'd lost part of my brain. I couldn't explain to her how frustrated I was feeling in St. Martin. I didn't know why, and I have no idea what it'll be like in Crosgrove practicing medicine. I know one thing for sure. I am about to find out.

CHAPTER 5

Old Mr. Darby lived on the side of town that the rich people never went. The streets were shabby, the yards unkempt. Windows were patched with aluminum foil or cardboard, and no kids were out playing in the yards. Mr. Darby had lived in his house for over sixty years and he was going to die in that house. He was a retired schoolteacher who was actually pretty brilliant, although he felt like there weren't many left in the town who remembered his school days. Some of his students had moved out of Crosgrove and gone on to college or married. But Mr. Darby remembered the way Crosgrove used to be—quiet, lazy, and untouched by the rapid progression of most towns. Now things were different. No more Sundays sitting on his porch watching cars go by. His neighborhood had turned into a rough, dangerous place to live. He didn't know his neighbors because they kept changing from year to year. He paid for someone to keep his yard and didn't go out much anymore. The children he'd taught hardly ever came to see him. He was lonely but hardened to his life. He was sickly but didn't like the doctors in town; he rarely read the paper, but kept up with the local and world news by watching television once a day. He was a curious old man who was kind and gentle, but people mistook that gentleness for ignorance. He did take his evening walk each day and waved at the neighbors if they were outside.

Something was bothering him and he'd made up his mind to get to the bottom of it. There was a man who lived at the end of the block who worried

Mr. Darby. He couldn't put his finger on why, but something about the man just didn't add up. He'd run into him from time to time at the gas station, and even though the man was congenial, he seemed like he was hiding behind his hat. Mr. Darby had asked around town but no one really knew anything about this man except that his name was Lucas Cunningham. He made up his mind that he was going to find out more about this man was if it was the last thing he did. Usually he wasn't nosey about people, but this time he couldn't get this guy off his mind.

One morning he picked up his cane and took an early walk and headed past Lucas Cunningham's house. The house looked rundown like the rest of the houses on the block, and the blinds were pulled closed. It looked like no one was home. He squinted in the light of the sun and thought he saw a light on in the kitchen, but he couldn't be certain. He slowly moved across the lawn to the next house and looked back. There in the window, for a split second, was the face of Lucas, peeking through the blinds. Mr. Darby was losing his eyesight, but he was dead sure he saw Lucas. For some reason it tickled Mr. Darby to death that he had spotted him home. One day he was going to uncover the mystery of this man. And he would do it without anyone knowing what he was doing. That tickled him even more.

"Mornin', Mr. Darby!" It was Jean, the principal of Crosgrove High, walking her dog.

"'Lo, Miss Jean. You been doin' all right?"

"Oh, I have my issues, Mr. Darby. But I can't believe I've run into you this morning! I was going to call on you this week to ask a favor of you. Have you got a second?"

"I got the rest of my life, Miss Jean. What can I do for ya?"

Jean laughed and cleared her throat. "We're holding seminars for students who are seniors each week until graduation, and we're asking different business people to come and talk to the kids. Your name came up at the last meeting, because you have the reputation of being one of the best teachers this school has ever had. I was wondering if you would consider talking to the students during one of these meetings."

Mr. Darby froze in his tracks. He stood there in his baggy beige pants, his wrinkled plaid shirt, and shoes that looked like they'd been in a war. He cleared his throat and looked Jean in the eyes. "I've been out of teaching for as long as you can remember, Miss Jean. Didn't think anyone remembered my even bein' at Crosgrove High anymore. I don't know quite what to say—"

"Just think about it a few days and give me a call. I think you would enjoy it, Mr. Darby, and I know the kids would get a lot out of hearing your story." Jean reached up and put her hand under his chin and raised his wrinkled stubbly face up where she could see his eyes. "I know you feel forgotten, Peter, but many of us still remember you. Please think about this, will you? I would love for you to do this for the kids."

A small tear came up in Mr. Darby's eye, and he looked back down at his shoes. "I reckon I better clean up a bit if I'm goin' to talk to those kids. I look pretty bad, Miss Jean."

"That's the spirit! Now, if you need anything from me at all, just give me a call. I'm so excited I don't know what to say. Thank you so much and I know you're going to love doing this. I'll talk to you soon and give you the exact day I want you to be at the school."

Jean walked away smiling. *This was going to be magic. No one would be ready for Mr. Darby.* If she was remembering right, he was quite a speaker in his day, and she knew somewhere down deep inside that old man there was still Mr. Darby the teacher waiting to come out. He was a brilliant man, graduating in the top ten in his class at the university. He had lived in this town all his life and given a rich education to many children who were now adults raising their own children. She made a mental note to get the local news involved in this event.

Peter Darby walked home slowly, scratching his head, and even had a little kick in his step. *So someone wants me to show up at the school and talk to the kids again. I never thought this day would come 'round again. I better get myself cleaned up and get to thinkin' about what I want to talk about. I'm only goin' to get one shot at this, so I better make it good."*

❧

Down the street, in that dark house that no one ever entered, was a woman living in a cold basement with one tiny window too high to see out of and a locked door. She listened every evening at dusk to the sound of someone walking past the house and what stuck in her mind that morning was a tapping noise that sounded like a cane.

CHAPTER 6

Walking home from a girlfriend's house on a cloudy day in October eighteen years ago, Charlotte Reeves was happy to be fifteen. As she stepped on the piles of leaves that were accumulating along the edge of the sidewalk, her mind was focused on the boy across the street. His name was Jeff Windsor and he was in her class at school. He was washing his father's car and whistling. Music was blaring from the radio in the car, and she was daydreaming about a kiss one day from Jeff. She had put lipstick on before leaving her friend's house, and looked pretty in her blue jeans and white shirt. Her long brown hair was blowing in the slight breeze, and her chocolate brown eyes were trying hard not to stare. He turned once and waved at her as she walked by, and then went back to rinsing off the car. Charlotte hurried past, and smiled to herself, thinking maybe there was a slight chance he might ask her out one day.

It was late afternoon and the sun was beginning to set below the tree tops. Not many cars were on the street as she got close to Middleton Avenue, where she would turn right and head home. She was lost in a daydream and didn't see the truck pull up beside her. It was a blue pickup truck with a large dent in the back bumper. There was rust along the edges of the truck and a pile of old blankets in the back. When she stopped to wait for the red light, a man in black clothes and a hat pulled down over his face grabbed her and threw her in the cab and drove off. It happened so quickly that she didn't make a sound. She sat up and stared at the man but didn't recognize him at all. She couldn't make out his face very clearly because of all the hair and the hat pulled over his eyes. She screamed and tried to open the door, nearly falling out of the truck, but his hand was too quick and he grabbed her arm and pulled her back in. He threatened to hurt her if she tried again to escape. Her heart was thumping in her chest and all she could think of was how she was going to get away from him.

He stopped at a stop sign, where he forced a scarf over her eyes and tied it behind her head. He took a rope and tied her hands, even though she fought him with all her might. He hit her a few times and muttered under his breath that he could kill her easily if she didn't stop struggling. She sat still in the seat and shuddered at the smell of his breath. Her mind was going at the speed of light, realizing she was in serious trouble. She panicked, knowing that the farther they went away from town, the harder it would be to find her.

It wasn't long before he pulled into a driveway and she heard him slam the door of the truck. He came around and opened the door on her side and grabbed her arm and pulled her out of the truck. He was strong and all she could see if she looked down was a pair of old work shoes on his feet. They walked up some steps and into a house, and the smell nearly knocked her down. It smelled musty and damp, and there was another smell she couldn't put her finger on. It almost made her vomit.

The man pulled Charlotte down some stairs into a cold cellar, where he untied her hands and took off the blindfold. One single light in the corner was turned on and she could barely see what was in the room. He pointed to a bed in the corner and some blankets, and shoved her down in a chair.

"This is where you're goin' to be stayin' for now. I don' want to hear one peep outta ya, do ya hear?" Charlotte nodded and started to cry. "Now, shut down them tears, 'cuz I ain't gonna have a baby 'round here. You might as well git used to bein' here, 'cuz nobody's gonna find ya for a long, long time. You and me gonna be good friends, girl. Real good friends. And do as I tell you, or you'll be dead, ya hear?"

Still as a mouse, Charlotte listened as he climbed the stairs and closed the door. She looked around the room and saw one window up high that didn't look like it was open. There was no other way out of the room. Her heart was beating so hard and fast that she was sure he could hear it. She was scared, hungry, and worried that her mother would never be able to find her. She had no idea what street she was on or what her surroundings were like. But the house seemed to be old, and the man who grabbed her was obviously dangerous. She tried to keep her mind clear so that she could have a plan of escape. But the last words she'd heard from him were echoing in her mind. "*We are going to be friends. Real good friends.*"What did he want from her? And why did he put her in the cellar?* She curled up in a ball and cried harder than she had ever cried. But no one could hear her. She felt so invisible, so hidden. She had no idea where she was.

The first night was the worst night of her life. She was afraid to go to sleep and yet she was mentally exhausted. She could hear him walking around upstairs and was petrified that he would come downstairs and hurt her somehow. She sat up in the smelly bed and cried for most of the night, hoping somehow someone saw her being dragged into the house. She tried to listen through the glass of the window, but it was too high for her to reach. She looked around the room for something to stand on, but even when she dragged the low chair over to the wall and stood on tiptoe, she still couldn't see out of the window. She did see the occasional lights of a car go by, which cast strange shadows across the walls of the cellar. All she could think of was getting away. Somehow she had to get enough nerve to go up the stairs. Maybe he would go out and that would give her time to get away. It was her only hope. And she clung to that hope like a rope pulling her out of quicksand. But as the days went by, she sank deeper into that quicksand and the rope that was going to pull her out got shorter and shorter.

Days turned into months and months turned into years. Charlotte lost track of time because one day ran into the next. She discovered in the most horrendous way what he'd meant by being "friends." He came down to bring her food and then made her do things she would've never dreamed of doing. Her childhood slipped away like a kite whose string was cut, floating away into the clouds so far that all she could see was a dot.

Charlotte felt small and forgotten. It felt like no one was even trying to find her. She suspected she was still in Crosgrove, but she had no clue where the house was located. As time passed she had no idea what day it was, or what year. All she knew was that her life had been reduced to a cellar and one man she hated more than anything in the world. Her meals consisted of one or two canned vegetables with an occasional meat that she couldn't recognize. Eventually he brought an old television downstairs and some books. There was no cable, so she could only see three fuzzy stations, but at least she could watch local channels. He bought her a comb and brush and toothbrush, toothpaste, and a change of clothes, which consisted of a flannel shirt, a pair of faded jeans that hung on her thin frame, and one pair of cheap underpants. He allowed her a small mirror, and sometimes when she looked at herself, it was like looking at a stranger.

She couldn't believe that no one had found her after all this time. And each day that went by just cemented the nightmare she kept having that this was going to be how she would spend the rest of her life; locked up in a basement and left for dead. She assumed that the police had given up ever finding her or even uncovering a clue to her sudden disappearance. *My mother probably thinks I am dead; I wish I knew.* She'd developed her own routine, as pathetic as it was, to pass the time she was alone. One of the things she did was listen to cars go by and occasionally people talking as they walked past the house. She could barely hear voices but that didn't keep her from straining to listen. She learned that every afternoon someone walked by the house who used a cane. She could hear it hitting the concrete in a rhythm, and she felt like it was a man. She could've been totally wrong, but she pretended that this person was looking for her. This small hope kept her going from day to day, month to month. Every once in a while there would be a day when she didn't hear the cane, and the silence scared her to death. The next day she would get up hoping to hear it again so her world would feel safer. It was a warped way of hoping, but it was all she had. She felt dirty and used up. The horror of her situation began to dim and she slowly adjusted to Lucas and his sick ways. It became her world; the only life she had.

๑๑

Lately, Charlotte could hear coughing upstairs. He was sounding terribly sick. He might go all day without coughing, but at night it got bad. Real bad. He came to the top of the stairs and would leave her meals there. He came down to see her less and less. This made it easier for her, but she wanted out. She wanted to find a way to escape. She hoped more than anything that he would die, so the coughing became music to her ears. And she prayed to a God that she barely believed in, that this horrific man would die. And she asked forgiveness at the same time for the hatred she felt. She wondered at night about her mother; how she could possibly breathe at all without her. Or ever smile again. For in her heart of hearts, she felt forgotten by the world beyond her window, except for the man with the cane. She tried to remember her mother's face and her laughter, but all she got was a blank dark picture. No face. Nothing. It was useless to try to remember for it had been so long she could barely remember her room, or what the house looked like. In her sleep sometimes a face would appear that seemed like her mother. So she held on to that with all that she could. Everything was slippery. Slipping away. And she was growing older in a dark cellar and no one was watching.

One night when she thought Lucas was asleep, she climbed the stairway and tried to open the door. Lucas always locked it when he left her meals, but this night, probably because he was so sick, he'd forgotten to lock it. She turned the knob and the door opened with a loud creak. She froze in her tracks, terrified that he might have heard the noise. For a moment Charlotte took a deep breath and looked around the room. It smelled and was so dirty. Dishes piled on the kitchen counter, papers on the floor. The carpet was filthy and the walls greasy. The air reeked of stale cigarettes. She tiptoed into the kitchen and was going near the back door when he came up behind her and grabbed her, putting his hand over her mouth. She tried to get away but he was suddenly as strong as Goliath. He pulled her hair and dragged her back down the stairs, screaming at her all the way.

"I told ya never to come up those stairs, didn't I? I told ya I would shoot you dead away if I caught ya tryin' to leave. And what did you do? First chance ya got when I'm near dead myself, you creep up those stairs and try to leave. Have ya lost your mind, what little ya have left? Do you want me to kill ya?"

Charlotte couldn't say a word because he had his hand over her mouth. He slowly let his hand loosen its grip on her face and she swallowed hard. She kept her eyes on the floor because she couldn't bear to look at his eyes. Not now. He shook her and made her promise she would never do it again. She swore she wouldn't, and she meant it. She knew he had a gun in his lap most of the time. It was a miracle she hadn't gotten shot this time. She would have to do better than this in planning an escape. He was just too quick for her to leave out the kitchen door. Her heart was racing and she was shaking from head to toe. *What was I thinking? How did I think he wasn't going to hear me open that door? I could've gotten myself killed. I'm losing my mind staying in this damn cellar all the time. I'm not even thinkin' straight.*

∽

Lucas turned and walked back up the stairs slowly. He was feeling weak and disappointed in her. *I'm goin' to have to keep my eyes on her; once she got out she would want to come out again so I'm goin' to have to be watchin' more closely. The desire to leave is buildin' and one day it's goin' to explode in her. Then she won't care if she gets killed or not. I don't want that day to come because I don't want her dead.*

He sat down in his chair and laid his head back. He was so tired of worrying. Tired of trying to hide from the law or anyone else. He had no life; that was exactly why he'd kidnapped Charlotte. He wanted a life.

༄

In the cellar, Charlotte sat on her bed crying. She was so close to getting out and she'd blown it. It would take years to get that chance again. How could she stay down here any longer? She was sick of it and was desperate to see her mother again. Her ray of hope had grown so dim she could barely see it. Charlotte was a strong young woman but he'd nearly broken her spirit. The Charlotte she used to be no longer existed. She had shed that girl like a burn victim sheds his dead skin, slowly and with much pain. The callous indifference he always showed toward her most basic needs, the intimidation he caused her to feel, and the things he made her do had slowly scraped off the girl she used to be. And all that was left was a raw resemblance of her, bleeding in a way no one could see.

CHAPTER 7

It was Monday morning and my first day in the office. I had run ads letting the town know that I'd opened a new practice here, but for a while I was prepared to feel invisible. This was totally new to me, and I was missing my friend Case terribly. A phone call was in order on my first day open.

"Hello?"

"Case, buddy! How's my man?"

I heard coughing and a pause. "Hey Mike! How in the world are ya?" More coughing.

"Well, I'm here on my first day at the new office feeling pretty lonely, if ya want to know the truth, Case. You sound terrible, by the way."

"Oh, stop it. You're diagnosing me from miles away. I'm fine, really. Just a fall cold or flu bug. So how's it goin,' Mike? You think you're goin' to like it there, huh?"

"Hard to say yet. But I do love this office. Can't wait for you to see it. The rooms are a perfect size for treatment rooms, and I really have space for one more doctor if I have enough patients comin' in."

"Sounds terrific. I knew you would find the right spot. Olivia and I want to come up soon to see you once I get over this darn bug I've gotten. I'm goin' in for some tests tomorrow but soon as I see the light, I'm comin' your way. Jill doing okay up there?"

"I haven't seen hide nor hair of her since we moved. I'm not jokin', man. She's at our daughter's house all the time, goin' shopping or I don't know what. But she did help me get moved into this office and I'm a lot more organized than I would've been, doin' it on my own."

Coughing fit again. "Well, Mike. I better be hangin' up here real soon. I'm a bit weak and haven't eaten much lately. Keep me posted on things; it sure did me good to hear your voice. Don't be a stranger, will ya? I miss the dog out of you."

"I miss you too, Case. Just doesn't seem right."

"Take care, Mike. I'll call ya soon and let ya know how I'm doin'. Bye now."

Something in the pit of my stomach was telling me that Case was real sick. I didn't like it one bit. Now how was I supposed to go work on people today with Case on my mind? I sure hoped it was a case of the flu and not something more serious. His heart had been giving him problems last year; I wondered if it was acting up again and he was just not telling me. I made a note to call Olivia that evening to find out the real truth. Darn that man. This was no time to be keeping secrets.

෬ා

My first patient was walking through the door, and my new secretary, Mary Beth, put him in the first treatment room. Even though I'd practiced for years and years, don't really remember how many, I still got nervous about my first patient of the day. I grabbed his chart and saw that his name was Lucas Cunningham. He lived across town on Amber Lane. Bad chest pains and cough. Sounded like Case!

Mr. Cunningham sat down in a chair and breathed in heavily. He looked nervous about coming to the doctor, probably because he hated talking about himself. Doctors ask way too many questions and that's something most people don't think they need in their lives; a nosey doctor. He cleared his throat and answered my first question. "I started this cough 'bout six weeks ago. Thought it'd clear up on its own, but guess not. My chest was hurtin' for the last week, so here I am. Need ya to tell me what's goin' on, I guess."

"Well, let me listen to your chest, Mr. Cunningham. How long since you went to a dentist? You remember?"

"I ain't never been to a dentist, Doc. I hate dentists."

"I see. Well you might try going once in your lifetime. Your teeth look pretty bad. Now open wide."

I don't know what in the world made me pick this profession, but today, working on Lucas Cunningham, I almost doubted my sanity. He was a total mess. His breath would stop a freight train, and that cough of his had a gravelly sound that screamed "pneumonia." He didn't want to take any medicine, but I wrote him out a prescription for an antibiotic, anyway. He balked at the X-ray request, but I insisted he get one if I was going to diagnose him correctly. His skin was dry, he had enough wax in his ears to make it impossible for him to hear most of what I said, and he limped on his left leg and winced every time I touched his ankle. I would bet my life that he hadn't bathed in months, and he seemed nervous when I asked him what he did for a living. My guess was that he didn't work at all.

As he was leaving, he looked back at me and I froze in my tracks. Don't know why, exactly. I don't remember ever seeing a look like that before, so I don't know what he was thinking. The hair stood on my arm, for one thing. And secondly, I had this weird sensation like he was trying to tell me something. I told him to come back on Thursday but he just nodded and walked out the door. It left me cold. I actually felt a cold draft on my neck. Probably nothing at all. Like I said, my first day in practice in this new town. But weird just the same.

༄

"Olivia, you have to promise me you won't talk to Jill about my illness just yet, all right?"

"I promise, Case. But you shouldn't keep this from Michael too much longer. He's smart and will figure it out, anyway. You already know that."

"Yeah, I know. But he's just moved into his new office and I don't want to drag him down just yet. I wanted to run up and see him, but darn, Olivia, I just don't have the energy now to go. It's not like me to feel this weak but I know my lungs are giving out. Years of smoking have finally caught up with me. I still don't believe it, honey. I knew I had a cough, but good gosh, this thing snowballed on me. I may not have long to live and I really felt pretty healthy up until a few months ago. My last X-ray wasn't that bad. I did have emphysema but I didn't think it was that far along. Glad I went to James Stanley, though. He's the best in his field. I'm worried about the tumor they saw in my lungs. Doesn't sound good, honey."

Tears ran down Olivia's face and she got choked up for a second. "Case, I can't live without you, so we need to check out all our options here. Don't you want a second opinion? It's not like you to just accept this diagnosis without looking into it more."

"I know what's going on, honey. I'm a doctor, remember? If you'll feel better, I'll call my friend Spence in Jackson Cove and get him to run some tests on me. But I feel sure he'll come up with the same diagnosis." He looked at Olivia's face and grimaced. He wasn't ready to leave this world. Not yet.

"I'm not saying James doesn't know what he's doing, Case. But I do think we need a second opinion. Michael would have a cow if he knew you were hiding this from him. It's been a couple of months since you've seen him, and now you're going to have to call him and tell him your days are numbered. How's he going to handle that, Case? Like the rest of us. Not very well at all."

I know you're right, Olivia. I'm surprised that he hasn't already sensed what's wrong. He has that ability to see things sometimes. It gets kind of creepy, you know? So it won't surprise me one bit if I get a call from him in the next few days asking me if it's cancer."

"You're right, Case. But still call your friend. It would make me feel better."

CHAPTER 8

Peyton Bridgeforth came walking in my office at three in the afternoon, sweating, pale, and angry. "How many times do we have to complain about the light at Fifth and Main? Every day last week that light was out, and yesterday morning in rush hour traffic, no light. As I'm heading your way just a few moments ago, the light is still out. What's the problem? Can't we get anything done around here?"

"Good afternoon, Peyton. Have a seat, and let's see what's going on with you. Don't you have an air conditioner in your car? Why are you sweating so badly?"

"I feel horrible, Dr. Lankford. My chest feels heavy, and I'm not sleeping worth a darn anymore. I mean, things at work are tough. Don't mean to complain, because things are hard for all of us now. But right now I feel overwhelmed about my life. I—"

"Hold on, Peyton. Take it easy. I know things are tough. Let me check you out a moment and see what's going on. Just sit down here on the table and let me listen to your heart."

I hadn't seen Peyton but once at a church social, but he looked pale and clammy, and he was obviously upset about something. He had hypertension, and his heart was beating faster than a speeding bullet. I made a note for Mary Beth to schedule some tests for him at the hospital and asked him into my office. I needed to find out what in the world was going on with him.

"Peyton, relax with me for a moment. Let's talk about what's going on in your life right now. Why are you so angry? Can you tell me that?"

"I—I don't exactly know, Dr. Lankford. I guess I feel frustrated. It's not easy to tell you why. My wife…"

"Is your wife having an affair, Peyton?"

Shocked and white as a sheet, Peyton sat up straight in this chair. "What? Is my wife what?"

I was dead sure for some reason that I was right about my assumption. I wanted to be careful because I hadn't known Peyton long and he was a new patient. "Is your wife having an affair, Peyton?"

Peyton started to shake and stood up abruptly. "Doc, I need to leave. I don't feel too well. I can't talk about it right now. You see, we've been having some problems lately. It's all too much to deal with and I . . ."

Peyton moved away from my desk and stumbled. I darted around my desk and caught him as he was going down. He got his balance and realized I had my arm around his back. He turned and looked me straight in the eyes and broke down in tears. I told him to have a seat and I ran across the hall and got some cold water in a glass and brought it to him.

"Peyton, take it easy now. It's going to be all right. I know this is a tough time for you, but things like this can be worked out. I have a name of a good marriage counselor, and I know he'll help you get this marriage back where it needs to be. Will you go see him?"

Blowing his nose, Peyton shook his head. "There's no way she'll go, Doc. No way."

"Well, you go then. See what this guy has to say. It might help you when you're talking to her."

Peyton stood up and shook my hand. "I'll take his card and give him a call. Sorry for the tears. I guess I'm more upset than I realized. It's totally out of character for her to do this. She cried when she told me about it. I still love her, but good gosh, how in the world do I get over an affair? How do we get past this ugly place?"

"That's why you need to call this counselor, Peyton. He'll help you sort through all of this."

"I shouldn't have left her alone so much. She's a bit younger than me and fragile. I should've paid attention. Say Doc, how did you know? How in the heck did you know about the affair?" He stood there looking at me, waiting.

I stood there with a blank look on my face. I didn't have an answer. At least the answer he wanted to hear. "Peyton, I don't really know. It just came to me when I was looking at you. I didn't mean to upset you or pry into your personal business. But if you don't deal with these emotions that are welling up inside of you, you're going to have a heart attack or something worse. I want you to have those tests run tomorrow, and call that counselor. I want to see you back in here as soon as I get the results of those tests. We'll call you and let you know when to come in."

Peyton stood there with a puzzled look on his face. "You just felt it? Did you hear about this in town or something? Doc, come on. You're not being honest here. How did you know about the affair? Are people talking about it around town?"

"Relax, Peyton. I'm being as honest as I can be. I don't know how I knew. I just knew. Now please don't let that upset you right now. I won't talk about it with anyone, you know that. This stays between you and me. Right here. It won't leave the room. Now go home and see what you can do to save your marriage. And remember Peyton, forgiveness goes a long way in restoring hearts."

When Peyton left my office, I just sat there thinking. *How in the world did I know about the affair? It's crazy. It just came to me like a thought but somehow I knew it was true. I would've bet my life on it. What the heck is going on? I've always been close to my patients but this was someone I barely knew. I've never met his wife. How did I know about the affair?*

I headed out the door and jogged to the car. It had been a long day and I was ready to talk to Jill about what just happened with Peyton. I knew if I told her I was taking a risk of having to listen to her comments about my going too far with my patients. But I also knew she understood that I had this sixth sense about things. *I think she is just concerned that I'll get too involved or make someone angry.* I missed Case more than ever and I was worried about his cough. Something was wrong there. I think he's in trouble, and I'm frustrated because he's holding out on me.

∽

Charlotte was sitting underneath the window waiting for the tap of the cane. It was raining so hard that she was convinced he wouldn't walk today. It was getting late and he always walked right at dusk. Lucas was upstairs in bed; he made it down to the top of the cellar stairs to bring her supper. She was beginning to think there might be a way to escape. However, he'd been sick before and recovered. She pulled out her mirror and looked at herself, trying to see her mother in the reflection.

I feel forgotten, used up. There's no one here but me all day long in this tiny cold damp cellar. People come near the house but no one ever stops. That keeps coming back to me as I sit here day after day. I have to find a way out of here or I'll lose my mind. Surely my mother can feel I'm alive. I can feel her. But I have lost her smell. . . .People must have forgotten about me by now. I don't even know how long I've been in this rotten house; how many years it's been. I can remember the day he grabbed me off the street. It was surreal. Like a dream. He was a sick, sick man; I guess he wanted me for his wife, only he's so messed up that he can't stand to be around anyone for long. I'm shocked that he went to the doctor. What I would love to know is what that doctor thought of him. His physical condition.

Charlotte turned on her television and leaned back against the wall above the window. Usually she watched a program for a little while and then let herself go into a foggy daydream of what life would be like if she were free. For a time Lucas kept her hair short and used dull scissors to chop it off, but now, since his health had grown worse over time, he had allowed her hair to be long. She had aged quickly from all the stress and poor nutrition, and her mind was as small as the room she was in. Perhaps one loses the ability to think past the situation they're in if they're confined long enough and the conditions are bad enough. Many nights she had to listen to his ranting about his life, his failures, and the blame he placed on everyone but himself. She couldn't really tell how old he was. There were times he was halfway nice to her and other times she feared for her life. That emotional roller coaster made it difficult for her to ever relax. There wasn't a day that went by that she didn't think about escaping; seeing her family again, living her life like a normal person. Yet in a way, she actually feared seeing everyone because life had gone on without her for so long. But most of all she feared that she'd go mad living in the cellar and not realize it. Others would notice it immediately and she'd be in the dark. Like now. Alone in her own world.

∽

Lucas was sitting in his favorite chair with the television on low. His mind was running rampant like it always did this time of day. It was dusk and the worst time of the day for him. Memories were flooding back of those nights when his father would come home drunk and beat up his mother. He sat with his fists clinched remembering her screams, knowing there was nothing he could do short of killing the one man he loved most of all in the world. This pattern began when he was a young boy and continued until he left home. But it pushed his tolerance and ability to rationalize the behavior over the slippery edge of insanity, and one day he totally left the road of youth and found his feet on the unfamiliar path of deception, murder, and darkness. It was a lonely path that he knew he couldn't share with a single person. Except for his mother, he was all alone in the knowledge that he'd killed his father with his own hands. At least he was smart enough to wear gloves; he'd seen enough on television to know better than to use his bare hands. The toughest part was dragging the old man out the door, into his trunk, and dumping him into the swamp. He never knew if the gators got him or what, because his body was never found. So luck was on his side in that one single moment in his life. His mother was mentally broken for the rest of her life and no matter how he tried to make things right, she never forgave him for killing his father. That love/hate relationship was all she had known and she just couldn't get past the fact that she had married the one man she ever loved and now he was dead. She never gave one thought to how it had affected her son to watch his mother being beaten to a pulp by his father. Night after night—the screams, the dishes thrown across the kitchen, the threats of death. It had just never ended.

Lucas stretched out in the chair and laid his head back on the worn, stained cushion. He rented the house he was in, owned an old beat-up pickup truck on its last leg, and worked enough odd jobs to feed himself and pay his bills. He listened to see if he could hear Charlotte moving around. She was the one thing he had, and he had been forced to steal her away from her family in order to have someone in his house. He hadn't intended to ever hurt her, but sometimes the memories got so bad that he went downstairs and made her scream. It was really a distraction to break his train of thought but sometimes it got out of hand.

She'd been down there way too long. He couldn't believe the years had passed so quickly. He had a gun sitting out on the edge of the table near his chair. He was prepared to shoot her if she tried to escape, but he never even had to load the gun after the first year. He had broken her spirit, which was a sick thing to do but it was the only way he could keep her with him. He convinced her there was no way out, and that her family had given up on ever finding her alive. She cried for weeks, but soon there was no sound from the cellar. She seemed to settle in to the life he was allowing her to have, which was pretty pathetic. He wanted to bring her upstairs so she could cook and move around more, but he was afraid she'd leave. Then he'd be alone in his fears and he wouldn't be able to face himself. They were civil to each other, but he knew better than to relax for one moment, or she'd be gone. The outside world was oblivious to her suffering, but once she got out, everyone would know. He couldn't have that, not now. Not ever. He wasn't going to kill her; he just wanted someone in his home. Someone like family.

CHAPTER 9

It has been proven that the best way for someone to meet people is to join a committee, or so I was told. So I joined the school board, Rotary Club, and the Chamber of Commerce. It may have been overkill but I did get a lot of patients after a few meetings. Crosgrove High School was holding a seminar for seniors that would go through the weekend but tonight a former teacher named Mr. Peter Darby was speaking. Word was that he was a phenomenal teacher and many of his students were given scholarships and ended up achieving more than they could have ever dreamed of. Most of the kids came from broken families who were barely able to put food on the table, so it was an even greater feat to motivate these children to want a higher education. During the last school board meeting, it was unanimous for us to have Mr. Darby speak to the seniors. I looked forward to hearing what he had to say. The auditorium was packed and noisy. It was a bit warm and I decided to remove my coat and take a risk at looking over at my wife and getting a raised eyebrow. Finally the principal walked up to the microphone and cleared her throat. She raised her hand and the room slowly began to quiet down. It took a few minutes for the kids in the back of the room to settle down, but after someone stood up and shouted, "Be Quiet!" the room was still.

"Ladies and gentlemen, seniors, and guests. This is a special night for Crosgrove; not only for the seniors who'll be leaving us shortly, but because we've been graced with one of the best teachers ever to walk the halls of Crosgrove

High School since it opened in 1955. Mr. Peter Darby taught here for many years, and all of his students grew to love him. He has agreed to come tonight to speak to us, and without further ado, I give the floor to Mr. Darby."

The applause was generous, and slowly a corner of the curtain moved and our eyes all focused on the right side of the stage. It seemed like a century before anything happened, and then I heard him coming before I saw him. He walked with a cane, hitting it on the floor before he took a step. He walked slow but deliberately, and he was dressed to the nines in his best suit. He had a hat on that was cocked to one side. As he approached the microphone, he removed his hat and laid it on a chair provided for him, in case his legs should tire. People were talking low and wondering who he was, and there was some laughter in the back of the auditorium. He did look quite the character standing there bent over, looking out at the crowd. We all were a bit worried watching him standing there so fragile, until he cleared his throat one last time and began to speak.

"I grew up on a farm in the middle of nowhere in Madisonville, Alabama. Both my brothers died from childhood illnesses, and my father and mother were killed in a car wreck by a drunk driver. I was left on that farm, overlooked by the state, alone and afraid. Somehow I slipped through the greasy cracks of society because nobody ever came down that long dusty road to see how I was. Or if I had food to eat. I learned very quickly that if I was going to survive, I'd better find a way of doing it by myself. I discovered that I couldn't count on anyone but myself, so I dug down deeper than I thought I could go and found the strength to live some kind of life that would take me out of the filthy hole I was living in at the time. My neighbors were miles away and stayed pretty much to themselves. I never felt so alone in my life as the day my parents died. I was invisible to the world, and no one was there to wipe my tears. It made me tough, and it could've made me bitter. But somehow, what my mother had taught me and my father had shown me took root in the middle of selfishness and self pity, and I rose above the pain and became a man at ten years old."

Peter walked to the edge of the stage and looked out across the room. His walk was so painful to watch that we were relieved when he went back to the microphone and placed one of his hands on the chair for balance.

"I decided to plant a garden on the farm so I could always have food. That sounds simple but it wasn't at the age of ten. I had to plow the land and plant the seeds. Then I had to water and weed it. When it was time to harvest, it was me and me alone who got out there in the heat and harvested the vegetables. I sold some on the street corner in town and made enough money from the summer vegetables to buy some meat for winter, and also some clothes. I had made up my mind that I had to go back to school if I was ever going to make something of myself. My hair needed cutting so I found my way to a local barbershop and had them give me my first hair cut. My shoes were too small and had holes in the bottom so I went to the local Salvation Army and bought clothes and shoes and a coat for next to nothing. They even let me have a television set that needed rabbit ears to work. The only problem was, I didn't have electricity. I couldn't afford to pay that bill so it was cut off. But I had dreams, so I hung on to those dreams like nothing you've ever seen, hoping for the day when I could have anything I needed to make my new life work."

The room was still. You could hear a pin drop. All eyes were on Mr. Darby, as he stood their sharing his life story with us. We weren't sure where this all was going, but he had us on the edge of our seats. Blowing our noses, of course. There wasn't a dry eye in the place.

"I started back to school in the fall and walked home every day. It took me an hour and a half to walk home from school. I was so tired when I got home, but nobody was there to fix my supper. Or help me with my homework. I was alone in this endeavor, and most days I made the best of it. But there were times, I want you to know, that I cried my eyes out. I yelled at the sky, shaking my fists in the air. I screamed at God, at my parents who had left me here alone, and at the people around me who still didn't see me. But after my pity party, I would go in and fix my supper, do my homework and go to bed. I was so tired I could hardly walk up the stairs to my bedroom, which was a loft. I learned not to require much, because there was no money to make things any different. I also was determined to make good grades, because that was the only way I was going to make it to college.

"The way I walked home every day was a winding path that led me into some woods before it found its way to my driveway. One day when I was headed into

the woods, I heard someone crying. I walked and walked and suddenly I ran up
on a young girl named Emily in the woods. She was so upset and I couldn't get a
word out of her. So I took her to my house, which was a mile away, and gave her
something to drink. Emily finally told me that her father was beating her mother
up. That he had a gun. She was afraid one day he would kill them all. Being
alone had made me hard. I felt like a man even though I was a child. So I walked
her home, wanting to see this guy who had frightened this young girl to death.
There he was on the porch sitting with a gun on his lap. I walked straight up to
him, too stupid to be scared, and told him in no uncertain terms that if he laid
a hand on his daughter or wife again, I would kill him. He threw his head back
and laughed and laughed. But he didn't know me. He didn't know the pain I'd
suffered that had turned my heart into something like the heart of a great lion.
I had the courage it would take to kill him if it would save the child and mother.
I had heard the story of David and Goliath, and that echoed in my mind when I
was looking at this man.

"Later in the fall, she came running up on my porch screaming, 'My daddy
has been beating my mom all morning. I came home from school to find her lyin'
across my bed. She won't talk to me. She won't say a word. I'm scared he killed
her, Peter.'

"Anger rose up in my throat, and I grabbed one of my father's rifles and
headed to her house. Emily was yelling at me to be careful but I couldn't hear
her. My mind was racing and I had only one thing on my mind; to stop this man
before he killed someone. He saw me coming. As though he could read my mind,
he stood up and aimed his gun at me but I couldn't see it. I was blinded by my
own hatred. He pulled the trigger and it hit me in my left side. I fell hard to the
ground, but I used the rifle to pull myself back up. He was about to take another
shot at me when I pulled the trigger and he fell to the ground like a rotten tree.
I don't think he moved a muscle after he fell. The police came and asked me a
lot of questions. I was taken in an ambulance to the hospital and stayed about a
week after surgery to remove the bullet. Emily's father was dead and no charges
were placed against me. He had a record with the law a mile long, and a prison
record. I couldn't wait to get out of the hospital so I could get back to school."

He paused and took a long drink of water and set the bottle carefully on the
small table.

"I'm sharing all of this with you because I know your lives aren't perfect. You may not have breakfast every morning, or a parent there when you get home from school. Life is tough and none of us have perfect parents. I also know you see more than you should on the street and in your school with all the drugs that are out there. I want you to understand that I've been where you are, and you can pull yourself through to a better place if you really want to be there.

"I graduated from high school with honors and got a full scholarship to college. Once I made it to college, I never looked back. I was away from that farm and the poverty-twisted life I was born into. I taught school here at Crosgrove High School for more years than I can count, but I tried to make an impression on each child that education matters. If I had given in to the sickness around me, I would've ended up on the street in trouble. But I pulled the goodness out of what my parents taught me and forced it into my own life, and then tried to give it to the students that were in my classes. I wanted to come tonight and speak to you because I came from nothing but I still had a good life. It's not where you're from that matters, it's where you're going."

The clapping was so loud I could hardly think. All the kids were standing up and clapping and the parents were dabbing their eyes. Mr. Darby stood a few moments at the microphone and then he smiled the biggest smile I've ever seen. He turned and took his cane and walked off the stage. No one wanted him to leave. In telling his story he'd woven a web that captured us and we weren't ready to let go. Jean Roberts stood and watched Mr. Darby leave the stage and turned to face the crowd. She motioned for us to sit down and be quiet again and asked Mr. Darby to wait. It took a few moments as everyone was still overwhelmed by his story, but after all the kids were in their seats, she spoke in a quiet voice.

"I know this was a surprise for most of you in this room. But it wasn't a surprise for me. I was one of the students that Mr. Darby taught here at Crosgrove High. I had problems at home and was unable to find my way out. He not only showed me how to rise above what I saw at home, but Mr. Darby gave me a dream. And I kept that dream alive in my heart until after I graduated from college and found my way back home. My dream was to be the principal of Crosgrove High School. That dream was made real in my life because of the tools that Mr. Darby instilled in me all the years he taught here. He not only talked to me after class, but even when I was no longer in his classes, he found the time to meet with me after school so I wouldn't get discouraged.

"I would like at this time for all those parents who were affected by Mr. Darby while they were at Crosgrove High to stand up."

The room got noisy and people were talking all at once. Suddenly more than half the audience stood up. Mr. Darby was at the edge of the stage where the curtain kept him hidden from the crowd. He peeked around the corner and looked at all the people standing up and heard the applause that was deafening. He had hoped that he'd affected a few in his lifetime, but this was overwhelming. He walked out on the stage and took a weak bow and waved to all of the parents standing. Then Miss Roberts walked over to him and kissed his forehead and thanked him for all he'd done in her life. He was so overcome that he turned and walked off the stage. His knees were weakening and he knew he had better head home. One of the teachers behind the curtain took his arm and as they were leaving the building Peter Darby could still hear the applause and loud cries of those he had left behind.

⌒〜⌒

I was hoping to get a chance to speak with Mr. Darby before he left. Since I wasn't able to, I made a mental note to give him a call. This might be a good opportunity for me to make a house call, which was unheard of these days, just to see how Mr. Darby was doing. I bet he had some stories to tell, and it might help me get a better picture of Crosgrove after talking to him. I might even get Case to sit in on this one. He would get a kick out of listening to old Peter Darby. Jill was by my side, quiet, allowing me to have my own thoughts. But I wanted to hear what she thought about what Mr. Darby had said.

"Honey, how did you like that speech?"

"Oh my gosh! I'm still wiping my eyes, to tell you the truth. That sweet man could hardly stand there, much less have the energy to speak to a room full of people. I wouldn't have missed this for anything in the world."

"I agree, angel. What a powerful message those kids heard tonight. And you saw how many people he'd affected while at Crosgrove. That was only a handful of the adults who had been taught by the man. Think of how many there really are, after all the years he taught school. You couldn't fit them all in that auditorium!"

"I know one thing; there isn't a teacher in the world that wouldn't want to have had that kind of impact on their students. He's a special little man. Someone that you could sit and listen to for hours. You know?"

"That's exactly what I plan to do, Jill. Sit and listen."

CHAPTER 10

Anna Grace was beginning to show and it was easier to believe that she was having a baby now that we could see her stomach growing. I still had to pinch myself when I thought about being a grandfather. It sounded weird but sort of nice at the same time. Jill and Anna had been working hard on the nursery and it was shaping up. Thomas and Anna had learned that the baby was a little boy, and now they were arguing over names every night after supper. Jill and I made our own list from time to time and passed it on to them. We really didn't want to get in the middle of this name search, but I would find myself thinking about it every time I woke up in the night. Already the baby was causing havoc in our lives.

Jill and I had settled into our home on Macon Avenue. It wasn't an overly large home, but it met our needs perfectly. There was a separate study for me so that I could have an office at home and a place for all my medical books. Jill had a sewing room and was already busy sewing clothes for the baby. She'd already made curtains for the nursery and had a list a mile long of things to do. I found myself wandering into my study at night, opening a window to let some fresh air in, and sitting at my desk letting my mind go. If I was working with a patient who had a difficult diagnosis, I would pull out my medical books and read until well into the night. It was a lovely home and we fell right into our own ruts pretty quickly. We are creatures of habit, and even in new surroundings we are forever seeking to make it our own.

This particular night I was sitting at my desk thinking of Case and wondering if he was fishing much anymore. I dialed his number hoping to hear the good news that he was feeling much better.

"Case, is that you, buddy?"

Coughing again. "Hey, Mike!" Case cleared his throat and took a sip of hot coffee to settle his throat.

"How are you? You still sound a bit rough. What's going on?"

"Aw, nothing much, man. Just working and trying to get myself back to feeling strong again. How's the new place? You busy yet?"

"There you go dodging my questions again, Case. I'm going to head your way if you don't tell me what the heck is going on with your health. I'm a doctor, remember? Now spit it out. Tell me what's wrong with you."

There was a pause that seemed long to me. "I didn't want to say anything until I knew more, Mike, but it looks like I have lung cancer. We're running lots of tests, but this thing sort of crept up on me all of a sudden, and pretty much without warning."

I was frozen in my seat. My mouth was dry as a cork and I flat didn't know what to say. Cancer? "Case, are you kidding me? Cancer? How in the world would you get lung cancer? You haven't smoked in ten years. What kind of cancer? Do you know yet?"

"Now calm down, Michael. I knew this would upset you and I was waiting to get up the courage to call. Don't go getting yourself all worked up. We don't know what type yet, but it's fast growing, I'd say that for sure. I've never seen anything like this in my life. In all my years of practice, I've never seen a cancer like this. I had no symptoms until you left. And then it hit me right between the eyes. Mike, I'm short of breath, have this dreadful cough, and am weak as a kitten. No warning, I'm telling you."

"I'm coming to see you. I want to go to the doctor with you to hear what he has to say. Are you seeing James Stanley? He's the best in the field, buddy."

"Now, Michael. I know you're concerned, but there's no need for you to drive all the way back here just to go to the doctor with me. I'm a grown man, and I have Olivia here. You're still building your practice and don't have the time to hover over me. I'll be fine, I'm sure. James is the best in his field, I agree, and I trust him explicitly. So relax, will you?"

"I'm not going to argue with you, Case. I'm really worried. I mean, this doesn't sound good at all. Will you let me know what James says? I might give him a call, myself. This was the last thing I thought I'd hear tonight when I called you. I was going to talk to you about fishing and the speaker last night at our meeting at the school. Now none of that's important. I want you well, Case. I feel like I've been sucker-punched."

There was a long silence at the other end of the phone. I heard Case sigh before he spoke again. I knew how tough this conversation must be for him and that he wanted to hang up knowing he had said the right things to me. I also knew his prognosis was not good and that he was processing the truth that this was going to be the end of the line for him.

"Listen, Mike. We know this isn't good. I realize all too well how fast you're putting all this together. I've never been able to hide anything from you, buddy, but this is the most life-altering issue you and I've ever had to deal with. We've always had each other, and in this one thing I'm alone. And when I die, you'll be alone. We've never gone a week without each other since we were kids, and I wasn't expecting this separation so early in our lives. We've lived a good life but we're considerably young and in good health except for this darn cancer that's taking over my lungs. I don't want this to happen any more than you do, Mike. Believe me, I'm sittin' here trying to figure out how I can stop the progress of this cancer in my body. I'm even reading up on the holistic approach. But if the cancer is the type I think it is, small cell lung cancer, then I don't have long."

I sat at my desk with tears falling down my face. I never cry. But this man was my best friend. Case was like my brother. A huge part of my life. How could I make it through the last years of my life without him? I don't want to even think about not having him around. He was so calm. Damn him! How can he be so calm? I've heard that God gives a person certain amount of grace to face death when it comes. Well, He's not giving me anything right now! This is the worst thing short of losing my wife or daughter, that I could face in my life. Case and I belong!

"Case, I want you to know I'm here for you. Please let me come. I want to be there when you hear what type the cancer is. I want to go through this with you."

Case sounded as if he could hardly speak, like he was holding back the tears. "Mike, don't do it. I think it's best that I find this out on my own. I know that sounds cold to you, but it's going to be nearly impossible for us to say goodbye as it is. Can you imagine you being here when I die? There's no way I would do that to you, man. Come on. Think about it. We can talk on the phone up until the end, but there's no way I can die with you sitting there on my bed bawling your eyes out. You have to be strong for me, Mike. I need that. I need to know I can call and gripe to you about how sick I feel. How tough it is. I can't do that to Olivia. She's already heard too much, you know? I need you to be there for me; can you do that?"

A lump the size of a basketball was in my throat. It felt tight; I could hardly swallow. I took a sip of water and blew all the air out of my lungs. I knew he was right, but I didn't want to tell him I agreed to stay here. I wanted more than anything else, more than breathing, to be near Case when he died. And he was telling me no. I don't think I can do it. I don't think I can stay away, no matter what he says.

"Case. You're asking too much of me. I'll be here for you to the end. I'll hold you up with my own strength. But don't ask me to stay here. I want to come now and see you before you go down. We've seen what cancer does to a person, and I don't want to wait until the very end when you're in a coma. At least give me that, will you?"

"All right, Mike. I'll keep you posted on things and tell you when to come. How's that? Feel any better? Just let me talk to the doctors and see what the prognosis is. The time line. I'll call you as soon as I walk out of their office. Is that a deal?"

"Sounds much better on this end. Keep in close contact with me, and know that I'm thinking of you every waking moment. I love you. Don't forget that, will you? I love you like a brother, Case."

"I love you, Mike. Now don't go gettin' soft on me. Take it easy and I'll be talking to you soon."

"I'll be waiting to hear from you, you hear?"

Silence. Coughing. "Mike, thanks for the life we had, you and I. All those times we laughed and talked and cried will carry me through this illness. I'll carry a part of you with me to the other side."

The line went dead. And I couldn't move. I don't even know how long I sat there at my desk staring out the window into the night. Hours went by and I just couldn't move. Those last words did me in.

"I'll take a part of you with me to the other side.". . . *Did he have to say that? My best friend was dying and I wasn't there with him.*.

CHAPTER 11

Jill hung up the phone and shook her head in disbelief. After a two-hour conversation with Olivia about Case, she was now wondering if the decision to
move was the right choice. Tears were streaming down her face and all she could
do was shake her head and cry.

*Case. A lifelong friend, and he was dying. How will Mike be able to deal with this?
Now I'm wondering if we made the right decision. We would be there now if Mike hadn't
felt so strongly about moving, and I hate to doubt him, but now what do we do? It's incon-
ceivable that Case is dying. My brain doesn't want to accept it, so I can only imagine what
Mike's going through.*

She got up slowly and walked into the living room of their new home. She
sat down on the sofa and looked out the window facing the street. The cars were
going by like nothing had changed. The world was unaware that their whole life
was changed now or would be soon. Olivia sounded almost numb on the phone,
talking like it was someone else's husband who was dying. *Maybe we better go home
so I can be there for her, too. She's going to need someone when Case gets close to death.
We're all going to need each other.*

☙

The office was packed when I went in to work. It made me feel good that we
were building a solid practice and that word was getting out that I even existed

on this street. I looked around to see if I had any new patients, as there seemed to be a lot of familiar faces in the room. I moved on to check out the charts and noticed that Lucas Cunningham was coming in. y first patient was a woman named Jessica Reeves. She lived on the outskirts of town alone. Her husband had been dead for several years. I looked at her chart and noticed under "children" there was one sentence. *Still waiting to find her.* What did that mean? I took a deep breath and walked towards Jessica, and she jumped almost like I had startled her.

"Good morning, Mrs. Reeves. I hope you're not feeling too poorly this lovely morning! What can I do for you today?"

Her eyes met mine for a moment and they were dead. I hadn't seen that in a person in a long time. Cold. Hard. Almost like she was no longer there.

"I'm here because I'm gettin' weak, wakin' up clammy, heart racing. I have no appetite, and sometimes get panicky. I hate doctors but I thought I best get in here to see what's goin' on."

I studied her for a minute while I was getting my stethoscope. "Here, let me listen to your chest; take a deep breath for me." A little raspy. "Now let me look into your eyes. Any problems seeing?"

"Nope. Nothing wrong with my eyes."

"Anything happen lately to rock your world? Are you upset about anything, Mrs. Reeves?"

"Nothin' new, Doc. My life is the same today as it was yesterday. Been that way for near 'bout eighteen years now. Except for Larry dying, my life remains unchanged."

Her pulse was calming down, and her breathing was normal. Her throat was clear, and I couldn't detect anything going on. No fever. "So when did you stop feeling hungry, Mrs. Reeves?"

"'Bout eighteen years ago." She laughed a hollow kind of laugh. Kind of eerie.

"Well, I guess I'm going to have to ask what happened eighteen years ago. That seems to be a significant number for you."

Jessica sat up straight and turned to look out the window near the examining table. It was a clear sunny day and the leaves were rustling in the wind, but her expression didn't show that she even noticed how pretty the day was. She looked lost in her own gray world. She took a deep breath and looked at me with the eyes of a broken woman. Her skin was yellow and deeply lined, yet she was only fifty five years old. Her hair was unkempt and her teeth were in bad shape. I looked at her nails and they were broken off and dirty. This woman was obviously depressed about something. "Oh, there's no point in goin' over what happened that long ago, Doc. There's nothin' you can do 'bout those times. I know that. Just wanted to make sure nothin' new was goin' on in this aging body of mine. I just don't feel good, is all."

"Well, I might be able to help you more if you shared with me a little about your life. Maybe that eighteen years is important in finding out about why you feel so rotten. Why don't you talk to me about it, and give me a chance to decide if there's something I can help you with. Is that fair?"

"I reckon it's fair, all right. But it's mighty painful for me to talk about, you see. My only daughter was fifteen years old and was out visitin' a friend. Apparently she was walking back home from a girlfriend's house. She disappeared into thin air; no one seemed to notice anything. I mean, absolutely nothin'. The police asked everyone in town, and no one saw anything. Can you imagine that? A young girl picked up off the street and no one saw it? I been sick ever since. There was about six months that every person in town was searchin' for Charlotte. But when nothin' was found, not even a shoe, the case grew cold. The police had other things to do. I used to walk to the police department every day to see if they'd found anything yet. But always the same answer. Nothin'. I still think it's odd that nobody saw anything. She just flat disappeared. It's been so long now that I wouldn't even recognize my own daughter. I sure doubt she'd know me if she walked by me on the street."

I was pretty much speechless at this point. Never dreamed this would be what caused this woman to go so far down that she was near dead inside. "So your only daughter was kidnapped and you've heard nothing at all from the kidnapper? Not one word?"

"Nope. Nothing at all. I was hoping they wanted money. But it seems they just wanted her. I hope to God she's dead so that she didn't have to go through any torture or anything. I've laid awake nights worryin' about what she might have gone through. I have since let go of it, because it doesn't look like we're ever goin' to find my daughter alive."

I'd read about this type of thing happening in the paper to families and I think I remember something on on the news about a case in California where a girl was abducted and later had two children by her abductor.. But never in all my years of practice had I met someone who'd lost a child to a kidnapper. I had the weirdest feeling in the pit of my stomach, and I couldn't quit staring at Jessica Reeves.

"Jessica, I'm going to put you on a depression drug called Prozac that'll help you immensely. It's fairly safe to take and has few side effects. Are you willing to take something that might make you feel better?"

"Don't like drugs, Doc. But I might try it for a while, if you think it'll make my heart calm down. It's hard for a mother to really ever let go of a child. Like I said, I pray she's dead so that I don't have to find out she was really hurtin' all this time. Sufferin'. I just don't think I could take that, Dr. Lankford. Fifteen years old. Her whole life ahead of her." Jessica shook her head and wiped a stray tear that found its way through the map of wrinkles and down her chin.

"I don't know what that's like, Mrs. Reeves. I can't imagine the torment you've gone through worrying about her. I'm so sorry. But I'll do what I can to help you get your strength back. Now take one of these a day and let me know if you have any problems with the medicine. Anything at all, okay?" He handed her the prescription of Prozac and shook her hand.

Jessica stood up and walked to the door. She turned and looked back at me with the most pitiful eyes I'd ever seen in my entire life. They drained all of the energy out of my body, as I stood there looking back at her. "If I had a grave to go to, I would visit her every single day of my life. But all I have is her bedroom, which I haven't touched since the day she was taken from me. You know, Doc, some days I can't go in that room. I just can't make myself go in that room. It's too strong, Doc. It makes me feel like I can't breathe."

"You're doing a great job of coping with this, Mrs. Reeves. Don't be so hard on yourself. Most people couldn't handle what you've had to deal with. And it's not my place to say this, but don't ever lose hope. Hope is what keeps us all going, did you know that? We all need hope. So let me know if you feel any better on this medicine. I want to see you in six weeks to assess how you're improving. We may need to adjust the dosage from time to time."

When she left, I knew I had a lot more patients to see for the day. But my energy was lying in a puddle on the floor. I could hardly move. My mind was on Charlotte Reeves. My receptionist brought in the next patient, Jeffrey Copperfield, and I tried to snap myself back to reality. I sat Mr. Copperfield down on the table and listened to his chest. He was talking to me about his last hunting trip and my mind was straining to focus on what he was saying. I looked into his eyes for a nanosecond and I felt something inside. A strange feeling about him. "Mr. Copperfield, how are things in your world? What brought you in here today?"

"Well, Doc, just feeling old is all. It was time for my annual physical so I thought I'd just come in and let you look at me. Things are tough right now, but I'm making it okay. My kids are here visiting from college and one of them wrecked their car—"

He was rambling on and on but my mind was on this one thought that had come to me. I was sensing that Mr. Copperfield had a gambling problem. I didn't know how I knew this, but I was dead sure of it. And I could see the toll the addiction had taken on his body. All of his words were covering up what was written on his body. And I had learned that the body doesn't lie. It told me what my patient could not force himself to say.

"So how's your job going, Mr. Copperfield? What do you do for a living?"

He hesitated. "Well, I repair watches. Been at Littlefield's Jewelers for twenty-five years now." He sat there chewing on a fingernail and laughed. "The economy has gone down so much that people aren't buying watches that much. There's talk of laying off some of the employees at the store and I sure hope I'm not one of 'em. With kids in college, that could really put me in a bind."

"Things are tough, that's for sure. You able to make ends meet, Mr. Copperfield? I mean, you're not having trouble paying your bills, are you?"

"That's a strange question, Doc. You hardly know me and you're asking about my bills! No, I'm not having trouble paying bills, but I hardly think that has anything to do with my physical, now does it?"

I was checking his heart and blood pressure while we were talking. He was in good shape, but I wanted to run the usual blood tests to check cholesterol and liver enzymes. It might be a good idea to run a stress test on him with all that was going on in his life. I knew he was lying to me. "Oh, I'm just asking. Always like to keep up with my patients. You ever been to the Casinos in Raven City? I've heard a lot of people like to go there on weekends."

A bead of sweat was developing on the edge of his brow. He began to fidget a little so I knew I'd hit a nerve. "Well, I've graced the doorway of that place a few times. But I know what I'm doin', Doc. I'm not stupid. A man could lose his whole paycheck bettin' on those games. I take just what I can afford to lose and then quit before it gets out hand."

My fear was justified. "Mr. Copperfield, you don't have a gambling problem, do you? Is that why you came in today? Because your problem is causing a lot of stress in your life? I'm just guessing here, but if I were a bettin' man, I would say the stress I see in your face is all from the strain that the gambling has placed on your pocketbook. Am I readin' you right?"

Fred Copperfield was blushing and got quiet all of a sudden. I watched him, knowing he was trying to figure out how I knew all of this. "I may have a small problem, Doc, but nothing that could destroy my life. Like I said, I'm not a stupid man. I know what I'm doing. So do I need to have any tests run? I need to head back to work."

"I'm scheduling standard stress tests at the hospital for you next week. Then we'll bring you back in to go over the results. I hope things work out for you, Mr. Copperfield. But don't be too sure that others don't know about your gambling habit. It's probably pretty obvious to your family and I imagine they're worried about you. Have a good day, will you? My receptionist will call when she has scheduled your tests. I'll see you soon."

∾

The day was passing pretty quickly and I was down to my last patient. That happened to be Lucas Cunningham, and he was obviously not feeling well. Sweat was pouring down the sides of his face and he was breathing heavily. Mary Beth brought him into the examining room and he plopped down on the table. "Hey, Doc. I feel sicker than the last time I came in. Can't you give me some more medicine? I need somethin', Doc."

"Let me check your lungs, Lucas. You don't look too good to me. How's your appetite? Any fever?"

"I'm eatin' all right. And I git chills in the night. Nothin' too bad. But it's happenin' pretty regular now."

"I'd like to put you in the hospital and run some tests on you, Lucas. Your chest sounds pretty rough and I hear fluid rattling around. Let's see what's going on in your lungs."

"Oh, no. I ain't goin' into no hospital now, Doc. There's no way I'm goin' into the hospital. If'n ya can't check me out right here, then I'll just go back home. I ain't goin' into no hospital. I feel pretty bad, Doc. All's I need is some drugs to help me."

He was really bothering me. There was something about him that was just nagging at me, but I couldn't put my finger on it. I could tell he wasn't going to budge about the tests so I decided to schedule them all outpatient. "We can do it on an outpatient basis, don't worry. You have a phone number where I can reach you?"

"I'll call ya, Doc. I don't give out my number to anybody. When you want me to call? Later today?"

"Yes, that'll be fine, Lucas. Call before five o'clock and Mary Beth will tell you when your tests are scheduled. We really need to get a handle on what's going on inside that chest of yours before this gets out of hand. I'm going to have some blood work done to see what else might be going on. You're a pretty sick man, you know?"

"I been sicker than this before, Doc."

"Say, Lucas. Where did you say you lived? What street was that?"

"Elmore Street. Why do you need to know that, Doc?"

"Just wondering. I just met someone who lives on that street. A Mr. Peter Darby. He's a retired teacher who taught at Crosgrove High. You know him?"

"No, never heard of him. I'm pretty much a recluse. Don't like people around. I'll call ya later for the test schedule. I'm not too happy about gettin' this done. I think I just need another round of meds."

"We'll see, Lucas. Stay in touch with me. We shouldn't let this go on or you'll end up in a place worse than a hospital, you hear, Lucas?"

I was talking to the air. Lucas was already walking out of the office door. He didn't look like he had bathed since the last time I saw him. It was time to head home and I was more than ready to see Jill and have dinner with Anna Grace and Thomas. Interesting group of patients, and my mind was still settling on Jessica Reeves. I knew better than to get too attached to patients and their stories, but this one was going to be a tough one to let go.

CHAPTER 12

The restaurant was packed and the band was playing '80s music that made me want to dance. I grabbed Jill's arm and tried to swing her around, but she was embarrassed and pulled me towards the table the waiter was preparing for us. I laughed when I saw Anna Grace roll her eyes. She never could stand to see her parents being playful or dancing. I guess we embarrassed her; but it sure was fun.

"So, Anna, my dear. How is pregnancy sitting with you?

"Dad, I love being pregnant. Even though I was sick at the beginning, things have settled down and now I can enjoy feeling the life within me. I don't know why any woman wouldn't want to have a baby!"

"Thomas, you getting nervous? Your life is about to change big time!"

They looked at each other and smiled. Thomas said, "Anna, you tell your dad."

Anna smiled at both of us. "Dad, all our lives are going to change big time. We're having twins! My doctor took another ultrasound and there are two babies in there. Is that unreal? A girl and a boy! The doctor thought I was only having one baby, but today in the ultrasound he saw two. Can you imagine picking names for two? Oh my gosh! We're going crazy at night in bed, sitting there going over names. It's a riot!"

"What? Twins? Are you joking? Jill, did you know this?" I looked at Jill and her face said everything. I was the blind man in the group. "So when were you going to let me in on this news? Huh?" I got up and hugged Anna and shook Thomas's hand. "You guys are going to love this. I'm so happy for you! Good thing Jill is here because you're going to need all the help you can get, Anna."

After dinner Jill and I were driving home, enjoying the evening. "This sure has been an adventure, Jill. Can you believe how things have played out? The practice is building, Anna and Thomas are going to be proud parents of two children, and we're slowly getting to know people in town. How do you feel about being here now?"

"Mike, I heard from Olivia today—the news is not good so I do have a few mixed feelings about moving—but I do love this town. The people seem warm and friendly, and Anna absolutely loves being here. My life certainly has gotten busier helping her get the nursery ready and buying baby clothes. Now with two babies coming, we're going to have to add to the nursery and the clothes too! In a way, they're having their family all at once. I still have to pinch myself about it being twins."

"I never dreamed she would have twins. Are their twins in your family? I don't think there are in mine."

"I did have twin cousins. So somewhere down the line there were twins."

"So, honey, what did Olivia tell you today—"

My cell phone rang. "Hello?"

There was a pause on the other end, and then someone spoke. The voice was so soft I could hardly hear it. I pulled over on the side of the road, thinking it was a patient calling. "Hello? This is Dr. Lankford. Can I help you?"

"Mike. This is Case." The voice died off. I froze.

"Case? Case! Talk to me! Are you okay?"

"Mike. I called to say goodbye. I'm not going to make it much longer. Things are pretty bad here. I don't want to drag you down with the details, buddy, but I promised you I'd call you when things got worse. Well, they couldn't get much worse."

I felt like I was going to lose my supper. I could barely hear him. "I'm coming over, Case. Jill and I will pack right now and head back to St. Martin. I want to be there, Case."

"No, Mike. Now don't go doing that. You won't make it in time. Trust me. I can barely talk now—and I just wanted to tell you I love you, Mike. . . .Please don't drive here. I'll get Olivia to call as soon as it happens so that you can be here for her. She's the one who will need you, Mike, not me. I'm too far gone. . . . My oxygen level is so low now that I'm about to go into coma. I love you, Mike. Remember that. I'll take a part of you with me, man. This is tougher—that I thought it would be—"

What could I say? "Case, I wish there was more time to talk about things. This is our worst nightmare and I can't be there with you. I love you, Case. Know one day I'll see you again. It'll seem like a moment has passed and I'll be right there with you. I hate this, man. I don't know what to say to you." My eyes filled with water.

"One more thing, Mike." His voice was so faint I could barely hear it. "Promise . . . you'll look out for Olivia for me. . . . Will you?"

"Of course I will. We'll stay in touch with her and maybe we'll bring her back here for a bit. Case. I love you—I'm going to miss you. You have no idea. Case—wait."

"Bye, Mike. Take. good care . . . of . . . Olivia. I'm gone Mike . . . goodbye . . ."

I turned off the car and sat there looking out the window. Tears were streaming down my face and I felt like I couldn't breathe. I wanted to run. I got out of the car and started running. I could hear Jill screaming at me as I ran farther away, but I just had to run. My best friend was gone. Nothing would ever be the same. I finally stopped running and stood there out of breath. Jill pulled the car up behind me and got out. "Mike, what in the world are you doing? What did he say?"

I was breathing so fast I could hardly answer. "Case is gone, Jill. He called to tell me goodbye. He was losing oxygen to his brain. He was slipping into coma. I can't accept this. I don't want to believe this is the end. It wasn't supposed to be this way, Jill. He was supposed to be around and grow old with us. Why would God take him so early? I'm a doctor and I have no answers. None." I didn't think I'd ever felt so hopeless in my entire life.

"I know this is going to be hard for you, Mike. He was your best friend. You loved him more than anyone in the world. But somehow you'll work through this. I'll help you, honey. We'll make it through this, I promise."

The words she said were like molasses moving sluggishly through the air. Somehow my brain wouldn't receive what she was saying. In fact, my brain was on hold. I didn't want to hear, because my friend was dying or already dead. I wanted to be with him. I could understand two people wanting to die at the same time. I could even understand suicide at that moment in time. I didn't care about anything else but being with Case, whatever that took. But in my heart I knew I couldn't get to him. Somehow the thought was taking root in my mind like a small stream of water that breaks through a dam and allows the whole river to burst through. I knew that I would have to learn to live without my friend. Feelings came rushing in and I cried hard for the longest time. I got into the car and let Jill drive us home. She didn't say a word, because she knew I wouldn't be able to hear it. I loved her for allowing me to grieve for my friend.

In that moment when I let go, I saw the past right in front of my eyes. All the times of sneaking out and going to the corner pool hall. The times we skipped school and went fishing. Or he went fishing; I sat on the bank watching and reading a book. The time we built a fort in the snow and made snow cream. How he was there for me when I lost Mava. How I was there for him when his father got sick. I realized at that moment that I still had Case with me in my memories. And for that moment, they would have to be enough. I got out of the car and went into the house and went straight to my desk. There on the top of my desk near the clock was a photo of me and Case. We were standing there with a glass of wine, smiling, being silly. He had his hat pulled down over one eye trying to look debonair. I whispered into the air, "Goodbye, my friend. I won't forget you."

I put the photo back in its special place on my desk and walked out of the office and turned out the light. Jill and I walked up the stairs and put our pajamas on and climbed into bed. This was a first for me. The first night without Case. I sure hoped it got easier, because the lump in my throat was the size of a football.

◦⁀◦

My feet felt like lead as I walked into the church with Jill and sat next to Olivia on the front pew. I was sweating and chilled at the same time and my neck was stiff from the tension of losing my best friend. The church was full of many of our patients and quite a few people from around St. Martins. People were whispering and dabbing their eyes; I wasn't going to even think about turning my head to look at anyone. It was all I could do to hold it together and I was beginning to wonder if I was going to be able to stand up and talk about Case to everyone. Jill had her arm through mine for support, and for the second time since he died, it was sinking in that I no longer had my friend. Not ever again. I felt a lump in my throat and coughed. Jill squeezed my hand and leaned over to kiss my shoulder. I couldn't feel it, but I did appreciate her caring. She knew I was pretty much worthless at this point.

Matt Hinson, the preacher, walked up to the podium and cleared his throat. He was having about as much trouble as I was dealing with Case's death. We were all close to Matt, so I knew he had to be dreading this funeral. He spoke quietly and looked around the room, saying a lot of wonderful things about Case. The neat thing was that all of them were true. A young girl came up and sang a beautiful song and I lost myself in it a few times.

Suddenly the church got quiet and I realized that it was my turn to head to the podium. My knees were weak and I felt shaky, but I had to do this for Case. I'd written down a few lines but my eyes didn't seem to want to focus on the words. I looked around the room and said a silent prayer, hoping I could get through this speech without breaking down. I decided to think of Olivia and that helped me have the strength and find the words.

"I'm going to be honest with you this afternoon. I don't have the ability on my own to stand here and talk to you about my best friend Case. It's hitting me pretty hard standing in this church looking out at all of you, that one of the best human beings we've ever known has left us. And I'm dealing with mixed emotions about my own decision to move away from St. Martins when I might have been able to be around for Case while he was suffering if I'd stayed a little longer. But God in his mercy probably spared me the sight of that great man going down. Since I lived most of my life with Case, I feel I knew him better than anyone. We shared almost everything together and I loved him like a brother.

"When I think back to when we were kids, I remember we were taught to play fair, play fast, and to run the race to win. Well, that is exactly how Case lived out his life. I'm certain Olivia would agree that he was a great husband, but first and foremost he was a doctor. There wasn't a day that went by that he didn't give one hundred percent to his patients. I think I learned more from him than anyone in my life, and I tell you right now, there's a huge hole in my life with him being gone. His smile and great laugh kept me going for days and I have some great memories to carry me through the rest of my life.

"On a lighter note, Case spent a lot of years trying to teach me to fly-fish, but I just didn't have it. He would get so frustrated that he'd snatch the rod away from me to show me how to do it right. I know he's sitting up there in heaven now, rolling his eyes at me for bringing that up, but I couldn't pass up the chance.

"In my practice now in Crosgrove I'll carry with me what I've learned from Case, and hopefully pass on to the people I meet every day the grace that was given me by Case. I thank God for his friendship and love in my life, as I know many of you do. Let's support Olivia and help her through these days of grieving. I love you all and I just wish I could have seen you under different circumstances."

The rest of the service was a blur as we went through the motions of burying Case. Olivia was amazing and her strength held us all up. Jill and I left town after begging Olivia to go back with us. She was adamant about staying in her house, wanting to cope with the loss on her own. Frankly, I couldn't get out of town fast enough because I needed time alone to settle things in my own mind. There were just too many people in St. Martins who knew Case and wanted to talk to me about him. It was just too soon for me, and I think Jill knew it without my saying a word. The trip home was pretty quiet, but we were both just fine with that. Again, I thanked God for a wife who got me, because if there was a time that I needed her to get me, it was now.

CHAPTER 13

My first visit with Peter Darby was set for Friday afternoon at three. I was looking forward to it and couldn't wait to hear what he had to say. For such a small man he had the character of a giant and had affected so many students; I just knew he had some stories to tell about Crosgrove. I'd done my homework and read all I could get my hands on about Crosgrove High and also about Peter. There was more history about him than I could read. He had only touched on a small amount of his life when he shared that night with the seniors and faculty.

Mr. Darby had been a busy man in his younger days! He'd started a Boys Club while at Crosgrove, and at first the town was not behind it. But his theory was that if he could give the kids a place to go after school, he could find a way to turn their lives around and give them more direction. After the first year, half the kids in the school under the age of fifteen were involved in the club. Once in the club, students were taught to work in the community to give back. They did yard work for those who were handicapped. They painted houses, worked in gardens, and cleaned up the school grounds. Once the town saw what was happening, they got behind the Boys Club and supported it one hundred percent. That wasn't all. He'd also started a band at Crosgrove and talked the school board into hiring a band director. Now Crosgrove High had the best band in a three state area. And it wasn't near as large a school as its competitors.

I discovered that Peter was a visionary in his own right. He knew there were many areas that were lacking where the youth were concerned. So he tried to develop activities that would strengthen them and show them a better way to live. Several of the children came from rough neighborhoods and poverty. He knew better than anyone that the only way out of poverty was education and having a direction. He tried to involve other teachers so that it was a team effort. He gained their respect because of his background and what he'd done with his own life. Mr. Darby came from nothing and without encouragement from anyone, he became the best teacher for miles around. He was voted teacher of the year almost every year he taught. But what spoke louder than all the accolades was how the kids talked about Mr. Darby as their teacher and friend. You could stop any child on the street and they knew Mr. Darby. They'd either been directly affected by him or knew someone who was. It was amazing, and I couldn't wait to spend an hour with this gentleman and pick his brain for as long as he would allow it. I had a feeling I would get some resistance, but I had the patience of Job.

∽

Lucas's tests were back from the lab and things were close to getting out of hand. I needed to get him on some pretty strong drugs to keep him out of the hospital. I knew I had a fight on my hands, but it pretty much boiled down to whether he wanted to live or not. Mary Beth set up an appointment for today at two o'clock. I was ready for the fight.

My last patient before lunch was Bobby Dunn. He was a new patient and Mary Beth had him fill out forms before he came into the exam room. I picked up his chart and was about to open it when he walked into the room.

"Hey, Doc! Bobby Dunn here. Couldn't wait to come in and meet the new doctor in town. So how's it going for you? You been busy? I heard you moved here from St. Martin. What made you come here? Do you have family here or somethin'? I mean, why else would you move to Crosgrove, unless you knew someone here?" His head fell back and he laughed loudly. So I used the moment to jump into the conversation.

"Good morning, Mr. Dunn. How are we feeling today? And what brings you here to see me?"

He stopped laughing long enough to hear the last part of my sentence. "Well, Doc, it was time for me to find a new doctor, and I decided that I might as well try the new one in town. Been here so long that I've been to all the other doctors at one time or another. So now it's your turn to see if you can fix me up."

"Let's check out your history, Mr. Dunn. It says here that you've had one heart attack, your cholesterol is off the chart, you have hypertension, and you're overweight. You smoke two packs a day, and you consume alcohol. I would say you're a walking time bomb, don't you agree?"

Bobby sat there scratching his head. "Uh, yeah, yeah. All that stuff is true. But hey, Doc, we only live once, and I'm all about living in the moment. We are goin' to die of something, aren't we?"

I turned and smiled at Bobby. "Oh yes, we're going to die all right. But you're going at the speed of light, my man. Why are you in such a hurry to die?"

"Well, uh, I'm not exactly in a hurry, Doc. But I do like to enjoy life, ya know?"

"I would suggest, without my knowing anything else about you, Bobby, that you try to slow this down just a smidge. You're playing Russian roulette here. You're fifty-five years old; just the age when things start happening in your body. All the years you've abused your body accumulate damage that will come to a head at some point. You can live this way only so long and then you're going to pay some huge consequences. Is that what you want? Because you're heading that direction like a freight train running wild on a track with no brakes."

"Gosh, Doc. When you put it that way, it doesn't sound too good. I know I need to back off a little. Other doctors have told me I need to slow it down. But it's hard to change my ways."

"I'm going to run a lot of tests on you to see where you are today with your cholesterol and blood pressure, and also order you a stress test. I'm concerned because you've already had one heart attack and even with that behind you, you haven't changed the way you live. Mr. Dunn, you're looking another heart attack right in the face, do you understand that?"

Bobby looked down at his feet and shook his head. "I guess I do. My wife has been nagging me for years to slow it down. I just couldn't do it. But when you put it this way, maybe I do need to change. What do I need to do?"

I cracked a smile. "For one thing, get rid of those cigarettes in your pocket. Just think, your car won't have white ashes all over the dash. Slow down the drinking, and lose about thirty pounds. That would go a long way in lengthening your life. Now let's get those tests set up. We can run the blood test here, but the stress test will be scheduled at the hospital. Listen, Bobby. I'm not joking about another heart attack. Just looking at you right now, I'd say it could happen anytime."

"I hear you loud and clear. When do you want me back here?"

"I should get those results by Monday. So make your appointment with Mary Beth for Monday afternoon. And I want to hear that you're on your way to quitting smoking, okay?"

Bobby didn't look too happy. "Okay, Doc. I'll see what I can do. Boy, you run a tight ship, don't you?"

"If I'm going to be your doctor, it's my responsibility to get you in the best shape possible. And I don't want you to ruin my record!"

Bobby grinned weakly. I called my new nurse, Louise, in to draw blood. His other tests would have to be done at the hospital after a fast. When I walked out of my office I had Mary Beth phone the hospital to schedule the stress test with one of the best heart men in Crosgrove, Tom Thornton. If Bobby thought I was tough, wait until he meets Tom—the thought made me chuckle a little. That man could cut through steel with his eyes.

⁊

Lucas was dreading his appointment with Dr. Lankford. He really hoped he'd be feeling much better so he didn't have to show up for this visit. In reality, he was much worse. His chills were now going on in the evening and all through the night. He had no appetite at all, and he'd lost a lot of weight. His eyes were sunken in, and he felt like he was going to die. He barely had time to fix food for Charlotte, and he was worried that she would try to come upstairs while he was sleeping in his chair. He was so weak he would've had a hard time stopping her without shooting her. He'd grown attached to having her around and that wasn't the way he wanted things to end. She was pretty pale and sickly herself. Maybe he could get some meds for her. But that would be difficult and he didn't want to send up any red flags. All these years no one had ever questioned him. Why start something now?

"Good morning, Lucas. Have a seat. How are things with you now that you've been on medication for a while?"

"Not too good, Dr. Lankford. I feel pretty rotten. I think I'm worse."

"Let's take your temperature and blood pressure. You look weak and you've lost weight."

I could tell Lucas was beginning to worry about his health. He was very pale and his lungs were full of fluid. I really wanted him in the hospital, but I knew the answer he'd give me. I couldn't force him to go, but that's where he would get the best care and also be put on oxygen. His oxygen level in his blood was ninety-six percent, but today it had dropped to ninety percent.

"Lucas, you need hospital care. I would like to suggest that we put you in for a week and see if that helps get this under control. Pneumonia is a tough thing to recover from without constant medical help. And you need to be put on oxygen for a while. What do you say?"

"No way. I'm not goin' to no hospital. I knew I shouldn't come in today. I knew you'd try to get me to go to that darn place again. Well, I'd rather die than go to the hospital."

"Okay, okay. Settle down, Lucas. We can try a few more drugs to see if it will knock this thing out. But I can't promise you anything. Did you take the whole prescription?"

"Took it all. You got to give me somethin' to make me feel better. I'm feeling pretty rotten here, Doc."

"I'm writing you several prescriptions, Lucas and giving you a nebulizer that you can use at your house. This should make your breathing better, since you won't let me put you in the hospital. I want you to take these drugs like I prescribe them, and don't drink while taking them. Can I count on you doing that?"

"I'll take the drugs, Doc. Can I go now?"

"Lucas, I'd like to make a house call and check in on you. If you won't go to the hospital, then you have to let me call on you at home. That's the only way I'm going to continue treating you. I can't be responsible for your health if you won't allow me to treat you the way you need to be treated to get well. That's fair, isn't it?"

"Yeah, yeah. I hear ya. I'll call and tell you when you can come. But don't' count on it bein' soon. Can I go? I have things to do."

"Go ahead, Lucas. But I'm noting on your chart that you are refusing my suggestion to go to the hospital. You call my office if you get worse. Then we can make a decision on what to do. You may have no choice but to check in to the hospital, Lucas. If you have difficulty breathing, call 911. Don't play around with this, Lucas. It's pretty serious, okay?"

Lucas looked down and shook his head. *How in the world did I get so sick? I can't leave the house for any reason, or Charlotte would not be able to eat. She would either die, or she'd find a way out of the house. I don't like either choice.* He walked out of the office with his head down, breathing slowly. This wasn't how things were supposed to turn out. All he wanted was a family. Someone around who loved him back. But Charlotte hardly ever spoke to him. He knew she hated him, but hate was better than nothing at all. And that was what he had all his life. Nothing.

∽

I was done for the day. Fried. Lucas for some reason drained me of every speck of energy. Just standing near him did me in. I was ready to see Peter Darby; my first visit with the man. In times like this that I really missed Case. I could still feel him around me, smiling, even laughing at me. I continued having issues with why he left so early. One of the best times of our lives and he was gone, and all those things that we shared had become almost sacred to me. Even though he was gone, it was still really new to me that he was gone for good, and I knew I'd never let go of him completely. I would try as long as I could to have a piece of him with me everywhere I went in life. And I knew for a fact that he took a part of me with him beyond the grave.

CHAPTER 14

Walking up the path to Peter's door, my heart was pounding in my chest. I wasn't sure why, but it must have been because I felt I was about to be in the presence of someone very unique. I stepped up to the door and knocked, knowing he was on the other side waiting for me.

"Come on in, Doctor. I was just walkin' to the kitchen to get us somethin' to drink. You okay with iced tea? Or would you rather have coffee?"

"Tea's great with me, Peter. Hey, it's a nice afternoon. What's say we sit out here on your porch?"

"You're my kind of man. Be right with you."

I wanted to be relaxed with Peter, and I wanted him to be able to open up to me. This was an important day and I might not get this opportunity again. We don't get this chance but maybe once in a lifetime to sit and talk to someone the caliber of Peter Darby. I picked the chair on the outside edge near the railing and propped my feet up. This was going to be a great afternoon.

"I see you made yourself comfortable. You were right. It's perfect out here. So how you been, Doc? Gettin' plenty of patients?"

"Yeah, I'm seein' my share of people. It takes time to build up a practice, but I'm gettin' my share. How are you feelin'? That's one reason I came by today."

"I'm gettin' old, Doc. So all the things I'm feelin' sort of go along with gettin' old. I have a bad back, I need a cane to keep my balance, I'm not hearin' too well, and my appetite isn't what it should be. You want to know anything else?" He laughed a great deep laugh and sat back in his chair.

I chuckled and looked over at him sitting in the chair. His hair was white and he had an old hat on that he pulled down on one side. His clothes were old and you'd think he didn't have a dime to his name. You would also surmise that he was an uneducated man at first glance. But you'd be wrong. Nothing could be farther from the truth.

"I want to check you out today to make sure everything]s okay. But I really want to hear about your life. I hope you feel comfortable in sharin' some things with me; I feel so fortunate to be able to sit here with you so I can learn more about your life."

"My pleasure. It's not every day that a doctor wants to sit on your porch and shoot the breeze, ya know? So, what's on your mind, Doc? What do you want to know about me?"

"I have millions of questions, but really I want to know about how you grew up. Your speech the other night really piqued my curiosity about you. How long have you lived in this house?"

"I moved into this neighborhood about thirty years ago. Back then it looked a lot better than it does today. People cared about how their yards looked and took care of things. I remember washin' cars for some quick money. Now, as you can see, people aren't taking care of their cars anymore. This neighborhood was one of the better ones, and there were kids everywhere. Do you see any now? Nope. Too rough around here. But I kept on here because it was the easiest thing to do. Never wanted a big house and this one fits me just fine."

"Were you ever married, Peter? Or in love?"

"The question of the century, huh, Doc? Everyone always wanted to know if I had a girlfriend. I got so tired of hearin' that question I thought I would puke. But now I'm so old it doesn't bother me anymore." He laughed again and I was liking Peter Darby more and more. "I fell in love when I was about twenty-eight years old. I was out of college and already had a teaching job at Crosgrove. She taught first grade at the elementary school down the street. She was young, pretty, and I couldn't talk when I was around her. So ya know she had to look good." He gave me a wink.

"So did you guys date? Or were you afraid to ask her out?"

He looked at me and smiled. "Oh, we dated all right. I fell head over heels in love with this girl. She really was the only girl I ever loved. A train ran smack into her car one night on her way home from work. I was right behind her, maybe a block back, and saw the train coming. I didn't realize she was so close to the tracks, but when the train hit, I got out of my car and went runnin' to see who it was. When I saw her car sittin' there all crashed to pieces, I fell to my knees. I don't remember much after that. I think I've blocked it out of my mind. But to answer your question, yes, I've been in love. I guess I never got over her. I dated some other girls but no one measured up."

"That's a pretty sad story. I have a hard time believin' you couldn't find another woman to spend your life with. You seem like such a nice guy."

"Oh, lots of women came knockin' on my door, Doc. But I guess I got caught up in my teaching and spent so much time with the kids that I really didn't have the time to date. I really locked in to the dream I had when I was young; that I wanted to make a difference in the kids around me. I wanted them to have a better life than I did. I pretty much lived for those kids, ya know?"

"I could tell that the other night. The whole room stood up when you were through with your talk. Pretty powerful moment. So if love wasn't on your agenda as you were growing up, what was on your agenda? Just teaching and affecting the kids in a good way?"

"I lived a rough life in my childhood. I lived alone and did everything I wanted to do. I answered to nobody. It felt good in a way, and I kinda got used to being alone. It's not a good thing because you get very selfish in your thinkin'. But I developed a survival instinct and carry it with me even today. Part of that plan was that you don't ever depend on anyone else. Just yourself. That way you're never disappointed. I learned the hard way that I could make anything happen if I wanted it bad enough. But I had to do it myself. I couldn't wait for someone else to do it for me or make it happen."

"I wish I'd learned that as a young boy. I dreamed of doing many things, but they never developed into reality. I think many people live their lives that way, don't you?"

"Heck, I believe most of the world lives that way. That's why the world is in such a mess. But don't get me started on that. So what else do you want to know, Doc?"

"Well how did you make it when your parents died? That had to be tough on you as a young kid."

"It was near impossible to get by back then. Things were tough. No one had any money and I was underneath the steps of poverty. But, ya know, when you don't have anything, ya don't have to have much money. All I needed was food and a way to plant crops. I discovered on my own the value of money and how to get it. But education was the biggest goal and the biggest challenge for me. I had to find a way to get myself in school and not just be average. I had to excel. I needed a scholarship if I wanted to go to college, and that was one goal I had to meet to reach my other goals. Like teaching. I guess I was a goal setter way back then. I was lonely, buddy. Oh yeah, I was lonelier than a stray cat." He paused and plucked a piece of straw from the broom standing in the corner of the porch and stuck it in his mouth. He sat back and looked off in the distance. I knew he was lost in his memories.

"I can't imagine being so young and not having anyone around to talk to. Or yell at you!"

"I didn't know a soul could get that lonely, but there was no one around for miles. I talked to God so much He turned off his hearing aid. I guarantee you He got sick of me whinin'. But I didn't know what else to do. I talked to Him when I was plowin' the fields and the sun was near set on the horizon. I talked to Him when the crops weren't gettin' enough rain; I yelled at Him when we got too much rain. I'm sure He doesn't like me much anymore, because I wore Him plumb out when I was young. But you know what, Doc? I think it helped some of the time. I think He actually heard me gripin' or cryin' and gave me a break. Or it sure seemed like it."

"I've been there before myself. I'm sure He did step in for you some of the time, Peter. He does that for all of us. So were you ever afraid of being alone?"

"Nope. After my parents died, I didn't have much to be afraid of. I just set my mind on what I had to do every day and got busy doin' it. I did have rats in the house and there were other animals outside that I had to keep an eye on. They would eat the crops and that meant I didn't eat. Some nights I sat outside with a gun just waitin' for them to show up."

"Sounds barbaric in a way, because in the city life was going on as usual. You were livin' pretty stripped down in the woods, Peter. But look where you ended up? No one would've ever believed you would end up being a highly respected teacher. You should be proud of yourself. You've achieved more in your life than most people, and yet you're so humble. That's the word I would use to describe you—'humble.'"

"I don't know about being humble, man. I'm not sure I really know what that word entails. But I learned that pride only got you in trouble. So I ran from anything that deterred me from reachin' my goals. You know, Doc, I was tempted often to steal. I needed food so many times, and I would walk right by the fruit stand close to town and never take one single piece of fruit. I was starvin' but I was determined not to steal my way up the ladder. I said I didn't have a fear, but I lied. I feared getting caught more than anything. No one really knew I lived alone as a young kid. And if I was found out, they would've tried to put me in a foster home or somethin' worse. So I remained invisible as long as I could so that nothin' would mess up my way of living." Peter yawned and I could tell he was ready for an afternoon nap.

"Well, I sure have enjoyed our talk, Peter. Let me listen to your chest and check you out for a moment." Surprisingly, he seemed in pretty good health.

"You won't find anything wrong with me, Doc. I'm too stubborn to be sick. I'm just flat out old. That's all that's wrong with me now." He was about right. But I did have another question I wanted to ask him before I left.

"Peter, do you know any of your neighbors here anymore? I mean, do you get out any and meet your neighbors on this street?"

"I don't get out much, Doc. But every day I do walk down the street and back. I know who lives in the houses, but I don't know the people at all. I guess you might consider me a recluse at this point, because I just feel I don't need people anymore. Why do you ask?"

"Oh, no real reason. I have a client that lives on your street. Just thought you might know who he is."

"Who is this guy, anyway?"

"Lucas Cunningham." I watched his face closely to see if I saw any recognition at all. He looked away and then back at me. His face had changed.

"I think I know who that is. He lives down the street in that house where the door is practically hanging off the hinges. When I walk by that house, sometimes he's looking out the window. His last name is on the mailbox. I get kind of uneasy feelings when I pass his house, but I don't have any reasons to give you as to why I feel that way."

"Well, he drains me of my energy every time he comes in for a checkup. I know nothing about him, except that he doesn't really want to leave his house. Just thought I would ask you if you knew him, is all." I stood up and walked to the steps. "Peter, I have enjoyed this visit immensely. Thanks so much for allowing me to come by. You have no idea what this meant to me today. I hope you'll allow me to return soon?"

"You don't have to hurry off, Doc. I've enjoyed myself more talkin' to you than I have anyone in a long time. Sorry if I talked too much. I get started on my past and sometimes I don't know when to shut up. Don't really have too many people come around that really care, I guess."

"Well, after that speech the other night, I'm sure you'll be getting some phone calls. You really touched a lot of people. I'll stop by again soon to see you. Take care, and if you need anything, Peter, give me a call. Not just sayin' that to be nice. Okay?"

"Means a lot. Don't wait too long. Just give me a heads up so I can have the tea made."

He smiled a weary smile and headed into his house. The porch was pretty run down and I made a mental note to try to bring some nails and a hammer to tighten the boards back down. That was as much for my safety as his. . .

I walked to my car thinking about the afternoon and all the words that Peter had said. He was quite a unique human being. Someone I was honored to know. This was one man I wouldn't mind helping; maybe I could make a small difference in his otherwise solitary life. That would make it all worthwhile.

CHAPTER 15

Thomas stood in the nursery shaking his head. I barely make enough money for one baby, and now we're having our whole family all at once. My company is downsizing because of the economy, and I'm worried sick I may be the next cut. I can't let on to Anna Grace that I'm worried. Not now. She needs to be able to enjoy this pregnancy, and I would love that more than anything in the world. We've talked about this for years. I may just have to take on a second job; a lot of men do that. I never thought I would be facing such a financial strain at this point in my life. It'll either make me or break me. Maybe Dad has some thoughts on the situation. I'll call him tonight . . .

∽

The nursery was almost finished. Two beds, two diaper pails, two of everything. One bed was done in blue and white and the other in pink and white. One had bows and lace and the other one had animals. The only thing lacking were the names over the beds, and that was the debate of the century. Anna Grace was sitting in the living room going through books and books on names. It had gotten way too complicated. She and Thomas nearly divorced last night arguing over names. *Why did it have to be so hard?* She hated all the names he picked, and he laughed at all the names she chose. It was ridiculous for two people who had gotten along so well until these two babies popped up. With only two months to go, Anna knew they had to get their act together and choose the names.

The phone rang and it was Jill. "Hello, honey. You feeling okay this morning?"

"Yeah, Mom. I'm okay, I guess. Really stressing over this name issue. Thomas is being stubborn and I just flat hate the names he comes up with. How will we ever settle on two names we both can live with?"

Jill laughed. "I remember the fights we had about naming you. It was a miracle we lived through them! Oh, baby. You'll pick names you can live with that the children won't hate you for! Just relax and be flexible. Listen, your father and I are heading back to St. Martin for the weekend to visit Olivia. It will be extremely hard on your father, but it's time we returned and spent some time with her to make sure she's all right. Michael promised Case that he would take care of her. The finances and real estate, you know? I think she has an appointment with a lawyer on Monday, so Michael may want to hang around and go with her to that meeting. He just has to know she's okay, and that things are manageable for her."

"How's she holding up, Mom?"

"I think she's done very well, actually. But there's a huge hole in her life. She loved Case since high school and never dreamed she would have to adjust to life without him at this age. But we just don't know, do we?"

"It doesn't seem like we can count on anything in life staying the same, Mom."

"That's pretty much how it is, honey. But don't sound so glum! Once you get those names picked out, you'll feel much better. I'll call you when we're headed home."

෩

I am sitting on the porch looking out at all the trees swaying in the gentle breeze. Summer used to be my favorite time of year when I was a kid. As I've gotten older it's become harder to take the heat, much as I hate to admit it. But that isn't what is bothering me on such a beautiful day. I'm having trouble even wanting to go to St. Martin in the morning. I need to go; I promised Case I would see to Olivia. But this would be the first time that I faced St. Martin without my best friend. I fear I'll see him everywhere I go, all the places we went together. I'm still adjusting to not having him in my life. I need to be a man about it; I know he would do it for me.

This has been a very busy year, setting up a new practice, buying a new home. Anna and Thomas expecting two children. When I think of all the patients I've seen, and the things I've heard in the exam room, it's overwhelming to think that things are moving in an entirely new direction as far as my practice is concerned . . . I'm accustomed to hearing about past illnesses and some marital issues. But lately people have been confiding in me their personal failures, their intimate marriage problems, even going so far as to ask me to speak to their wife or husband about problems they are dealing with. No matter how many times I state that I'm not a marriage counselor, more and more people want counsel. Secrets. Family secrets that have never been let out of the box, are being spoken quietly in my exam room. I'm profoundly aware of the difficulty with which they let these filthy little secrets out of the dusty box they've placed way back in their hearts. I don't take it lightly that they find solace in talking with me. But I wonder at times how I'll come up with a solution that's right for their life. I already have their health in my hands; now I'm dealing with their minds. Their hearts. The very core of their being. I'm learning to weigh my words and say as few as possible. I'm listening more than anything else.

I'm personally amazed at the coping skills a human being can develop when they are put through a certain level of stress. Some of these people have kept secrets and tolerated inhumane behavior all their lives. It has become their normal. Their minds have become twisted and their ability to process truth and a better way to live doesn't exist. I can tell when I give them a solution, a way out…they aren't so eager to grab it and run. For the sickness they have lived in for so long has become a safety net in a way. It has kept them from having to do anything for so long, that they are incapable of moving forward. They are caught in a quicksand that is slowly eating them alive.

I struggle with how much to get involved; when to talk to the police about something, and when to leave well enough alone. The one story that haunts me in the early hours of the morning when I'm sitting at my desk going over medical journals is that of Jessica Reeves and her missing daughter. For some reason that has stuck in my craw and I can't seem to dismiss it. I'm not personally responsible for anything to do with Jessica Reeves except her health, but I can't get the look on that woman's face out of my mind. I have a daughter. I can't wrap my mind around the thought of someone kidnapping her when she was fifteen and not ever finding her. Not ever hearing from the kidnapper. Something just doesn't add up and I don't know why I can't stop thinking about her. After all these years the case has grown cold... there has been no trace of her in all these years. I hate to think it but the girl is probably dead by now or across the country where no one will ever find her. There are hundreds of these cases in police files, I'm certain. They just get stored away and forgotten like the child who was taken.

With Case gone out of my life, my determination is even stronger to develop a way to help more people in my medical practice. Already I'm seeing a change but I want more. I guess if my eyes are open, I'll see the way. It has become more difficult over the years to diagnose the illness and prescribe the right mediations. The side effects are often worse than the disease, and somehow I'm supposed to issue these prescriptions without a thought about what effect they can have on the patient. The pills I prescribe, I wouldn't want to take myself. That says something; and that alone is almost enough to make me look for a new career. However, the drive to help people get well is stronger than ever. It is a fight I'll have as long as I stay in practice. The good must outweigh the bad, or there is no point.

Things have turned a corner at the office, so much so that I had to hire a nurse and even then work piles up. It might be time to add another physician in the office even though I never thought I'd work with anyone else but Case. I just may need to make a few friends and put some feelers out for a partner in crime. Jill has settled in and made friends, gotten involved on a few committees, and really enjoys being closer to Anna. I'm networking and talking to new friends I've made, learning more and more about the town and how it's run. Met a police officer the other night at a gathering at the church, and he seemed like a nice guy. I think I'll ask him about the Charlotte Reeves case and see what he has to say. But I'm not saying a word to Jill about it; she would frown on my getting so involved in a patient's life. I have to follow my heart; and I'm too stubborn to let a frown from my wife keep me from checking into this case. She'll get over it, but Jessica Reeves never will. That's enough for me to continue my interest in this case.

CHAPTER 16

The trip to St. Martin was like being in a time capsule. It hadn't been that long ago, but so much had changed in my life that I felt like I didn't belong in St. Martin anymore. For one thing, I'd lost my partner, my best friend, and half my heart. We don't realize how much someone means to us until they are gone. Oh we think we know, but we have no idea. I feel a vacancy in my life, a hole that cannot be filled no matter how much work I do, how late I stay up at night pouring over medical journals, or how many people I talk to. It is a rare thing to have such a friend, and I will cherish it until I die. But I don't like going through it one bit. In fact, I feel angry inside about losing Case. And now we're pulling into St. Martin to visit Olivia and I have no idea what in the heck I'm going to say to her. A part of me doesn't want to even look into her eyes, for I know sure as shootin' I'll see Case in them. And a lot of pain. We all are sorting through this as best we can, but it's harder than I ever thought it would be to let go of someone you love so much. It makes me more determined than ever to make my life matter in these next ten years as a physician.

∽

"Olivia. It's so good to see you, honey." Jill was the first to speak up. Thank heavens because I was swallowing a lump the size of Nebraska in my throat.

"I'm so glad to see you two, you have no idea. Come here, Michael. Give me a hug. I need it now more than ever."

I stepped up to the plate and held Olivia in my arms. She was thinner and looked tired. I guess we all looked pretty rough these days. But she'd been Case's sweetheart since high school, so I frankly didn't know how she was breathing.

"I been meanin' to call you, Olivia. This has been difficult for all of us, and I really haven't been able to speak about it too much. I keep thinking I'm handling it pretty well, and then it hits me in the face like a line drive standing on the pitcher's mound. It has flat taken the wind out of me. How are you holdin' up ?"

"Oh, Mike. I'm just now able to sleep in our bed again. This came upon us so quickly, so unexpected, that he was gone before I really got an opportunity to accept he was going to die. The doctors did all they could. James went out of his way to make Case comfortable. But the cancer just swallowed him up, literally." She put her head on my shoulder and cried for a moment quietly. Then we all walked into the house and sat down in the living room.

"Olivia, we were thinking. Maybe you'd like to come to Crosgrove for a few weeks. It would break your routine, and maybe it will feel good to get out of town. What do you think?"

Jill stepped in, putting her hand on Olivia's arm. "Yeah, Liv. Come back with us and spend some time in Crosgrove. I know all the great boutiques to shop and we'll eat lunch out every day. We can sit up at night talking about old times; don't you think it would feel good to get away?"

Olivia got up and walked to the window. She turned to look at us, and we knew her answer before she spoke. "You're so sweet to me. I know Case asked you to look after me, Michael. But I'm really happiest right here where we were together all these years. I'm not going to run away from dealing with his death. I think it's best for me to stay and work through it. That's not to say I won't visit soon. But right now, at this point in my grieving, I think I'd feel better here at home. Plenty of people come by during the week to see how I am. You wouldn't believe how many of your old patients come to visit me, Michael!"

"Oh I bet they do, Olivia. They loved Case. All of them did. Well, you know what's best for you. We just wanted to give you the choice, is all. Are you hungry? We're starving and I'm thinking we should eat at Mason's Café. He has the best key lime pie in the world, and it was Case's favorite pie. My mouth is watering just thinking about it."

The women laughed and we got up and walked to the car. It was a lovely afternoon and there was a nice breeze blowing. I was ready for good conversation but the thought of food was nauseating at the moment. I was just trying to get the conversation off Case so I could breathe. My legs felt like lead and as strong as I'd been since his death, I felt like I was going to fall apart when we pulled up at the restaurant. I was certain that Case would be listening in if at all possible. I was pretending to be up for Olivia, but inside I felt the weight of not having Case around. It really didn't feel like the same place at all. There was a huge emptiness that was hard to describe; I could only guess what Olivia was feeling. Our lives don't make much of an impact on this earth, and it's an odd comparison, because to our loved ones there is a hole as large as the moon after we go. To the rest of the world, dust and leaves gather over our grave and we become like the others who have gone before us. A grave marker is all we have to leave behind. That's the very reason why I'm convinced we should do all we can do while we're here, affecting as many people as we can for good. Otherwise, what's the point? For those who knew Case, he was powerful, gentle, and always thinking of others. He could diagnose better than any doctor I'd ever known. He worked long hours and gave medical care to many who could not afford to pay. But in the long scheme of things, who would remember he lived? The three of us standing there . . . how very small we were in the universe. A dot. I guess that's how life is. It didn't feel good to be walking around here without him. But I vowed that all the days I have left on this earth would be spent in a way that would make Case proud to know me. And I prayed that God would give me the strength to do this, because at that moment I felt like I'd lost my right leg and half my heart.

I looked at Olivia and wondered how she could go on with her life. But I knew somehow she would gather the strength and courage to do it. Just looking at her calmness that night made me want to be a better man.

CHAPTER 17

The girls were settled down for the afternoon on the sofa chatting about old times, and I decided to wander outside for a short walk. I found myself on an old dirt path that would lead me to the lake where Case fished most of the time. It took longer than I remembered to get there, but when I turned the corner and looked through a stretch of oak trees, I could see the water glistening in the afternoon sun. It took my breath away to see this sight, knowing Case would never see it again.

Walking up to the lake I bent down and stuck my hand in the water. It was hot outside and the water was warm. It would be a hard time fishing this time of year, as the fish always go to the bottom of the lake to stay cool. I know Case always said we had to keep our lines near the bottom to ever catch anything in the hot summer. I let the sun shine directly on my face, hoping it would warm my confused heart. I sat on a fallen tree near the water's edge and just took in the surroundings. I felt so close to Case it wouldn't have surprised me at all if he'd walked up. I had learned a lot from him, and I vowed more than once to use it as I lived out the rest of my time as a physician. *One thing for certain, I look forward to what's ahead, and I'll hold everything that has come before very dear to my heart.* I'm a lucky man to have known him, and coming back here to St. Martin has confirmed that I made the right choice in moving to Crosgrove. Hard as it was to make that decision. My life is changing before my eyes, and I realize now that there's nothing I can do to stop it. Nor do I want to anymore.

❧

Charlotte could hear Lucas coughing upstairs. This had been going on for a few months now and it didn't sound much better. She tiptoed up the stairs and got to the door. She knew it would be locked, but it made her feel closer to getting out of this hell she was in. She put her ear to the door and listened. She could hear him breathing; that was how bad sick he was. She got brave for a moment and called out his name. "Lucas! Lucas! Are you okay?"

Lucas was sitting in his chair laying back trying to rest. The fever had broken and he was weak from the coughing. He'd been sipping on some hot tea and had just closed his eyes when he thought he heard his name called out. He sat up and listened again.

"Lucas! Can you hear me?"

❧

He did hear his name this time. Loud and clear. It was Charlotte! *What in the world is she calling me for? Boy, this is a first.* "What you want, girl? I told you never to come up those stairs."

Charlotte backed down a few steps and called out through the cracks of the door. "I was just wondering how you were. I can hear you coughing. Are you okay?"

"Sure, I'm fine. Now go back down there or I'll get my gun out again. I'm bringing your food to you in a minute. Just sittin' here restin', is all."

She tiptoed down the steps and lay down on her bed, crying softly in her pillow. *I was hoping he was dead. How much longer can he live with this stuff? He sounds horrific. I pray to God that he dies. That's my only way out of this mess. I wouldn't be so lucky as to have him die. That would just be too easy. My luck's not that good. I'm here for the rest of my life if he doesn't die first. I've got to find a way to escape when he drifts off to sleep. But he's such a light sleeper I'm petrified he'll wake up and shoot me. I wouldn't put it past him one bit. Not to mention the trivial fact that I'm locked in the cellar with no key.*

She sat up and dried her eyes and reached for a Kleenex to blow her nose. She was so tired of being alone. Of having no one to care what she was going through or thinking. It was about dusk and just when she was about to go to the bathroom—she heard a faint tapping sound. She walked over to the window and strained to hear. She thought she heard someone walking with a cane, but it was so faint she wasn't sure. Her heart raced as she listened. She leaned into the cool concrete wall and listened with all her might. There it was. The tapping of that cane. He hadn't forgotten about her. She smiled in the cold, near empty room and that smile would've melted the heart of anyone. But no one was watching. No one had seen her smile in years. She felt sad tonight, more than usual. But she still loved hearing that cane.

Just when she was about to lie back down on the bed, Lucas opened the door and set her tray down. Her heart jumped up into her throat and she panicked. She always panicked when he opened the door, because she wasn't sure if he would come down the stairs or not.

"Don't get any ideas about that window, baby. Cause you ain't goin' nowhere. I wish I could let you outta here, but there's no way I can do that right now You'd run away for sure. I wanted you to be able to come upstairs, Charlotte. But how can I ever trust you? How do I know you won't try to kill me or run away?"

"Oh, you won't have to worry about that, Lucas. I have no family now. You're the only family I know anymore. They're probably all dead by now, anyways."

"You're right there, girl. I'm the only family you have. And don't forget it. When I get to feeling better, and I will, I'm comin' back down there and prove it to ya."

Charlotte shuddered at those words and covered her mouth. She stood dead still and waited for him to shut the door and lock it, and then she climbed the stairs quietly and picked up the tray. She was so hungry she would've eaten almost anything. Tonight her supper consisted of potatoes, peas, and chicken. *No tellin' how old this food is,* she thought. *But miraculously I haven't gotten sick from eatin' what he fixes.* She laughed out loud and sat down and began to eat slowly, chewing each bite as though it was filet mignon. She had no idea what time it was, or what day. It really didn't matter much, anyway. Every day was the same. The only sun she ever felt on her face was a tiny ray of sun that came through the window above her. It shot out across the room like an arrow and she often went over to it and let her face feel the warmth. Her skin was yellowing and she was aging fast. It wasn't healthy, the way she was living, and she knew it. But what could she do? Her mind was running out of ideas, and she was getting tired of dreaming about getting out. Resignation was an ugly bedfellow. It was winning over against the frail hope she had held on to for years. That hope was getting worn and tattered like an old pair of shoes. And resignation was showing up on her face in the frown lines that were forming at each end of her mouth. She had begun to feel herself slipping away. Giving up. Almost not caring anymore. That was dangerous because then he would win, and she'd made a vow in the beginning that she would never give up. She hated him with a vengeance and at the same time had grown to feel sorry for him. He was pretty pitiful and had no life. He was a prisoner in his own home, like she was. They lived their lives doing the same things, which never included the rest of the world.

∽

Lucas was feeling a tad hungry after losing the fever, so he ate some of what he'd fixed for Charlotte. It made him feel stronger just eating again. He smiled to himself at the thought of going back down those stairs to her. He loved her in a sick sort of way. Not like a wife, but like a friend. Only he knew he treated her badly when he went to the cellar. He never wanted her to think she had any effect on him at all. He never wanted to lose ground with her. For if he turned his back for one single second, she would be gone, and he would spend the rest of his life running. He knew they would find him somehow, and he wasn't going to spend the rest of his life in prison for kidnapping. He'd kill her and himself first before he would let them take him to prison. This relationship had lasted longer than he thought it ever would. In the beginning he had no idea how long he would keep her prisoner in his home. But as time went on, he got attached to having someone in the house.

∽

Peter Darby walked by the house every single afternoon unless it was pouring down raining. He hadn't seen Lucas peeking through the window in quite some time. He wanted to call Dr, Lankford and ask him some questions about Lucas, but he was hesitant. If Lucas was his patient, he wouldn't be able to tell him much, anyway. Peter was growing weaker and knew his time wasn't too far off. He'd been pretty healthy all his life, but living alone had taken its toll on him. It was in this time of his life that he felt he'd made a mistake by not marrying. He not only had no wife, but no children to look after him in his old age. No grand-children to keep him young. He kept up with the people he taught in high school, but their children were grown now. It was a lonely life and not very fulfilling. He enjoyed speaking at Crosgrove, but it was hard on him physically. Maybe it was time to give Dr. Lankford a call for another visit on the porch, sipping tea. He had enjoyed that day immensely and he decided to make a call in the morning.

༄

Charlotte sat on her narrow bed thinking that there might be a way she could break that window or find out if she could open it. If she moved her bed to the window and put the chair on top, she just might be tall enough to see out of the window. Of course, if Lucas found out or had even an inkling of what she was doing, there was no telling what he'd do to her. She'd thought about this for years but was petrified to take a chance again. She'd tried early on to move her bed across the room but he was ready and waiting at the top of the stairs. It's uncanny how intimidation and fear can immobilize a person until they are afraid to move in any direction. And she knew full well what would happen if he came back down into the cellar. The window seemed illusive to her and he'd put fear into her so early on that she dare not crack that door open without a good plan. He was so ill right now that it might be the perfect time to try again. She had to get her mind set on the fact that if he heard her moving the bed across the floor, he would come down those stairs with his gun aimed right at her head. Maybe death would be a welcome reprieve to how she was living. This was certainly not living. Not like the rest of mankind. She was living like a caged dog, only she had a larger cage to walk around in. She was getting so weary of this situation that she was just about willing to risk it all to find a way of escape. Her heart was pounding in her chest as she tried to scoot the bed across the concrete floor. It made a scraping sound that was louder because of the echo in the room. She moved it an inch at a time and stopped to listen. Nothing yet. Her eye was on the door at the top of the stairs. If she saw any movement of the doorknob, she would stop and lie on the bed and pretend to be asleep. She was successful in moving the bed near the window, so she grabbed the low chair and struggled to put it on the bed. It was heavy and not stable at all, and she knew if she tried to climb on the chair it might topple over and she would fall. That noise would bring him down those stairs in a flash.

Sweat was forming on her brow as she stepped up on the chair. It moved back and forth, wobbling so much that she could barely keep her balance. This was the closest she'd ever gotten to the window. She tried to stand straight up to see if she could look out, but the chair just wouldn't stay still. She looked around and decided to climb down and get a few books to put under the legs of the chair. That worked well, and she smiled to herself. *I've been down here so long my brain is dulled. Any idiot would have known to put books under the legs.*

She climbed up on the chair again without even the slightest wobble. *Oh my gosh! I'm so close to the window it's unreal. I hope I can see out.* She stretched herself as tall as she could go and stood on her tiptoes. . Her head came to the edge of the bottom of the window, but she did see grass and the trunk of a tree. That was enough to make her smile and gave her courage to try harder to find a way to see more. She couldn't tell by looking if the window could be opened or not. It seemed like it was sealed shut, but she couldn't be certain. She climbed down and looked around the room to see if there was anything she could put in the chair to raise her up higher. There was a pile of books on the floor but they were thin books. She grabbed a handful of them, anyway, and climbed on the chair again. This time she could see better, so she just stood there looking around for what seemed like an hour. Actually it was only a few moments, but she was lost in her own thoughts. Tears rolled down her face as she looked at the sky and green grass. The leaves were full and green and the trees were beautiful to her. It had been so long since she had seen anything that it was like seeing it for the first time. *Thank God I got a chance to see this. I have to get out! I feel like I can breathe again. Somehow I have to find a way to get out of this house or I'll die here and nobody will ever know. They think I'm already dead anyway.*

Just as she was climbing down, the door to the stairway opened and Lucas looked her square in the eyes. The look she saw was not anger. In fact that surprised her more than anything. What she saw on his face was the look of fear. He was too sick to come down but the words he spoke shot through her like an arrow, blowing out the flame of hope in her heart. She jumped down and moved the bed away from the window, put the chair back in its place, and lay down in her bed. Her heart was pounding so hard that she knew he could hear it. And all the joy she had felt about seeing outside rose up to the ceiling and turned to smoke.

⁂

Lucas was so shocked he nearly fell down the stairs. *How dare she try to see out of that window? How many times have I told her the consequences? She is ungrateful that I allowed her to live. And now I'm dependent upon her bein' here . . . it would be difficult for me to kill her. What she's tellin' me is that I mean nothin' to her. Nothing. I guess I expected that, but it still hurts. I have to get stronger so that she doesn't take advantage of me while I'm sick and weak. She could probably push me down right now.* He cleared his throat and told her if she moved he would kill her. He turned out the lights in the cellar and locked the door. He was shaking so hard he nearly fell. *That window is sealed shut. But what if she found a way out? I may have to board it up because it has become too much of a temptation to her. And to think I wanted to bring her upstairs.*

⁂

Charlotte lay in bed shaking and crying. She was elated at seeing out of the window. She would do it again no matter what. But even though he looked afraid he sounded furious. His words were wicked. She knew his mind was so sick that he would kill her in a second. She pushed him too far tonight. Her only hope was that he felt so bad he wouldn't come downstairs for a week or so. By then maybe he would have mellowed out a little. Somehow she found sleep coming up on her like a blanket nestling over her eyes. She was exhausted from the strain and fell into a deep sleep, dreaming of another world she no longer knew.

⁂

What she didn't know was that Peter Darby had just walked by her house a few moments before she was able to look out the window. She was making so much noise moving the bed that she failed to hear his cane tapping on the sidewalk. And he failed to see her face peeking out of the cellar window. A few minutes that seemed irrelevant to millions, but in those few moments, her life could have changed drastically. For Peter was always looking at the house when he walked by. If he had seen a woman's face looking out of that cellar window, the next phone call he would have made would have been to Dr. Michael Lankford. He wouldn't have known it was Charlotte Reeves looking back at him, but it would have been enough for him to be more curious than he was already about Lucas Cunningham. No one in Crosgrove was thinking about finding Charlotte Reeves anymore. They'd given up hope. But Peter was feeling uneasy and had for years on his walk past that house. To see a face in the cellar window would've been enough to trigger action on his part.

∽

Sleep comes to those who are happy and those who are sad, bringing rest to the mind and spirit. And it allows us to dream of a land where there are no closed doors separating us from what we love the most. Freedom. So Charlotte dreamed of being able to fly out the window and never look back. And she dreamed someone was waiting on the other side.

CHAPTER 18

Over the last few months word was spreading about the newest doctor in town. My phone was ringing every morning with calls from people who needed an appointment. It seemed that my efforts to care about the health and welfare of my patients was paying off. All in all, I'm getting busier and need another doctor to help with the increased patient load.

Gregory Hinson seemed like the perfect match for my practice. He was forthright, intelligent, and had years of medical experience. He'd been chief of staff at Ohio Medical Center, but had moved to Crosgrove for much the same reason as I had, to get away from the hustle and bustle of a big city and to be near his daughter and her husband. He wanted to practice medicine in a unique way, smaller office, with the ability to give the patient more time. He was tired of keeping up with the numbers in a large practice. Malpractice insurance was out the roof, and he was getting older and didn't want to the hassle.

"Gregory, what say we take a break from our talk and go to lunch? I'd love to show you my favorite café in town."

"Sounds good to me, Michael. I loved this place as soon as I drove into it, and after meeting you, I'm actually excited about being here. Lunch sounds great."

Sarah's Café was on the corner of Morgan Avenue and Second Street. All the businessmen ate there for lunch, so I knew it was going to be a hit. Ever since the first time I had lunch there, I never went anywhere else. Old Sarah had my number when I walk in the door. That could be good or bad, depending on how you look at it.

"Let's sit against the wall over there so we can have some privacy in here, Gregory. You hungry? Cause the menu is enough to kill you, but you'll get hooked like I did. The lemon ice box pie will absolutely do you in!"

"I realize that what you're saying is that this isn't the healthiest place to eat but the food tastes fabulous!"

"You got that right, my man. So tell me about yourself, Greg. Where were you born?"

The afternoon flew like an eagle over Northridge Mountain. And I was more than certain that Gregory would join me in my practice. It felt like a good fit, but he said he had to mull it over and would get back to me in a day or two. I was excited about having someone else in my office; number one: I could get a day off. Number two: we could see more patients and actually make some money. Gregory was tall, bald, and had the greatest smile I'd seen in a long time. His laugh rumbled out of his great chest and he looked you right in the eye when he was talking to you. That impressed me, for a doctor. Even though I am one, it's difficult most of the time to get a doctor to really listen. I was convinced that this man would really work with me hand in hand to create an atmosphere of caring and healthy living. We both needed to take off a few pounds, but I thought we were pretty good examples of what we were tryin' to get across.

☙

Heading home on Park Avenue, there was a bad wreck in the left lane of oncoming traffic. I pulled over to the side of the road and got out of my car. It looked like a head-on collision so I grabbed my cell and called for an ambulance. When I approached the two cars my mouth flew open. In the dark blue Honda I could barely make out the face of the woman but I could tell it was Jessica Reeves. She was bleeding profusely from her nose and was unconscious. I ran to her first to see if I could stabilize her before the ambulance got there, and pulled out my stethoscope to see if I could check her heart. She looked bad, but I didn't think she was dying. Her heart sounded strong and not erratic, but her pulse was up. Her windshield was busted so I assumed she had not worn a seatbelt.

It wasn't three minutes and I heard the sound of the ambulance coming. I slipped over to the other car and didn't recognize the other driver. He was already gone; it looked like his neck was broken. By the look of the position of the two cars, it appeared that he'd come across his lane into hers and hit her head on. The police were arriving and I walked up to the first officer that got out of the patrol car.

"Dr. Lankford here, officer. I called the ambulance immediately after I pulled off the road. If I can be of any help, let me know."

"I think the EMTs can take care of things now, Doctor. But thanks for your help. My wife really likes having you as her doctor. Maybe I need to make an appointment myself. I'll call you soon."

I walked back to Jessica Reeves and nodded to one of the EMTs. "She's my patient. I'm on my way to the hospital."

An hour later, Jessica was laying in a bed in ER, trying to get up, and struggling with the nurses. That made me feel better about her condition. I had checked her vital signs, but X-rays were forthcoming and I wanted to see what they looked like. I leaned over and spoke to her gently. "Mrs. Reeves, I want you to know they're going to take good care of you here. I already know you don't want to be in the hospital, but we need to make sure nothing serious is wrong with you. Be patient and let them do what they need to do to make you more comfortable."

She mumbled something but had a frown on her face. She was still in shock and looked a little dazed. I walked out into the main hallway of the ER and ran into Martin Payne, the doctor on duty. "Martin, how in the heck have you been? Haven't seen you in a few months. Things busy around here?"

"Been pretty busy. Kids drinking and driving. Roads get slippery this time of year with all the rain. Just wait until the snows come. Better not plan any vacations in the winter, Lankford."

"I'll wait around for the X-rays on Jessica Reeves; I want to see what's going on inside. She has some contusions on her forehead, but it doesn't look too bad considering she hit the windshield. What is it with seat belts? People just don't get it until they're in a bad wreck."

"Tell me about it. Looks like the X-rays are coming down now. Let's take a look and see what's going on, if anything. She's a tough cookie. She just may pull out of this with a broken nose and nothing else."

I smiled and followed him to his office to see the X-rays. He was right. She was clean except for a broken nose. Very fortunate. She could have easily been killed in that accident.

I hurried in to the office the next morning and found patients lined up in the waiting room. I moved through the most of them, thinking that the flu must have settled on Crosgrove. Everyone in the waiting room was coughing and blowing their nose. I swallowed some echinacea capsules, which would have made Case roll his eyes in disbelief. I swore by them and he argued that they were nothing but a placebo. We had that argument every winter; however, I never got the flu and he always did. I loved that part of the argument. My patients were happy to get a B12 shot and a shot of penicillin. I told them to rest and drink plenty of fluids and that nothing I could give them would hasten the course of the virus. We always kept juice in the office so they walked out with a glass of OJ and Kleenex.

My nurse spent a lot of her time in the winter months sterilizing the office and all the exam rooms. It seemed like a losing battle, but we had to make an attempt. The waiting room was the worst. So every morning before we opened, all the chairs were wiped down with disinfectant. It made the room smell good and we all felt better. I'm not sure it did much good in keeping the germs down.

Jill and I were having dinner tonight with a couple who'd lived in Crosgrove all their lives. They knew everyone in town and all the latest gossip. Paul and Sandra Holcomb were good people, hard working, and trustworthy. But they loved to talk about other people. I was going to use this questionable habit to find out about Lucas Cunningham. I wasn't even sure if they knew him or not, but that question was going to work its way into the conversation at some point. I still had a burning desire to find out about that man; maybe this would prove to be an advantageous opportunity. No one else seemed to know that much about him, and I was ready for some fresh gossip or at the very least, a lead. If I'm honest, I don't even know why I'm curious about Lucas. He's nothing special, has a forgettable face, and I've heard nothing negative about him. Actually, that's one of the problems. I've not heard anything at all about him. Good or bad. Yet when he comes into my office, there's something about him that just bothers me. Can't put my finger on it, but one day something will surface. It always does.

The phone rang late in the afternoon and the receptionist buzzed my office. "Peter Darby is on the phone. You want to talk to him now?"

"Yes, I'll take the call. Thanks, Mary Beth."

"Peter? How's it going, buddy?"

Peter smiled and cleared his throat. "Oh, gettin' along pretty good. I can tell I'm goin' down a bit, Doc. Just wondered if you cared to come by again and have a visit on my porch again?"

"Of course I would! I'm glad you called. When were you thinking about, Peter?"

"Maybe on Sunday. That's such a peaceful day and I'd really like you to see the lake behind my house. I love fly fishing and thought maybe we could go back there and try to catch a few."

I laughed and thought of Case. Boy, he would love this conversation for sure. "Sounds good to me, buddy. What time?"

"Oh, come over around one o'clock. Really means a lot to me, Doc."

"I look forward to it! See you on Sunday. And thanks for calling. I'll bring my black bag and check you out while I'm there. You aren't feeling too poorly, are you?"

"Nope. It's nothin' like that, Doc. Just feel like I'm goin' down is all. I'll wait until you check me over. Probably nothin' but the cold."

"Well, bundle up and stay warm. If you need me sooner, let me know, will you?"

"I'll be fine. See ya soon."

CHAPTER 19

When I walked into the hospital room, Jessica Reeves was sitting up in bed watching television. She turned and looked at me and smiled a crooked smile, and that made my day. I was worried she'd resist any help from the doctors because she had such an aversion to hospitals. The sun was coming into the room and even though it was a cold day outside, she was warm and cozy in her bed, sipping on some coffee.

"Good morning, lady. How's my favorite patient feeling this morning? They taking good care of you here?"

"Oh my, yes, Dr. Lankford. They couldn't have been nicer to me, ya know? I'm so grateful for what they've done for me, and really it's changed my feelings about doctors. You started that, of course."

"Well, I'm thrilled you're feeling better. I've talked to Dr. Lockhart and he said you're going to be fine. Your nose will heal quickly, even though I know it's sore. You're already blessed with two black eyes, Jessica! But I might add they don't look as bad as I thought they would."

"I haven't bothered with a mirror this mornin'. Just thankful to be sittin' up and drinkin' some coffee. Do you know when I might be goin' home?"

"I'll check at the desk, but probably tomorrow I would guess. Do you need a ride home from the hospital? I know your car looked pretty bad the other day."

Jessica smiled and looked out of the window. She shook her head slowly and turned to look at me with sad eyes. "No, Doc. I can get home on my own. I do have a neighbor who came by to see me. She said she'd be glad to take me home. Thanks, though. I really appreciate the offer. You've been swell to me and I don't take it for granted."

There was something about this woman that just grabbed at my heart. She was so broken inside, and it made me want to do something to make her world better. "It's nice to have a neighbor like that, Jessica. You let me know if that situation changes, and I'll be glad to pick you up and take you home. Give me a call soon and make another appointment after your nose has healed some. I want to keep a close eye on your health and how you're feeling with the meds I put you on. Okay?"

"Sure, Doc. Thanks for stoppin' by to see me. I'll call you soon."

I walked out of her room still thinking about her daughter who had been gone so long. I would give anything to know if that girl was still alive. It would be nothing short of a miracle if she was, but stranger things have happened. It sounded so final when the police stated that the case had been closed. The trail had gone cold. What if she was still waiting somewhere, still hoping to be found?

I made myself stop dwelling on Charlotte Reeves, and called Anna on my way back to the office. Her voice stopped me cold in my tracks. "Hey, honey. How's my favorite girl doing this morning?"

She responded weakly. "Hey, Dad. Well, not too good this morning. My stomach is hurting and Thomas is going to take me to the doctor. Have you met my doctor yet, Dad? His name is Josh Murphy. I really like him; he seems to know what he's doing and is into natural childbirth. I'm so glad I have him for a doctor, because I'm really nervous about this pregnancy. Something's wrong, Dad. I don't feel good at all."

"What's wrong, honey? Do you need me to go with you to the doctor?"

"My stomach feels weird and I feel like I'm going to be sick. I'm hurting, and I don't think I'm supposed to hurt, Dad."

"Now don't overreact, Anna. Try not to overanalyze what's happening. It could be anything at this point. I know Thomas is taking you, but do you want Mom and I to go with you?"

"No, I'll be okay with Thomas with me. But we'll call you if it's anything serious. Will you be home?"

"Yes. We have no plans to go out tonight. Just call me and let me know how you are."

When I walked in the door, Jill could tell by the look on my face that I was worried.

"Honey, what's going on? You don't look too happy tonight. Did you have a bad day at the office?"

"It's Anna, Jill. I just got off the phone with her and she's not feeling well. Thomas is taking her to the doctor right now. She's going to call us as soon as she knows anything. I'm worried that she may be having labor pains and it's too early for her to deliver. The babies wouldn't be fully developed yet. There's no way they would make it at four months." I walked over to Jill and hugged her.

"Oh no, Michael! Why didn't she call me? She can't lose those babies! They both were looking forward to this so much; it's going to kill her if she miscarries."

I shook my head and sat down at the table. "I imagine she was panicked and on the phone with her doctor all morning. We just have to wait and see what the doctor finds when he examines her. He'll know immediately. We should hear something pretty quick, as she was leaving right after we hung up the phone."

෴

ER was hopping as Thomas and Anna Grace headed in the door. They walked up and registered and told the nurse behind the desk that she was possibly in pre-mature labor. Someone came through the double doors and ushered them to the back and put Anna Grace in a side room. A nurse came in immediately and took her blood pressure and asked a lot of questions. Thomas pulled up a chair and took her hand.

"Are you having labor pains, Mrs. Miller?'

"It feels like labor, I guess."

"When did it start?"

"Well, it's been going on since yesterday. Only it got worse tonight and that's why I had Thomas bring me in."

"I see. Anything happen that you know of that would bring this on? Did you fall?"

"No, nothing. I was shopping yesterday, working around the house. Nothing unusual. It just started on its own. I knew something didn't feel right. There's a tightening in my lower abdomen."

"Sure, sure. Let's get an ultrasound done and see what's going on."

The doctor on duty came in and smiled, reassuring Anna that she would be okay." I'm Dr. Smithson. Now tell me what's going on, Mrs. Miller."

"Well, I was telling the nurse here that these labor pains started yesterday and got increasingly worse tonight. That's why I'm here. I'm not due until December. I can't have these babies at four months. They'll never make it." Anna started crying and Thomas squeezed her hand.

"Now, now, Mrs. Miller. Don't get upset. That'll only make things worse. Let me examine you and we'll do the ultrasound to see what's going on." He pulled his stool up close and put on a glove. The exam was done very carefully and he could easily tell she was in labor. The uterus was intact but he couldn't really tell what had brought on the labor.

After the ultrasound, he turned to look at Anna. 'You're definitely in labor. I can give you a drug to try to stop it. But I'm going to put you in for the night to see if we can calm this thing down. You must relax and try not to get so upset. And you've also got to trust me that we're going to do all we can to stop this labor. Who's your obstetrician?"

"Dr. Josh Murphy. Do I need to get in touch with him?"

"No, we'll do that now."

After he walked out of the room, Anna looked at Thomas and burst out crying. "There's no way I'm going to lose these babies, Thomas. They are a part of us. I couldn't handle it, do you understand? This can't be happening to us."

Thomas took her in his arms and held her, wiping her tears. His throat had a lump in it and he had no words to say that would make this any better. "Honey, we're going to have to trust the Dr. Smithson here and hope for the best. You have to try to stay calm, Anna, or it will make things worse. Remember what he said?"

"Yeah, I remember. I'll try to calm down but I'm so scared, Thomas."

"Let's call your parents and let them know you're going to be here for the night. They might want to come over and spend some time with you."

"I'll call Dad in a moment. I want to get in a room first and then I'll call."

∞

When the phone rang at 10:00 I knew it had to be Anna. "Hello, honey. Tell me what's going on?"

"Dad." Anna burst into tears again. "Dad, I'm in the hospital. My labor has started and the doctor is going to give me a drug that will try to stop it. He wants me here overnight so he can watch things and keep an eye on the babies. His name is Dr. Smithson. Do you know him?"

"Yeah, I know him. He's pretty good from what I hear. He'll call your gynecologist and let him know what's going on. I'm sure he'll come up and check on you tomorrow." He looked over at Jill and raised his eyebrows.

Jill shrugged her shoulders at me hopelessly and added, "We can go in the morning to see her, Michael. Unless you think we need to go tonight."

"I think she's all right tonight. Anna, your mom and I'll come in the morning. Now you call us tonight if anything happens. I have the phone right next to me, do you hear? And don't be afraid, angel. Dr. Smithson will take care of you, I'm sure. Remember to try to relax your muscles and not stay tense. I'll call in the morning if I've not heard from you by then."

"Okay, Dad. Thanks. Talk to you in the morning."

I hung up the phone and looked at Jill. She could tell by the look on my face that this wasn't good. "You know what, Jill? If she loses these babies, you and I are going to the house before she gets home and take down those baby beds. She doesn't need to come home and see that room all set up to be a nursery. You agree?"

"Oh, honey. Do you really think there's a big chance she'll lose them now?"

"I can't be sure, Jill. But just a gut feeling; it doesn't look good to me. She's only four months. We'll see what happens in the night. Her gynecologist will see her tomorrow and then we'll have a better chance of knowing how things are."

"Okay. I agree about taking the beds down and getting that nursery taken apart. Maybe we should send her and Thomas on a cruise or something to get her away from here for a while. That is, if she loses those babies. Oh, Michael, I think I'll die if she loses them. The poor thing. Surely that medicine will work."

"We can pray, Jill. We can pray it will."

CHAPTER 20

I was in a dead sleep when the phone rang. I jumped up and checked the clock to see what time it was. 4:30 a.m. This can't be good. "Hello, Dr Lankford here."

"Michael, it's Thomas. She lost the babies an hour ago. The doctor is with her now, so I took this time to call you. You might want to come up; I think she's going to need you."

"We'll be right there. Now things are going to be tough for you for a while, and we'll be here if you need us, Thomas. She's going to be depressed and her emotions will be like a rollercoaster. I'll see you in a few minutes."

I hung up the phone and felt sick. My only daughter has lost her babies. This was going to be a tough day that none of us would forget. I looked at Jill and she was crying. She'd heard the conversation and was already getting up to get dressed. The silence in the car on the way to the hospital was deafening. We both were lost in our thoughts, hoping Anna could handle the loss of her babies. She was young and I knew she could have more children, but this was her first pregnancy. And she had felt life in her stomach. They were very real to her. It wasn't going to be easy to come home and not be pregnant anymore. That's why Jill and I had to get that nursery taken apart.

When I walked into the room, Anna was lying there quiet and unmoving. Her eyes were closed and she seemed to be resting pretty well. Thomas came up and I hugged him. "How is she?"

"She's sleeping now, but she took it pretty hard. She did try to prepare herself last night in case she lost the babies. But nothing prepares you for this, Doc. Nothing."

"I know, Thomas. I know. Let's give her time and maybe she'll be stronger tomorrow. You're going to have to be strong for the two of you for a time. It will get easier, Thomas. I promise you that."

Jill was standing by the bed shaking her head. I hated to see her in such pain, hurting for her daughter. It broke my heart. I pulled two chairs up and we sat and talked with Thomas for a while, letting Anna rest. I suggested that we all go downstairs to the cafeteria and have breakfast so we could talk without disturbing Anna. This was going to be a long day and I felt useless. I'm a doctor, and there was nothing I could do to save my grandchildren or make my daughter feel better. It makes you wonder sometimes how far we've really come in the world of medicine that we can't save the babies that didn't ask to be born. As fragile as life really is, it's a miracle any of us make it through childbirth. *I suppose that's a miracle we'll never understand. Somehow there has to be a way for us to make it through this unforeseen time. And I know without a doubt that nothing will stop the flow of tears my daughter will cry when she wakes up.*

⁓

We got home about 10:00 and I was sitting at my desk looking at the photo of Case when my phone rang. It startled me as I was still unnerved from being at the hospital with Anna. "Hello, Dr. Lankford here."

"Michael, this is Gregory. How are you?"

"Pretty emotional right now, Gregory. My daughter miscarried early this morning so we were called to the hospital around four-thirty. I'm exhausted from the stress of it all, on top of not being able to do anything to help her. How are things going at your end?"

"I'm doing pretty good. I'm sorry to hear about your daughter; is there anything you need me to do?"

"No thanks, Gregory. It's just going to be a tough thing to go through. She's pretty upset."

"I can only imagine. Say Michael, I think I'm ready to come on board with you, if you're still interested in having me. I liked the way you spoke about your practice and how you want your patients handled. I really think we make a good team."

"Well this phone call sure makes my day, Gregory! You couldn't have phoned at a better time, frankly. I need another physician in my office and you're the man for the job. When can you start?"

"No point in putting it off, I'd say. How about Monday morning, if that works for you?"

"Monday's perfect. Just come right in and I'll be in my office. We can discuss the details and you can fill out some paperwork. I have an extra office for you and we can get your name on the door in two days. I know the guy at Andy's Signs and he'll do it faster than anyone else. How's that sound?"

"Sounds good to me. I look forward to it, Mike. See you on Monday."

I pushed my chair back and propped my legs on the desk. It was time to head into the office; I was certain I had patients waiting for me. But just for a moment I needed a second to reflect on the morning and my precious Anna lying up in a bed in the hospital after losing something so precious to her. I said a quick prayer that her heart would heal quickly and headed out the door. Jill was going to spend the day at a local fundraiser and that would keep her mind off things for a while. We still had to go to Anna's house and take down the cribs and get that room straight, but we could do that in the afternoon when I got off work.

It was Friday and the office was full. Mary Beth was beside herself trying to explain why I was late. I smiled at the familiar faces in the waiting room and headed back to my office. I grabbed the first file and my nurse Louise called the name of my first patient. It happened to be Malcolm Anderson and he was coughing and sneezing all the way to the exam room. He was short, overweight, but had a great laugh. It was always good to see him in spite of the fact that he was always sick when I saw him.

"Good morning, Malcolm. Thank you for being so patient. Tell me what's going on with you today?"

"Well, Doc, I probably caught this cold at the deli, with all those people coming in. Everyone is sneezing and there I am taking their money. I use hand sanitizer but I guess it doesn't get all the germs. Obviously!" He leaned his head back and laughed.

"It is that time of year, Malcolm, for sure. You had any fever?"

"Nope. Just feel crummy, Doc. Ya know?"

"Well, let's take your temperature and get your blood pressure. You given any thought to slowing down on your eating? Your blood pressure is up a bit today."

"Aw, Doc. I know I'm overweight. But for some reason I can't get motivated to lose the weight. After Annie died, I ate poorly. I don't want to cook meals just for myself, ya know? So I eat anytime I get hungry, and usually not something good for me. I'm a mess all right—" He laughed again, and looked to see if I was laughing, too.

"You need to be thinking about what you're eating, Malcolm. You aren't getting any younger and now is the time to prevent heart problems. I'm going to give you a supplement that curbs your appetite. Give it a try and maybe come off so much bread at your meals. You have a bad cold but it'll run its course. Just drink plenty of fluids and eat a lot of fruit. I'd love to see you take fifty pounds off if you could."

Malcolm got up and took the bottle of supplements and shook my hand. "I'll give it my best shot, Doc. Can't promise anything. I've been large all my life, and it will be difficult for me to imagine being anything else. If there's a smaller man trying to get out, he's sure not trying very hard!" With that, he laughed all the way out of the office.

I was looking forward to seeing Peter tomorrow. My mind was on him when I walked into the exam room and saw Jessica Reeves sitting there. "Hey, lady! How are you feeling? Does it feel good to be home?"

"It sure does, Doc. My nose is still bruised but that's to be expected. Could have killed me in that wreck; I thank God everyday that I lived through that collision."

"You've healed very quickly and I love your new attitude about doctors. So they treated you right in the hospital, did they?"

"Oh yes, I hated to leave! Good meals everyday and someone comin' in to check on me several times a day. I could ring a bell and someone would answer immediately. It was amazin', Doc."

I laughed and patted her back. "Let's listen to your lungs and see how we're doing today."

Everything sounded so much better that I told her I didn't want to see her for a month or so. "How you doing on the Prozac I prescribed for you? You feeling happier about your world or do I need to up the dose?'

"Oh, I won't go so far as to say I'm happy. But I'll say that I'm not thinkin' about drivin' off the bridge anymore. So that's sayin' somethin', Doc."

"Well, I'd say that was a huge improvement, Mrs. Reeves."

"Oh, call me Jesse, Doc. No point in that proper stuff anymore. Seein' as how I trust you now, you might as well call me by my name."

"That's an honor, Jesse. I'll remember to do that. Now you take care of yourself and if you have any problems at all, let me know."

CHAPTER 21

I left the office a little early and headed over to Anna's house. Jill was already there working on the nursery. "Hey, honey. Thought you'd never get here. Let's get these beds down before Thomas walks through that door with Anna."

I put down my coat and began taking one of the cribs down. It was a sad thing but I tried to keep the conversation going on something else. Jill didn't need to be red-eyed when her daughter came through the door. The focus had to be on getting her back to a normal routine as soon as possible. I was thinking more about sending her on a short cruise and that was sounding better and better.

"You know, Jill, let's encourage Anna to take that cruise with Thomas, if he can take a little time off work. It would be so good for her to get away for a week and think about something healthy. It's going to take a while for her to get over this, but right now she needs time away from everything that reminds her of those babies."

"You're always right. That would be the best thing in the world for her. I hope she's open to it but we'll find out soon enough. Losing two babies will be so hard emotionally for her to deal with. I don't even know if I could do it. I wish this hadn't happened, Mike. She was so excited about this pregnancy. I hate this for her!" She pulled her already wet Kleenex out of her pocket and dabbed at her eyes.

We put the beds up in the attic and cleaned up the rest of the room. As soon as we walked out of the room and turned off the light, in walked Thomas and Anna. She was a little weak and walking slow, but had a smile on her face when she saw us.

"Hey, honey. You want to lie down in your bed, or do you want to go to the sofa?" I grabbed Anna's arm and held her up.

Anna pointed towards the sofa and we got pillows and propped her up so she would be comfortable. "I'm tired and I don't know why. All I've done is sleep."

"Well, you've been through something quite traumatic, Anna. Your body needs that rest."

Thomas sat down and leaned his head on the back of the sofa. He rubbed Anna's feet and asked her if she wanted anything to drink. I sat down in my favorite chair across the room and Jill picked the chair closest to the sofa, so that she could talk to Anna.

"How are you feeling, angel? Are you sore?"

"No, actually I don't hurt anywhere, Momma. But mentally I'm exhausted. We don't have to tiptoe around the subject, Mom. We all know what happened two nights ago and actually it would feel better if we just kept it out in the open. We all wanted these babies to be born and now they're gone. Only God knows why. I still feel pregnant. I still feel like I'm going to be a mom. But there's no movement in my stomach anymore and it's a shock to my body and mind. It'll take me some time to catch up with what's happened. I'm sure that's normal but it doesn't feel normal to me."

"None of us can even begin to understand what you're feeling, Anna. but we just want to give you time to heal. You and Thomas need time to work through this, and we hope to make that as easy as possible. Your father and I've been talking about sending you on a cruise for a week. What do you guys think of that?"

Thomas grinned but looked at Anna Grace. "I think that would be an excellent idea! I just need to see if I can get off work for a week. What do you think, Anna? Are you up to it?"

Anna didn't look as excited as I was hoping. "Well, I'm weak right now and going on an ocean liner doesn't seem too appealing at the moment. Maybe tomorrow or the next day, when I'm stronger, I'll be in the mood to discuss it."

We all laughed and I could tell she really didn't think it was too funny. I knew she wanted to lie back and rest so I took the cue and stood up. "We'll go,

Anna. But just let us know what you need, and you know to call me if you have any issues concerning your health. It's nice to have a Dad who's a doctor. I'm at your beck and call."

Anna smiled weakly and moved her long brown hair off her face. "I get it, Dad. And thanks so much for all you've done. You've taken care of me all my life and I know you won't stop now. It feels good to have you and Mom around. I'm so thankful you moved here, even though I realize it's been a great adjustment for you both."

We got up after talking for a few minutes and left. The ride home was pretty quiet, Jill lost in her own thoughts, and me thinking about where to send the kids. Maybe the Bahamas would be a good place; not too far, and they would have a ball. I'd like to get away myself before too long. Jill and I hadn't taken a vacation just for us in years.

When we drove in the driveway we both realized we hadn't eaten supper. I dropped Jill off and picked up some barbeque sandwiches around the corner from the house. We sat in the living room staring at the local news, eating and talking about our day. We both were worn out from worrying about Anna Grace and getting up so early. It was going to be an early night tonight. I remembered suddenly about the meeting with Peter. *Hard to keep things straight with so much going on around here.*

CHAPTER 22

Standing on my back porch looking out across that lawn, the morning sun was casting its rays across the wet grass. There were some birds playing in the birdbath in the front bed, and a dog was barking off in the distance. The neighborhood was quiet and I breathed in the morning air, wanting to feel refreshed after the last couple of days. It seemed like we'd been under some type of stress ever since we made the move to Crosgrove. I sat down in one of the chairs on the porch and pulled out my pipe. I rarely smoked, but when I was stressed out or real tired, I absolutely loved to smoke a pipe. This came from my father, who had a grand collection of pipes he'd purchased from all over the world.

I hadn't forgotten Case. His death had taken a toll on my life big time. I missed him like I would miss seeing the sun come up across the horizon. He made such an impact on my life, and it was sad that he'd never know that. I'd acquired several patients that I worried too much about, and now Anna has lost her two babies. *I know this is life; I counsel my patients about it all the time.* It's clinically impossible to deal with one's own issues the same way that we tell others to do. For I know in my own life, I can't see past my nose in dealing with the pain of loss or the adjustment it has taken to accept that I've lost my best friend. We all go on emotions instead of logic. It's so easy to tell another person how to manage their life; the flaw in that logic is that we hardly can manage our own. People need time to feel all the emotions that come with love, loss, and death, and those emotions make others uncomfortable. They are filled with the desire, and rightly so, to fix the problem. The problem with that desire is that the "fixing" will come with time and healing. No words or actions can hurry that along.

And that brings me to Jessica Reeves, how she's dealt with the fact that her daughter was taken from her one sunny day with no word since, no sign of hope that she's alive, is beyond human comprehension. This town is virtually without crime, and yet this horrific crime happened in broad daylight and no one seems to have seen anything. Crosgrove isn't a largely populated town. The residents know each other pretty well. Although there are those on the outskirts of town that stay to themselves, as is found in any town, for the most part it would be difficult to hide anything in Crosgrove. I'm thinking that perhaps someone saw something and is afraid to speak up. And now years have passed and the importance of what they saw has dimmed. Most people don't want to get involved, anyway.

Peter is another good example of how someone can get lost in the system and go unnoticed for years. Surely people saw him around town; but nobody spoke up. No one paid attention. We are forever lost in our own thoughts and worlds that we have created and are shockingly selfish if we were to admit it. That young boy raised himself, went to school in rags, and nearly starved to death trying to pull himself out of a hole. I know the teachers were aware of his physical condition and yet nothing was done. It's hard to conceive this could happen in such a seemingly caring town.

As a doctor, it's human behavior that's the most shocking and interesting, to say the least. I've observed the most barbaric behavior under the slightest bit of stress, and it never ceases to amaze me. Human beings trying to cope can turn into unrecognizable individuals because of their inability to manage their stress. It can be the smallest of things that tips the scale and brings out the bizarre behavior. And then you find someone else that's carrying stress the size and weight of an elephant on their back, and they smile and carry on, looking for ways to give to others when they can barely make it themselves. It certainly sets people apart, defining their character, when you place them under stress and watch their behavior and ability or inability to cope. Peter Darby rose above and pulled himself out of a dark hole, and has spent the most of his life showing others the way out. Most people wallow in the mire, blaming everyone else for their misfortune, and grow old with the mud they were stuck in all their lives, not noticing the rope lying near that would have pulled them out. I've loved practicing medicine mainly because I want to help the masses live a healthy life. But secondly, I enjoy encouraging people to step out of their comfort zone and consider a simple change that might turn their life completely around. I've learned that the very thing that people complain about the most is likely to be an area that they wouldn't consider changing even if you showed them the way. People who complain a lot don't actually like advice; they simply want an ear to bend. They really don't want change, they want sympathy. They are stuck forever on a merry-go-round of self pity and a craving for attention and sympathy. They erroneously feel no one could possibly understand what they've gone through.

This afternoon I'm going to see Peter, who has no idea how many people he's inspired. I can't wait to pick his brain again and watch those eyes twinkle. No matter how much he shares with me about his life, I'll never be able to really grasp what it took for him to walk in worn shoes that were too small, with clothes that were tattered and worn and a stomach that was always empty, and never complain about the situation he found himself in. He carried that attitude all through his school years and into adulthood. He made his life what he wanted it to be without the help of anyone. He never felt he was owed something from society. If that one attitude could be taught in school or bottled and sold, the inventor of that would be the wealthiest man in the world. Peter Darby is like a grand old oak tree whose branches spread out over the ground. And if you are fortunate enough to stand under his tree, the things you'll learn will change you forever. The sad thing is, a lot of it can't be taught. It has to come from the core of the person. And when all of us struggle, we find out who we really are, and what we're made of.

CHAPTER 23

I could hear Peter whistling when I walked up the path to his house. I knocked on the door and he came out smiling, carrying glasses of tea. It was warm on the porch but we decided to last as long as we could. The chairs were warm from the sun beaming down, so it felt good for a while.

"Been thinkin' about you a lot lately, Doc. How've you been doin' in your practice?"

"It's good to see you, Peter! I have more work than I can handle, so I've actually just hired another doctor to work with me. I'm real excited about him comin' on board."

"Sounds like a plan, Doc. I been feelin' like I'm goin' down a bit, and wanted to talk to you about it. I know I'm getting' old but nothin' major is wrong with me. So how come I can feel so poorly?"

"We all have aches and pains. Your body's wearing out. That's basically all that's wrong. How old are you, anyway? Do you mind my asking?"

"Well, if I'm correct, I'm about eighty-one by now. I could be off a year or two. Not sure when my real birthday is. It's felt weird all these years not to know that much about myself or my parents. I still miss 'em even today, but their faces are gone from my mind. I have no recollection of my brothers except the color of their hair. Wish I'd been able to have some photographs so that I could look at them from time to time."

"That's tough, I'm sure. You have few memories of your past life with your family, but you made new memories, Peter. And I'm glad to be a tiny part of those memories."

"Say Doc, would you like to go 'round to the backyard for a few minutes. I got something back there I'd like to show you."

We got up and walked around the house and there in front of us was a huge fishing pond. Standing against the shed were two fly reels. I laughed and shook my head and Peter looked at me with a raised eyebrow.

"What's so funny, Doc?"

"Well, my former partner always tried to get me to fly fish but I just wasn't interested. Now you bring me back here and want to fly fish with me. I know Case is busting a gut now!"

"Well, maybe you're supposed to learn how to fly fish. You ever thought of that? It might be somethin' that doesn't come naturally, but maybe it'll help you de-stress. You might as well get to learnin' now, cause it's gonna come up again somewhere in your life."

I rubbed my chin and looked at him. "You may have a point there. So let's get this over with so I can move on to something else I'm supposed to learn!"

"Attitude is everything in life. And in fishin'. So calm yourself down, Doc, and relax. This is a very graceful way of fishin' but you'll get the hang of it if you let yourself go. Now pick up that reel and watch me. I'm bent over and crooked, but I can fish like nothin' you've ever seen."

Well, Peter wasn't just whistlin' "Dixie." He picked up his reel and when he started the rhythm of swaying with the line, I was lost in the magic of it all. He had lost his height but he looked taller out there with the line in motion over his head. He eventually set the line on the water so light that it barely disturbed the water. In a few minutes he had a fish. He turned and looked at my face, which was a mixture of amazement and awe.

"Now, Doc, you ain't gonna get anything standin' there watchin' me. Come on over here and start practicin' the swaying motion. Get in a rhythm and just let your wrist stay straight, and keep your arm under control. You're casting with your right arm and doin' it slowly so that you give the line time to make a loop. Just stand near the water and practice the casting motion. It's kinda hypnotic, but you'll find that you love this motion and you'll get lost in it. After you practice that a bit and are comfortable with the rod, then lay the line on the water. You don't want any drag."

I did what I was told, but it took me a while to relax and let the line sway. I got it right a few times and it felt good, and I got a small taste of why Case loved it so much. After about ten minutes of practicing the cast I laid the line on the water. I watched Peter and pulled out line with my left hand. He was a patient teacher and I learned quicker than I thought I would.

"Now, you're gettin' it, Doc. How does that feel? You gettin' hooked yet?"

I let out a laugh and smiled at him. "Yeah, with your help. I guess Case sent you to me to teach me this. One way or another he was goin' to make a fly fisherman out of me."

"It won't hurt you none, Doc. And when you leave work uptight about a patient, just come here in my back yard or find a river somewhere nearby and fly fish for about an hour. It'll straighten your day out, I'm tellin' you."

We put our rods up against the side of the house and walked back to the porch. I sipped on the lukewarm tea that was on the table between the chairs. "So what would you like to do with the rest of your days, Peter?"

"Mainly stay alive, Doc," he chuckled. I really have no plans right now, except stayin' healthy."

"I'll bring you some vitamins. I don't think your diet is what it should be. If you take the supplements it will fill in where your diet is lacking. I don't want you to stress out too much about your health. You're doing pretty well for your age and the best thing you can do is not worry. You still walking every day?"

"Yep. I wouldn't miss that for anything. I look forward every evening to walkin' down the street a few blocks and back. May have to change my time when it gets colder out. But I'll walk as long as my legs will hold me up."

"Tell me about this town, Peter. I was thinking this morning about Jessica Reeves and her daughter who has been missing for years. It's just hard for me to swallow that no one saw anything. That she was grabbed right off a street corner without anyone noticing. The police don't even want to discuss it with me. They say the case has been cold for years and they consider her dead. I can't explain why this is haunting me, Peter, but it is. You have any light to shed on this subject?"

Peter scratched his head. He barely remembered the newspaper article about Charlotte Reeves being kidnapped. It was a long time ago. Maybe eighteen years. He would've been sixty-two years old back then. "I guess it could've happened that way, Doc. But it does seem odd that after all these years nothin's been found. You'd think the police would have uncovered some trace of her by now. But they don't look long, Doc. I think the department has gotten lazy over the years because there isn't much crime here, and never has been. You'd think it would be the other way around; that they would've tried to solve this case because it was rare."

"I agree. Maybe they did look long and hard, but I'm really puzzled that no one has stepped up at some point to say they saw something. She had to have been seen that day when she was walking home. It was later in the afternoon, but the sun was up. People were out and about. I'd love to run into somebody who saw her that day. Why, I'd pick their brain until they were ready to shoot me. Have you ever met Jessica Reeves, Charlotte's mother?"

"I think I did meet her through the school. I'm sure I did, Doc. But I've been out of teaching for at least twenty years now. That girl may have even been one of my students. I know it can get to ya, Doc. But don't dwell on it. It makes it tough because Mrs. Reeves is one of your patients. Maybe you can be kind to her and help her get her health back. That would be a kind thing to do, Doc. She's suffered enough."

"I'm watching out for her, Peter. But really there isn't much else I can do for her. I just wondered if you'd heard of the case, is all. Don't want to drive you crazy talkin' about it. I've enjoyed being with you immensely and hope we can do this again soon. Will you call and let me know if you want to get together again?"

"Oh, I'm gonna be checking on your fly fishin', buddy. Don't think you just get one lesson and it's done. No way. We're goin' to a lake when spring comes and catch some real fish. Your ole' buddy Case would be proud of you then."

"That sounds like a deal, Peter. Take care of yourself and call me if you need anything." This fly fishing thing was getting ridiculous. I laughed to myself as I walked to my car. I have to admit it felt great to get into a rhythm and get lost in the swaying of that line. I might like it more than I care to admit. Even to myself.

༄

It was mid-afternoon and I needed to run some errands. I decided to stop by and see Anna on my way home. Jill was at an auction for the fundraiser she was working on, so it was a perfect time for me to check on my daughter.

"Dad! What a nice surprise! Come on in. How are you?"

"The question is, how are you? You feeling better, Anna? How's your mood been?"

"Well . . . I have my days, Dad. It hasn't been very long and I'm still recovering from the miscarriage. What are you up to?" She looked tired and there were dark circles under her eyes.

"I was wondering if you'd given any thought about going on that cruise? I need to get the tickets if you decide to go."

"Thomas and I've talked about it, and he's really pushing me to say yes. I know it would be good for me, Dad. But I'm a bit emotional and tend to want to stay around the house. I don't feel like being around a lot of people just yet. Can you understand that?"

"Sure I can, honey. But you would have a private room on the cruise and it would be so relaxing for you. It wouldn't hurt you to get some sun, either."

"I know. I know. I'll make up my mind in a couple of days. Mother at the auction?"

"Yes, I'm on my way home. Just wanted to stop by and check in on you." I reached over and hugged her hard. I was worried about her; real worried.

"I'll give you a call on Wednesday of next week, Dad. One way or the other I'll call you."

"Sounds good, baby. Get plenty of rest, now. Talk to you soon."

As I walked out of her house, I decided to book the trip, anyway. Then she couldn't renege on me. I really thought she needed to get out and get some fresh air.

⁓

On the other side of the door, Anna was crying and holding her stomach. She just couldn't believe the babies were gone. No one seemed to understand how difficult this had been for her. This was her first pregnancy and now the babies were gone. She walked into the room that used to be the nursery. It was empty now, which described how she felt at the moment. Empty. How was she supposed to live after losing those babies? She wanted them so badly. She could remember how they felt moving in her stomach and how much in love she was with them. Their feet pressing against her ribs . . . she didn't get to smell them. That sweet smell of a newborn. Her heart was heavy and she felt so depressed. The thought of going on that cruise made her nervous. She had absolutely no desire to be around people, much less act happy like she was enjoying the cruise. Thomas really wanted to go which made her feel even worse for turning down the offer.

She had some pills that the doctor gave her to take if she needed help sleeping. She opened the lid and poured them out. There were about twenty pills in the bottle. Tiny pills. She knew from having a father who was a doctor that these pills were dangerous if you took too many. She was so tempted to take the whole bottle and just go to sleep. Then everything would go away. Thomas wouldn't be home for hours and no one else was coming by.

Anna walked into her bedroom where it was cool and dark. She suddenly felt weak and lay down on the bed. In her hand were the twenty pills. Tears were streaming down her face as she laid there and thought about the two babies that were her children. The thought of being with them was overpowering her. She suddenly became hysterical and grabbed the water beside her bed. She took one look at the photo on her bedside table of Thomas and her on her wedding day. She was so happy then. That was two years ago and now all she felt was darkness. *Oh, Thomas. Why can't you be home with me now, to help me get over this feeling. I feel so full of despair. So dark. I don't want to live anymore. Thomas . . . please understand that I just want to be with the children. Our babies. They didn't have a chance, Thomas. Not a chance. You all seem to be getting over it so quickly and I feel like I'm drowning. I carried them inside me and suddenly they're gone. There was no time to adjust. Maybe if I'd seen them . . . to see they were real . . . their little bodies. I can't take it. I just can't take it, Thomas.*

Anna got up and looked out the window. It was grey and cloudy. The sun had gone behind a dark cloud. *My father would die if he knew what I was thinking. My mother will never get over it. Why doesn't that matter to me now? I feel like I'm walking in a daze, in another world. Everything is in slow motion now.*

She lay on the bed, crying and put all the pills in her mouth. She sat up long enough to grab the water by her bed and swallowed the pills. It was too late now. She pulled the covers back and got in bed. She closed her eyes, with tears pouring down her cheeks, and prayed to God to forgive her. Somehow her father would have to understand. He was a doctor and he knew how broken she was. But her mother . . . Anna drifted into a deep sleep thinking of her babies. She would lay there undiscovered until Thomas came home at five thirty. The house was quiet; only the sound of the clock ticking in the hallway. Anna stopped breathing at 4:00.

CHAPTER 24

Jill and I were having an early dinner at 5:30. Jill was sharing with me how well the auction went and how much money they had raised for the local women's shelter in town. She really had a heart for those young women and it made her feel good to finally do something that might help them get their lives straightened out. I was just about to tell her about my visit with Peter Darby when the phone rang.

"Dad! It's Thomas. You've got to come over! I can't wake Anna up. Dad! I can't wake her up!" Thomas was screaming into the phone. My heart jumped into my throat and I ran and grabbed my black bag, telling Jill to get in the car.

"Jill, don't ask any questions. I'll fill you in on the way to Anna's. That was Thomas. Something's happened. Dear God, Jill, something's happened."

The drive to Anna's house seemed to take an hour even though I was speeding through town. I ran all the lights just trying to get there faster. Jill was already crying, because I told her that Thomas couldn't wake Anna up. It didn't sound good, but I was trying hard not to overreact. It was gray outside and starting to rain. I turned the wipers on in the car and tore down Anna's street. I couldn't get there fast enough. It seemed like we were moving in slow motion. We ran up to the door and burst into the house, screaming at Thomas.

"Where is she? Thomas! Where is she?" We ran head on into Thomas at the bedroom door.

"She's in here, Dad. She's not breathing! I can't feel a pulse anywhere."

My heart was racing and I pulled out my stethoscope. She was cold and clammy. Her body temperature had dropped. I felt no pulse and heard no heartbeat. She was gone. I turned her over and saw one tiny pill that had fallen down by the pillow's edge. I looked at the nightstand and there was an empty pill bottle for sleeping pills. I was horrified. I looked at Jill and she was already screaming at Anna. I grabbed her and pulled her away.

"Jill! Jill! She's gone. She took sleeping pills. Jill, listen to me, baby. She's gone."

It was like she couldn't hear me. She kept pushing me to get to Anna. I finally gave up and let her go, so that she could see for herself. Thomas was white as a sheet and shaking. I went over to him and told him to get something to drink in the kitchen. I picked up the phone and called 911. It was an obvious suicide but I phoned the police, anyway. I was in shock; it was my own daughter laying there dead. *I just saw you, Anna. I hugged you and we talked about the cruise. How could this have happened? How could we have missed this? I'm a doctor, for heaven's sake. Don't I know my own child? Was she that depressed over losing the babies that she wanted to die? How could I miss this?*

I went to Jill and pulled her away from the body. Anna was gone. The ambulance was there in minutes and the EMTs came in the door. The police came right behind them and asked Thomas a lot of questions. They checked her body closely to make sure there was no foul play involved. After about thirty minutes they allowed the EMTs to take her to the hospital. We climbed into my car and followed the ambulance. I felt dead inside; my mind couldn't function. I was stuck with a vision of seeing Anna lying on the bed like she was sleeping. I kept thinking she would wake up. We didn't say a word to each other 'til we got close to the hospital. We were overwhelmed with grief and just couldn't accept the fact that Anna had been so depressed and none of us saw it. This happened to other families, not to ours. I wanted to know how all of us missed this.

Shock is a funny thing that happens to the body during crisis. It sort of puts you in a place where you're floating. Nothing really sinks in. Our brains were not functioning normally at all. I could hardly talk intelligently to the nurses in ER, and Jill was speechless. Tears were pouring down her face as she stood there with Thomas. I don't really remember all that happened in the ER. We were numb. But one thing I remember well; we had to leave our daughter at the hospital and come home without her. And the hollow thought that I had running through my mind was that she would never come home again. Our daughter was gone forever. I prayed to God that we'd have the strength to go through this nightmare. I felt like I couldn't breathe.

⌒◦

For two weeks our lives were a blur; nothing really mattered. We went through the motions of the funeral and burial of our daughter but we were far from our normal lives. I was pulled back and couldn't reach Jill for days. Thomas stayed with us, as I was afraid for him to be alone. We all clung to each other in a silent slow motion dance that was orchestrated by our fear and tremendous sense of loss. For a while it felt like we couldn't count on anything. Every single aspect of our lives was subject to scrutiny, because nothing we knew before could be counted on as truth. All of us thought we had covered the ground of taking care of Anna's emotions. Thomas above all had remained by her side twenty-four hours a day, making sure she was okay emotionally. Her doctors had not picked up on any extreme emotions that needed to be dealt with. My feeling after five days of pure hell was that an extremely strong emotion came up randomly and caught her off guard. She was swallowed up in the loss of her babies and no longer could think clearly about anything. What was irrational suddenly became very rational. It became her way out of the pain and sorrow that was taking her down. I do believe the mind can reach a place outside the normal range of thinking and feeling, where it becomes difficult to discern what's real and what's not. Anna was floating between both realms, and slid down the icy slope of insanity for a brief moment. I can see how that could happen after losing the babies she wanted so much. She'd already fallen in love with them. They were a part of her body. She felt ripped apart both physically and mentally.

When the three of us came out of the stupor we were in, we sat down and tried to make some kind of sense of what had happened. It took us a while to sort through all of our emotions and we cried, laughed, and hugged each other, hoping to find our way back to a life without Anna Grace. That was a struggle for Thomas for his whole world was wrapped around her. We tried to reassure him that we were there for him, and that we'd help any way we could to get his life back to some form of a routine. He decided to head north to his parents' home in Washington so he would have a support group around him. I agreed it would be a good thing, even though we would've loved to have Thomas stay with us. He called his parents for support and they offered to fly him home. They called later and told him what his flight time was—he would leave tomorrow at 3:30.

We drove Thomas to his house and he packed his clothes, looked around for anything he might want to take, and then came back to our house. It was late when we all went to bed, but somehow I felt like we'd made progress in coping with this loss. Gregory had managed my patients for the last two weeks; I don't know what I would've done without him. He was a trooper and figured the mechanics of the office out all on his own. It felt good knowing he was there, and after phoning Mary Beth, I was told that the patients took to him right away.

Even though we all had turned a corner in a very short time, right on the edge of our consciousness was the haunting knowledge that Anna was gone. Out of our daily lives. But there wasn't a moment that went by that I didn't think of her. I looked for her on the streets when I was heading into work. I would wake up at night panicked because I couldn't remember her face, and I would get up and rummage through the photos on my desk until I found one of her. Jill was going through her own hell, trying to put the pieces together. I watched her closely and we slept against each other at night. Sometimes I would wake in the middle of the night and find her sitting in a chair rocking back and forth. I'd get up and go to her and ask her what she was thinking about. She always said the same thing. "I'm trying to find out where she is so I can go to her." I knew that Jill understood where Anna was, but that feeling of loss was so great. Nothing was taken for granted now. We knew one thing for sure. None of us would ever be the same again.

CHAPTER 25

In the early part of the morning, before the sun was completely above the horizon, Charlotte could hear Lucas stirring around upstairs. Things hadn't been good between them since he caught her looking out the window. She tried to reassure him that all she wanted to do was see out. She had no intentions of escaping. But he didn't swallow any of it. His greatest fear was that she would escape, and that kept him from giving her any freedom at all. He was coughing less and less, so she knew his health was improving. He was cooking more and bringing her better meals, so that meant he was working odd jobs again. This always excited her, because it meant he was gone some of the day and if she could figure out how to unlock that door at the top of the stairs she could get out of the house before he returned.

∾

Lucas was feeling stronger every day. The last dose of medicine seemed to be the magic bullet, because his throat wasn't so sore and he hadn't had a fever in several days. He was elated because that meant he didn't have to hear about going to the hospital. Dr. Lankford had mentioned coming to his house, but that wouldn't have happened. No one had ever been to his house, but he was certain Dr. Lankford would've tried. It felt good to be doing odd jobs again, and it also was nice to have some money in his bank account. He had thought about bringing Charlotte a present today but decided against it. Somehow he had to create a better atmosphere so she wouldn't think about leaving. He still had it in him to shoot her if she tried. It would kill him to do it, but he had made a promise to himself when he kidnapped her that if she tried to escape and it was real close, he'd take her down. When it came down to actually pulling the trigger he was not sure he could do it. But he'd have to face that when and if the time came. He did kill his father, but that was to save his mother. This would be outright cold-blooded murder.

∽

Charlotte had been depressed since she looked out the window and saw the world again. It almost made things worse because she was reminded of what she was missing being locked up in the cellar. She had adjusted after years of being down there and had accepted that this was her world. She constantly was thinking of ways to escape, but none of them ever came to fruition. The risk of Lucas shooting her was so great that she knew her plan had to be seamless. No holes. She had actually put on some weight since he was preparing better meals. Often there was a dessert and she really loved that. He also brought her some books to read from the used book store. That really excited her because there were only so many shows she could stand to watch on television. She found that she could lose herself in the books she read, and that was her one safe way of escape.

At night, when she was about to fall asleep, she would make herself go over that day when she first looked out of the window. She went over what the sky and grass and trees looked like. It was like seeing heaven, and she never wanted to forget it.

The last thing she thought about when she closed her eyes was her mother. She whispered into the darkness of the room, "Mother, please don't forget me. Don't lose the hope of finding me. I'll find my way back to you somehow. Please Mother, don't give up on me."

Twelve streets over, in another area of town, Jessica Reeves was about to go to sleep. She closed her eyes and whispered into the darkness, "Charlotte, I love you with all my heart. I pray you are dead, but my heart wants you alive. I'll never stop hopin' that you'll come back to me." And in the darkness the face she had forgotten years ago came in front of her eyes as clear as day. And then it was gone.

CHAPTER 26

It felt good to be back to work. On the drive in, I rolled my window down for a moment to feel the wind blowing in my face and took a deep breath, letting it roll around in my lungs. I needed to be awakened. I felt like I'd been in a dream; actually the worst nightmare I could've ever imagined. It was going to be difficult for us all not to slip back into that nightmare over and over, trying to figure out why. The why would never be fully solved, but it'll be the one thing that we pull with us through the muck and mire of that day, that will continually haunt us. Suicide may be a relief to the one who achieves it, but those who are left behind are forever tormented not by the life of the one who left, but the why of how they left.

When I walked in, Gregory greeted me with a hug. What a nice guy he was. I shook his hand and thanked him for stepping up to the plate when I really needed someone. He smiled his great smile, and said he hoped we all were feeling better. We walked into my office and sat down; he'd already put a cup of hot coffee on my desk and the files of the patients that were coming in today. Frankly, that was unexpected, and more than my receptionist or nurse had done since they came to work for me.

"Gregory, you're turning out to be a breath of fresh air around here. Thanks for the coffee and the files. How have things been around here?" I pushed away from my desk and propped my feet up.

"Nothing major, Mike. A lot of flu cases coming in the door. It's that time of year and it's spreading into the schools now. So we'll be seeing a lot of children soon. Not much news to tell you, except that we have a full day today. Are there patients that you would like to personally see, Mike? How are we dividing them up for now?"

"I will tag the folders of the patients that I would like to keep, and the rest we can divide as the day goes on. The nurse can alternate them and that way neither one of us is overloaded. You'll quickly develop patients who only want to see you, and that's fine. So we'll take it one day at a time until you've accumulated your own set of patients. It sort of takes care of itself in time, you know?"

"I agree. Here's the first patient of the day. A Jeff Windsor. Does that sound familiar to you?"

"Nope. Never heard of him before. I'll take him, so you can grab the second file and go to work. Have a great morning, Gregory. I know you've made mine!"

I went into the exam room and looked at the patient sitting on the table. He was a young man perhaps in his thirties, nice looking, texting hurriedly on his cell phone. He looked up at me sheepishly and closed his phone, tucked it in his pocket and cleared his throat.

"Good morning, Mr. Windsor. I'm Dr. Lankford. How can I help you this morning?"

"Nice to meet you, Dr. Lankford. I've heard good things about you. You're pretty new in town aren't you?"

"I've been here nearly a year, young man. I do love Crosgrove and am very happy my wife and I made the move."

"I've been having low back pain for several years and its gotten worse. Just wanted to come in and let you check it out to see if there was something we could do about it. This pain is driving me nuts."

"Sure, Mr. Windsor. May I call you Jeff?"

"That would be great!"

"Cool. Now stand up and let me see where that back's bothering you. Can you raise your arms without pain?"

"Yep."

"Can you bend over to reach your toes slowly without pain?"

Jeff tried to bed over but couldn't make it very far without wincing. "Not too good, Doc."

"How about raising your right knee up?"

"No pain here."

"Now raise your left knee."

"No pain, Doc."

"Good. Now you can sit back down. Did you do anything to reinjure your back recently?"

"I was washing my car and bent over to pick up the hose, and suddenly I had a sharp pain in my lower back."

"That sounds like fun. Let's get some X-rays so we can see what's going on with your back. I suggest we get an MRI so that we can see disc issues."

"That sounds serious, Doc. Is it?"

"No. But we need to make sure you haven't ruptured a disc. Say, how long have you lived in Crosgrove, Jeff?" I noticed that he was about the same age as Charlotte Reeves. A shot in the dark that he might know her.

"All my life."

"You attend Crosgrove High?"

"I sure did! Went there from elementary through high school."

Something popped into my mind out of nowhere. "Did you happen to have Peter Darby for a teacher when you were in high school?"

"Peter Darby? Of course! Who didn't have him for a teacher? If you went to Crosgrove, you had Mr. Darby at some point. He was one of my favorite teachers. Always made class interesting."

"Did you ever know a girl named Charlotte Reeves, Jeff?"

"Charlotte Reeves? Let's see. That name sounds familiar. Let me think."

"She would be about your age, I think. I heard that she was kidnapped years ago. Just wondered if you ever knew her."

Jeff got up from the table. "Seems like I do remember her name, Doc. We weren't best friends but her name sounds very familiar."

"Well, don't worry, Jeff. I was just wondering. It's a shame that nothing's ever turned up about her. I have a hard time believing that nobody ever saw anything that day when she was kidnapped. Her mother's one of my patients, and that woman is broken over losing her daughter. You can imagine, Jeff."

"Now that you mention it, I do remember Charlotte Reeves. I saw where she was kidnapped on the local news. It shocked the whole town. Everyone was upset that they couldn't find her. It was so sad to think that young girl was just gone. Like she was snatched off the face of the earth."

"Well, her mother told me she was walking home that day and was kidnapped. No one seems to know anything else about that day."

Jeff sat there in a daze. I could tell he was struggling to remember. "She was walking home. . . That rings a bell somewhere in my memory. In fact I think I remember seeing her walking on my street several times on her way home from somewhere. It's been so long ago that it's hard to remember anything at all about those years. I know her mother has probably given up hope of ever finding her daughter. It's too bad, Dr. Lankford."

"So you never knew her, Jeff?"

"Well, I'm sure I saw her around town or at school. But we never really talked to each other. It seems like I can remember her walking down my street on her way home from a girlfriend's house several times. But all she ever did was wave. I was pretty shy back then, and so was she. It would have taken something pretty monumental for us to get the nerve to speak to each other."

I laughed and shrugged my shoulders. "I was pretty shy, myself. Well if you ever think of anything, or know anyone you could ask about Charlotte Reeves, I sure would appreciate it. I really feel for her mother and wish Crosgrove could do something to help her out."

"Sure, Doc. If I think of anything, or ever hear anyone bring her name up, I'll let you know."

"Check with the front desk on your way out, Jeff. The nurse will make your appointment for the MRI. We'll call you when the results are back from the hospital. Let's hope it's good news!"

"Thanks, Doc. Nice to meet you."

I watched Jeff walk away with a hopeful feeling in my gut. Maybe somehow he'll remember something about her. Or talk to someone who knew her. It would be nothing short of a miracle if anything at all turned up. It could be that too much time had passed for anyone to remember much of anything.

I peeked in on Gregory and he was working with an old man who sounded pretty sick. I checked my watch and went back to my office to get the next file. I went into the exam room and closed the door. It was going to be a long day, but it felt good to have my mind busy on something besides Anna's death. Just thinking about it now made me sick and weak inside. I only hoped Jill could hold herself together until I get home from work.

In the middle of an exam with a patient it suddenly occurred to me that now I could relate to Jessica Reeves more than ever. She feared she had lost her daughter, and my only daughter had just died. The hope of ever finding Charlotte was very slim, but at least there was a slight chance. For me, there was none. Anna was gone. It made me even more determined to find out something about Charlotte.

CHAPTER 27

An odd thing happened on the way home from work tonight. I was driving slowly because traffic had backed up on Elm Street. Must have been a wreck or they were working on the road. My mind was wandering and I had the radio on. Suddenly I found myself thinking about Mava. It hadn't thought of her for a long, long time, since before Case died. I missed her tremendously. She was so young when she died that she missed most of our lives. I wondered what Mava would've looked like as a grown woman. Maybe like our mother . . . She was lovely as a little girl; always laughing. Her eyes would twinkle and she had a bit of mischief in her. She looked up to me as her big brother, and would do anything I asked her to do. Dear Mava. I'll be forever sorry for not watching her more closely. *And now my own daughter is gone because we didn't catch her brokenness.* How do things like this happen? People slipping through invisible cracks that swallow them up before we even realize they're gone. In a moment our lives can change so drastically and we're never ready to take such a leap.

All the years in medical school and all the years of treating patients haven't taught me how to deal with the loss of my own daughter. Nor have they helped me to know what to say when I walk through the door of our house and see my wife crying in a way I've never heard her cry before. What can I possibly say to her to make anything better? Nothing.

It has been a good day, but now I'm home and have to face the reality of our loss. I'm sure each day that goes by will shed its leaves and the pile will grow higher and higher. In the end, we will strain to remember this moment in time that seems so overwhelming. We will argue the points of how we found her, and what she could've possibly been thinking, until there are no more words to say about it. The harshness of the event will dim in our memories and hearts, but not the face of our daughter. And it may sound cruel because I do love Jill more than anything in the world, but I pray to God that the face of Anna is the last thing to go in my memory. I would love to carry that face with me when I close my eyes and see God Himself coming to take me home.

∽

Lucas had stepped out for about an hour to do some shopping. He'd left the porch light on and had locked all the doors. The last thing he did before he left was to check on Charlotte. She was reading a book, lost in her own thoughts. He'd left her a meal, and told her he was going. But he had to add that if she tried to look out of that window again, he would be forced to do something that he didn't want to do. She knew without further explanation what he meant. She could hear him leaving as the door shut behind him. She waited long enough and jumped off the sofa. She'd decided earlier that she was going to look out of the window one more time even if it meant she died. Because this life she'd lived in the cellar of his house wasn't worth trying to save. She had to be willing to take some risks or she would never know if she could escape or not.

She pushed the sofa under the window again and grabbed the chair. This time she put her book underneath the legs of the chair to stabilize it and added a few books in the seat to stand on. She hurriedly stood on the chair and looked out the dirty window. It was about dusk but she could still see pretty clearly. She looked around and took in the feeling of being outdoors; the wind was blowing and she could feel the air through the glass.

Suddenly she heard the tapping of a cane and looked to the right of the house. There coming down the sidewalk was a man, bent over, walking with a cane. It was too good to be true. She was looking at the man who always walked by her window every evening! The light in the sky was getting hazy and she could hardly see his face. He looked over towards the house and for a moment she thought he saw her. But he kept on walking and passed by the window without making any sign that he saw anything. Tears started streaming down her face, and she was angry for a moment. *How could he not see* me? *Maybe the window is too small . . .and the light is very dim in the cellar.* He would be walking back this way soon, and she would have to try to wave at him. The glass was very thick on the window, so there was no way to break it. She looked around the edges of the window but it appeared to be sealed shut.

She waited as long as she dared to wait for the old man to walk past the house again, and then she jumped down and moved the sofa back in its place against the wall. It took her a few minutes to get the chair down and all the books in their place on the bookshelf. She had to be sure that she left no trace of what she'd done. He would kill her this time if he knew she'd seen someone outside. She would have to pace herself. The more she went to the window, the higher the risk of getting caught. But one day she might find a way to get the attention of the old man with the cane. That was the closest she'd come to anyone on the outside all these years.

Charlotte sat down and thought about what it would mean if he saw her. She would have to have a plan or things could go all wrong. Slow was better. She couldn't do anything quickly or he would find out.

It wasn't long before Lucas came home. He had stopped at a local bar to get a few drinks, so he was feeling crazy inside. His thoughts were on Charlotte and how much he had grown attached to her. He had no real idea what love was, for he had never felt loved by anyone. But he felt like he owned her. That was a good feeling, and he felt proud of himself for accomplishing this feat of kidnapping a woman and keeping her to himself all these years. The community probably thought he was a recluse, but he could care less. He didn't trust any of them except Dr. Lankford, and even he was questionable. He sauntered up the steps to the front door of his house and unlocked the door. He was feeling romantic and had wicked thoughts of what he'd like to do to Charlotte. It'd been a long time since he had touched her and even though he was still frail, he could feel a warmth spreading through his body. She was his. She had to do what he said.

Once inside the house he put his groceries up and took off his coat and hat. The house felt cold so he dared to turn up the heat just to knock the chill out of the air. He put his ear to the cellar door and heard nothing, so he slowly turned the knob. Charlotte was sitting on the sofa in a daydream and didn't hear him on the stairs. She jumped with a start and her heart went up in her throat. *What is*

he doing coming down the stairs? He hasn't been down here in such a long time. It can't
be good.

"So what's my woman doin' tonight, huh? I come home to find you sittin' on
the sofa lookin' sad."

"I'm fine, Lucas. How was your day?"

"My day is of no consequence to you, remember? I'm feeling better and
wanting to get close to——"

He stopped short and looked at the window. His eyes were drawn to one
small book on the floor next to the window. It was almost hidden by the shadow
of the chair. "You trying to get out Charlotte? I told you not to go to that window
again!"

Charlotte turned ashen and stood up. "Oh no, Lucas. No way! I know you
don't want me to see outside and I promised I'd never do it again."

"Then what's this book doing on the floor next to this chair then? You know
you're supposed to keep those books on the bookshelf. You've never left one
out before." He walked up to her and put his hands on her throat. She looked
into his eyes and her heart started racing. He was furious. "Let me explain again,
missy. It seems you don't get it about the damn window. I'll kill you if you try to
escape. I promise you, Charlotte. Won't hesitate one minute to kill you. If you
haven't noticed, I own you. And when I tell you not to do somethin', I mean it."
His hands tightened on her throat and she tried to pull away from him. He threw
his head back and laughed.

"You won't be able to dodge the bullet, lady. And just to let you know a thing
or two about me——I killed my own father because he abused my mother one too
many times. So I do have a limit of what I will take from you. And your about to
push me over an edge that I can't pull myself back from. Do you get it? Go pick
up that book and don't let me see anything out of place down here again. I may
have to take the chair out of here if it's too much of a temptation to you. The
damn window is sealed shut. You can't get out, do you hear me? There is no way
out. You should know that by now, after all these years of living in this hole. I'd
have you upstairs but I can't trust you. If this happens again, I won't come downstairs; I'll simply aim from the stairs and shoot. Do what I say, or die."

He stomped up the stairs and slammed the door.

∾

Charlotte threw herself on the bed and cried. *How could I have been so stupid? I thought I put all the books up! He almost took my chair that I waited years for. My chance of getting that old man to see me would disappear and so would I. But what other option do I have? If I die, I die. I'm never going to stop trying to get out.*

CHAPTER 28

It was lightly raining when I got off work, but when I looked out across the sky I could see huge thunderheads forming at the edge of the horizon. It looked like it was going to pour, and there was the slightest feeling of fall in the air. I had asked Gregory to meet me for dinner, but first I was going to stop by the Memorial Park Cemetery to talk to Anna. I've never been much for graveyards but then I'd never had a daughter in one, either. All my beliefs and opinions about the dead went flying out the window the day Anna died. I may not come often, but tonight I wanted to sit with her even though I know it's just her body in the ground. It's odd how I know without a doubt that she isn't here. Her spirit. But yet there's this deep need to still talk to her. To let her know how I feel.

I walked a block and turned up towards a great oak tree that spread its arms out over many graves. Anna's was one of those graves that was graced by the large oak. When I came up to her grave I looked down and saw her name on the grave marker. It still took my breath away. It hadn't been that long ago that she was talking to me on the phone. Or that I hugged her and we laughed together. It seemed all wrong that her name was on the ground and that I was standing over her body buried six feet down. All these thoughts came in seconds as I approached the grave. I knelt down and placed my hand on the marker. Tears flowed down my face and dropped on the marker, mixed with the light rain falling. I could hear thunder in the distance, so I didn't have much time.

"Anna, baby, it's real difficult to be here with my knee on your grave. I still can't believe you're gone. My insides scream words that my mouth can't say, for it's insane that you're not here with your mother and me. You don't know the suffering your death has brought into all our lives. Thomas has no clue what to do with his life. You were his world, honey. You were our world. And you had no idea that in taking your life, ours would be forever damaged. Empty. A void so huge the moon couldn't fill it.

"Baby, I miss you. I keep looking for you to show up somewhere, but I know you won't. It's just me trying to cope. I——" I got so choked up I couldn't talk or think. I could hardly breathe. I stood up, forced myself to calm down, and then took a deep breath and looked around me. For a moment I got chilled and wanted to just run out of the cemetery. But I looked down and tried to deal with the feelings I was having. This was the toughest thing I'd ever been through in my life. I just didn't want to do it. I wiped my eyes on my shirtsleeve and cleared my throat.

"Anna, I won't come here often. I know you understand. Life goes on when we die, but it's not the same without you. All I can say is that we miss you so much and the only thing that gives us any comfort is to know you're with God. I have no doubt about that, angel. But I selfishly want you here with me. For whatever reason you left this world, I'm ever thankful you're at peace now. I love you, baby. I just don't know how I'm going to make it without you." I bent down on both knees and leaned over and kissed her grave and then I laid on top of the ground over her for a few moments. It was difficult to walk away from her, but I bit my lip and turned and headed down the hill. I foolishly felt like I was leaving her there. I knew different in my heart.

The sky was just about to explode when I got into my car. Gregory was waiting for me at Piccolo's and I needed to get a different look on my face before I walked into that restaurant. I straightened my shirt and wiped my eyes one more time. On the outside I looked fairly happy, meeting my new partner to eat a nice dinner. But inside, my guts were like Jello. And if it wouldn't scare the heck out of everyone in the restaurant, I wanted to scream as loud as humanly possible. But I didn't. I only smiled and shook Gregory's hand, and took my seat next to him at a table in the corner. Gregory looked at me and nodded. He didn't say anything, but he knew. I don't know to this day how he knew, but he knew. I owe him for not saying a word to me about it, because if he had, I would have lost it right there in the restaurant.

"Hey, buddy. What's good in this restaurant? You ever eaten the ribs here?"

"Heck no! I always get the prime rib, Gregory. And it'll melt in your mouth!"

He stretched in his chair and yawned. "I worked hard today, Mike. Can't believe how many patients we saw today. Good gosh."

I laughed and looked around the room. "Yeah, we had 'em in there today. Piled up in the waiting room. I thought Mary Beth was going to have a breakdown trying to fit them all in before 5:00. Oddly, we didn't make anyone wait too long today. Don't know how it happened, but I felt good about that."

"Oh, I forgot to tell you, Mike. You got a call from Peter Darby today. He was just checking on you. I told him you were doin' pretty well under the circumstances. He wanted to see you when you felt like it. Said somethin' about fly fishing."

That made me smile. "You've got to meet that guy, Greg. He's something else. Next time I see him I want you to go. You'll get the biggest kick out of listening to him talk. And he'll have you fly fishing in no time!"

Gregory laughed and slapped me on the back. "Good to see you smile. Worried about you guys, Mike. It's been a rough month for y'all but I think things are settling down a bit, don't you?"

"I sure do! And it's a good thing because I don't think I could take much more. Jill's pretty much at the end of her rope, too. Maybe we need to take a short trip somewhere. A long weekend, even. You got any great ideas?"

"Let me think on that, Mike. I'm sure I can come up with somewhere relaxing you guys can go. Winter is headed our way, though. You want to go south where it's warmer?"

"That might be nice, buddy. I'll check with her tonight and see what her frame of mind is. Normally I would surprise her with tickets, but not this time."

We ordered our meals and ate in silence. The greatest thing about our new friendship was that we didn't have to talk all the time. Gregory was reminding me more and more of Case, but I never spoke that out loud. After we ate, we covered all the topics we could think of about work, politics, and religion, without missing a beat. It was an invigorating conversation and worked my mind past what took place before dinner. When I arrived home I was in a much better frame of mind, which was needed because Jill was having a meltdown. She'd heard from Thomas.

"Honey, Thomas is struggling. It hasn't been long enough and he just doesn't know what to do with himself. He's moved his work up there and has made a couple of guy friends. But he's lost without her. I don't know what to say to him anymore."

"The fact is that we're all trying hard to cope, Jill. In our own pitiful ways we're trying to put our lives back together without Anna. It isn't going to be easy, I'm telling you that right now. I'm going through the same ridiculous dance that has no music. If I'm not extremely busy during my day, my thoughts go straight to our daughter. I know you're going through the same thing. So all we can do is support each other and be there for each other. There are no words that will fix this. That's the hell of it all. But we'll get through it. Does Thomas need therapy? I can check to see if any of my buddies know someone in Washington that could help him."

I walked over to Jill and put my arms around her. "Honey, we're going to calm down tonight and relax. It's normal to feel this way but let's take a break tonight. Anna wouldn't want our lives so torn apart, Jill. You know that as well as I do. Come on, let's sit down on the sofa and talk. I brought you some dessert from Piccolo's."

Jill smiled and laid her head on my shoulder. She was quiet a moment and then looked up at me with a solemn face. "Okay, honey. I know you're right. I've never been through this before. None of us have. There's no way to prepare for losing a child. The gamut of emotions is so hard to cope with. I'm angry, sad, frustrated, hurt, and missing her so badly. I can only imagine what Thomas must be going through; she was his wife, Mike. I imagine he could use some counseling. If I didn't have you I would have already lost my mind. You check to see if there's someone in Washington we can refer Thomas to."

I decided right then not to mention that I'd been to the cemetery earlier today . Some things were better left unsaid.

CHAPTER 29

The morning was just beginning with a cool October wind blowing across the crisp brown grass on the front lawn. Not too many people were about and the streets were quiet. The sun's rays were peeping low through the barren trees and the sky was full of white thin clouds moving at the pace of a snail. The north side of the house was still shaded and as I turned the corner of the porch past the front door, I found Jill sitting, wrapped in a quilt, a sweatshirt hoodie over her head. I hesitated to disturb her, for she looked so peaceful sitting there. She had a cup of coffee in her hands to keep her warm, and a journal sitting on the table next to her chair. I could see her breath turning white in the cold morning air. She was lost in her own thoughts, off somewhere I wasn't allowed to go, so I tiptoed back into the house. Sometimes it was easier to sort through things on our own, and I wanted to give her that time.

The phone rang and I jumped up to answer it.

"Michael? It's Olivia! How in the world are you?"

"We're making it pretty well, lady. Struggling to cope without our Anna."

"My heart has been sick worrying about you and Jill. She talked to me early on and I haven't been able to think of anything else since."

"It's a tough thing to go through, as you well know, Liv."

"Yes, and don't be surprised if it takes a long time. I still miss Case so much in my everyday life. I really don't want to get over him, but I have to tell myself that he's unaware of my suffering."

"I can relate to that. I went by her grave the other evening on my way to meet my new partner for a quick supper. It swallowed me up seeing her name on the ground. It made it so real. So permanent. I didn't want to leave, Liv. I felt like I was walking away from her. But in reality I know she isn't there."

"You'll feel that way for a time, Mike. But soon it'll be a little lighter for you and you'll find yourself going less and less to the cemetery. I felt at first like I was betraying Case, but now I know it really was for me, not him, that I went."

"Exactly. Well what's going on in your world?"

"I wanted to head your way, Mike. Stay with Jill for a few days. What do you think?"

"I think it's exactly what the doctor ordered! That's a great idea. When are you coming?"

"Tomorrow! I didn't want to give you much chance to say no. Can I come?"

"Jill would be angry if you didn't. In fact, let's surprise her. She could use a good surprise, you know?"

"Okay, I won't say a word. Expect me around dinnertime. When you hear a knock at the door, it's me."

"Mum's the word. See you tomorrow, Liv. It'll be good for all three of us."

◌~◌

Jeff was heading out the door for work and opened the garage. He stood by his car and looked out across the street at the trees that had lost their leaves. He glanced around his neighborhood and smiled. His parents had moved to a retirement community on the other side of town, and he was left with the family home to live in until he was ready to sell it and buy his own house. He was thinking about Charlotte Reeves this morning, remembering the times he saw her out on the street, walking home. She was a pretty girl, if he remembered correctly. But back then, he couldn't have spoken to her if his life had depended on it. And she was just as shy. He strained to remember the last time he saw her on his street. It was tough because it had been so long ago. He wished he could do something to help Dr. Lankford find a clue to her disappearance. But at the moment he was drawing a blank.

He pulled out of his driveway and drove to work, turning on Lewis Lane and pulling up to a red light. He looked to his left and there was an old pickup truck that was faded blue, with the paint chipping off. The driver had a cap on and had his head turned the other way. On the back window was an old sticker half torn off that said "I'd rather be fishing than —"The rest of the words were gone. Jeff smiled and turned to check the light.

Suddenly something came up in his memory. The sticker was orange with black lettering. He'd swear he had seen that before somewhere . . . He strained to remember where he'd seen that sticker, and he turned to look one more time at the truck. The light turned green and the truck pulled away, rumbling with dark smoke pouring out of the muffler, and Jeff watched mindlessly while he pulled out ahead of traffic. *I know I've seen that before. Where in the world was it? Had to be a long time ago. That truck is old. Maybe twenty years old. In fact, I think I've seen that truck before.*

He pulled into the parking lot, locked his car, and walked into his office. He spoke to Linda, his receptionist, put his briefcase down on his desk, and took off his coat and threw it up on the coat rack near his door. He sat down and turned on his computer and checked his schedule for the day. Since he'd opened his computer consulting company, he'd been busy from day one. Word spread fast and he had more business than he could handle, so he hired two other guys to go out and work on computers. He also had to hire a woman to answer the phone. He was making pretty good money and wanted to expand, but decided to take things slow. Better to be too busy than to expand and get in debt up to his eyebrows.

He got caught up in his work and the day flew by. He had snagged a good account on his own by contacting an old friend who worked at the college in Crosgrove. After getting connected with the director of computer science, the rest was history. That account kept him so busy that he could hardly keep up. But the money was good and it was practically hassle free. Finishing a scheduled service call on the director, he was walking out of the college when he ran into the friend, a old school buddy named John Hammond. They sat down on a bench and caught up on each other's lives. "It's been great seeing you, John, and it sounds like you have a full life. I'd better get going, it's getting late. Let's have lunch sometime soon."

"Sounds like a plan. Take it easy, man. Don't work so hard."

Jeff got back into his car and headed back to the office. He was still thinking about that faded blue pickup truck, and there was something in the back of his mind that was bugging him but he just couldn't put his finger on it. He was going to have to let it go for a while or he'd get nothing else accomplished. When he got back to the office Linda gave him a list of calls and he laid them on his desk. She also had two tickets to the concert in the park that evening and stuck them in his face. "You want to go to this concert tonight? I've got an extra ticket."

"Sure, I'll go with you. Let's get something to eat first; we'll have plenty of time to get to the park on time." He was glad she asked him to go. He needed to get out of the house more. He watched her walk away and smiled. She wasn't too bad to look at, and he sure didn't have anyone else on the horizon to go with. *I'm not getting any younger. I need to get my act together and look for some women to date. I'm too wrapped up in my work and life is passing me by. Linda's been dropping hints left and right and I've ignored them. But really, she's not my type and I don't want to lead her on. I'm too old to play games. I guess one date won't start anything. At least I hope it won't.*

He made a note on his desk to remind himself to call Dr. Lankford's office for an appointment. He had had to cancel the last appointment and that was when he would've found out about his MRI results. The night was young and he was starving. So he grabbed his coat and motioned to Linda, and they headed out of the office to eat. The temperature was dropping fast and he pulled his coat up around his neck. *The concert in the park may not last too long tonight. It's just too darn cold.*

CHAPTER 30

The doorbell rang at 6:00 and Jill looked over at Michael. "Who in the world would be ringing our doorbell at this time of night? Were you expecting anyone?"

"Let's go see who it is, Jill. What a great meal that was; I was enjoying the peace and quiet!"

Jill reached the door first and opened it, and found herself looking right into the face of her best friend Olivia. "What in the world? Olivia! What're you doing here this time of night? Is everything okay? Michael, did you know about this?"

Olivia grabbed her and held her a long time, both of them sobbing, and then they pulled away and looked at each other. "Jill, I just had to come! I hope you'll forgive me for popping in like this, but I really wanted to be here for you. It feels so good to see you!"

"I needed you here, Liv. But I didn't want you to have to drive all the way here by yourself. I see you made it just fine, though. Come, let's sit down. Are you hungry?"

"No, I stopped and ate a bite on the way. I just want to sit with you for the next few days and catch up. I want to know how you and Michael are doing with all that you've been through. And I want to go to the cemetery with you, Jill. I really do."

Jill paused and looked down. "Well, Liv, I haven't been to the cemetery since the funeral. I've been afraid to go, actually. I don't know if I can take it or not, seeing that grave marker with her name on it. It's just too new. You know?"

"Oh I know only too well, honey. We'll see how things go. Don't worry about that now. I just want to sit and look at you for awhile.

Michael gave Olivia a hug and winked at her. "You girls have a good visit. I think I'm gonna to run to the office a moment to check on a couple of things. I'll be back in a hour or so. Liv, I'm so glad you're here. Jill's been missing you, and this is a perfect time for a visit from you!"

⌒〜⌒

My phone rang when I got into the car to head to the office. I answered and it was Peter. "How's my favorite fishin' buddy doing tonight?"

"Not too good, I'm afraid. I know it's after supper, and you're probably ready to relax with your wife, but I sure would like you to check on me tonight. I'm not feeling good at all, Doc. Is that a possibility? I mean, don't be afraid to tell me no."

I smiled and shook my head. *Even when he feels bad he's a character.* "I'll be right over, Peter."

"You're sure, Doc?"

"Yep, be right there. Was goin' out, anyway."

"Okay. See ya in a minute. Really appreciate it."

The phone call worried me a little because he seemed to be going down fast all of a sudden. His health was basically good, but his body was just wearing out. I was eager to see how he was and maybe schedule some tests if needed. Old age has a way of soaking up all the youth in us until we are nothing but wrinkles and bones. It took me about ten minutes to get to his house, but I pulled into the driveway to find him sitting out on the porch waiting for me.

"Hey, Doc. That was pretty fast there. You run some red lights or somethin'?"

"I thought about it, man. But the traffic wasn't bad at all and I sailed right through those lights. So what's going on? You feelin' bad tonight?"

"Yeah, achin' everywhere, hard to breathe good. I just feel worn out all the time. Reckon I need some iron or somethin', Doc?"

"I'd like to meet him. Maybe when I get my test results you can introduce me to him. That is, if I live that long." He laughed his great laugh and that made me smile.

"Oh, you're too stubborn to die yet. Okay, I'm heading to the office for a few hours. You feeling any better about things?"

"Yep, as usual. All you have to do is show up and I feel better. Thanks for comin' by, and I'll call you on Monday to see about the test schedule. Not lookin' forward to that at all. But I'll do what I have to do. Don't want you to be disappointed in me."

"You couldn't disappoint me if you tried. Talk to you soon. If you get to feelin' worse, give me a call. I mean it, Peter."

CHAPTER 31

Sitting at my desk with the files in front of me, I began to go over Jessica Reeves' files. There wasn't much about her background for me to look at. I went on the Internet and looked in old newspaper articles about the kidnapping of her daughter, and read as much as I could read on it. There just weren't any clues at all showing up but I didn't want to let it go. It helped that Jeff Windsor was the same age as Charlotte. That meant they probably did know each other. And he did say he remembered her walking down his street on her way home several times. I forgot to ask him if he knew Lucas Cunningham; that would've been a great question for me to ask. If he said yes, then we might get somewhere about knowing more about the guy. Peter had already told me he felt uneasy about Lucas. I just don't know if that's a justifiable emotion to have towards Lucas or not. There's so much unknown.

I printed out all the articles there were on the kidnapping and put them in Jessica Reeves' file. For some reason I felt like I was going to run up on something that would give us all a clue as to what happened to that girl. It was bugging me that the police just dropped the case. Let it grow cold. This was a young girl that a lot of people knew. How could the town just turn their heads and go back to their lives, knowing she might still be alive?

I straightened my desk, put the files back and headed out the door. Out of the corner of my eye I saw the message light blinking on my phone. I'd been so preoccupied that I'd missed seeing it when I sat down at my desk. I pushed the button and listened to the message someone had left. "Dr. Lankford? This is Martha Johnston, one of your patients. Hope I'm not steppin' out here on a limb, but just wanted to ask you a question about one of your patients. I had a man workin' on my house for the last week and his name was Lucas Cunningham. He was nice enough but a little rough around the edges, if you know what I mean. Anyway, he did a pretty good job and I went to pay him and he wouldn't accept a check. He wanted straight cash. So I told him right out I'd have to bring the money to him tomorrow. I asked where he lived and he said he'd rather meet me somewhere to get it. I asked him why I couldn't just drop the money by his house and he just wouldn't have it. I guess I wanted to know if you knew this man 'cause I'm feeling a bit distrustful now about him. Anyways, Doc, give me a call when you get this message. It may not be anything in the world, but it seemed mighty strange to me."

I sat there listening to Martha's message thinking about what she was saying about Lucas. He was a strange bird. So he's been doin' work at her house . . . and doesn't want her to come by his home to bring the money. I can't imagine why that is, but maybe I can find out for her. I made up my mind I was going to call on Lucas Cunningham at his house on Monday afternoon. I'd wanted to know more about him myself, and now I had reason to go.

I headed out of the office, turned out the lights, and drove home. My mind was racing ninety miles an hour about a man who looked like he lived on the railroad tracks. Someone like Lucas could drive you crazy trying to figure him out. I do better face to face with a person, and even though he's been in my exam room more than once, that wasn't enough time. His home would be the perfect environment to see what he's really like.

ᗡᖇ

Lucas was heading towards the stairway door to take Charlotte her meal. He thought he heard her crying again. It was getting old for both of them for her to be locked up in the bottom of his house. He really wanted to bring her upstairs but just couldn't figure out how to keep her from trying to escape. He opened the door and walked partially down the steps, looking for her in the room. She was standing under the window just looking at him with a defiant look. Because she'd been able to look out the window several times, she no longer seemed beaten down or weak. She was much stronger than she'd been in a long time. Determined.

"I'm not scared of you anymore, Lucas. You can kill me if you choose, but I'm going to look out this window every single day that I'm alive. And I don't care what you do to me, I'll find a way to do it."

He saw fire in her eyes and he sort of liked it. He came close to her and she spit at him. He was so shocked that he dropped the tray with her food on it and it went flying across the concrete floor. He turned and slapped her as hard as he could muster, and she fell back against the wall. He hit her hard enough to knock her down, but she got right back up and stood there with her arms folded.

"Don't you ever do that again, do you hear me?" He was so mad he could hardly talk. *How dare she spit at him!*

"That won't be all I do to you if you try to come close to me. I've had enough of you touching me. I hate it! You might as well kill me 'cause you're never going to do those things to me again, Lucas. Better find you another young girl to abuse, because I'm over it. I have nothing to fear from you. You've done it all. Killing me would actually be a relief if I'm never going to get out of this hole. I'm sick of your smell and of being treated like a dog. People's dogs live better than I do. You say I'm family. That's a joke. You don't treat family like this, if I remember correctly."

Her words hung in the air like heavy stones, and he turned his head away from her. He knew what he'd done to her was wrong. But he tried hard not to think about it. He'd kept her here longer than she'd been with her mother. He turned to go upstairs and looked back at her. "Don't forget I do have a gun. Don't try anything stupid. You talk big now, but you'll change your tune. If you ever want out of this cellar, you'll have to be much nicer to me. And I'll have to be able to trust you. That's a stretch from how you are now, don't ya think? You've been here with me for eighteen years, most of which you were pretty pathetic. You should know by now that we're family, like I told ya the first day I kidnapped you. Remember? I know you remember that day."

"I remember every second of that day. The sheer terror of it all. But what bothers me the most is that I can't remember the face of my mother. You've stolen all of my memories and I hate you for that. It feels so good after all these years to really tell you how I feel. I was so afraid of you and now I realize that

I was really afraid of dying. Now I understand that at least by dying, I would be free."

Lucas couldn't think of anything to say, so he turned and walked the rest of the way up the stairs and locked the door. He leaned against it, thinking. *What in the world has changed her so much? Is it because I've been gone a lot and she's had time to think? Or that she's been watching the window and seeing what the world is now? I was stupid to think I could keep her cooped up in the cellar all these years and not pay a price. She's turning on me now. Big time. How do I turn this around so I can bring her upstairs. I can't put a chain around her neck. I need to make money to pay bills and buy food. I can't just stay here all day checking on her. I may have created something too big to solve. She's getting stronger and I'm the weaker one now.*

૦૦

Downstairs, Charlotte was sitting on the bed shaking. It had taken all she had to talk to him like that. He could have really hurt her, but he didn't. He almost seemed shocked that she stood up to him. Her heart was still racing from the adrenalin and she had a few hours before she would go to bed. *I didn't hear the old man walking tonight. He must not feel well. He hasn't missed many nights passing the window. If he only knew that I lived to hear him walk by, he would die. If he only knew how attached I've become to him. I wish I could find a way to let him know that I've seen him. That I need help. I will think of something. I have to, to survive this nightmare.*

CHAPTER 32

Monday morning was busy. We had a full schedule and Gregory and I didn't have a moment to catch up with each other until around noon. Mary Beth had scheduled Jeff Windsor for Tuesday, so I could share with him the MRI results. I looked forward to seeing him for several reasons. Peter Darby's tests were scheduled and she contacted him to tell him when and where to go. Peyton Bridgeforth was coming in at one o'clock for a checkup, and so was Jeffrey Copperfield. I had returned Martha Johnston's phone call and told her to be careful around Lucas. I didn't think he would hurt her, but I also didn't want her to meet him somewhere alone to pay him. I told her I thought it might be best to just mail it to him if he wouldn't take a check. I had just hung up the phone when Gregory walked through the door, closed it quietly, and plopped down in a chair across from my desk.

"Michael, I've heard it all now."

"I'm not sure I want to hear this, but go!"

"A Mrs. Wellington came in this morning saying she wanted to know if it was okay for her to have another baby. Now mind you, Michael, this woman is fifty-five years old. She's starting menopause, for heaven's sake. I had to hold back a chuckle, because she was dead serious."

I wiped my brow and rolled my eyes at Gregory. "What in the world did you say to her?"

"I told her that physically it would be extremely difficult for her at fifty years old; that's assuming she could conceive in the first place. And even more important, the baby would be at extreme risk for deformity, Down syndrome and who knows what else. Then she proceeds to tell me that she has no husband and wants a donor. It was just too much!"

"Well, I hope you convinced her that it was absolutely not in her best interest to have a baby at this stage of her life. She could adopt. Did you suggest that?"

"Oh, yes. She wouldn't hear of it. I think she's going through a mid-life crisis. I told her this was a very important time in her life. Her children are grown and she has plenty of time to devote to a charity, or tackle something that she's always wanted to do."

"I know it's difficult for some people, male and female alike, to move into their mid fifties and not know what their life's all about. Their children grow up and they feel abandoned or unimportant. Some men feel that way when they retire. I've had men come in here that were so depressed I had to put them on Prozac just to have an intelligent conversation where I thought we could make any progress at all. They begin to over control other areas of their lives because they aren't running companies anymore. It's a strange phenomenon but we all have to face it at some point. Some do it better than others, it seems."

"Well, I hope she calms down. I felt sorry for her, but a baby isn't what she needs at this time in her life. I'm sure it's been done before, but I wouldn't advise it." He paused and looked at his watch. "How's your morning been?"

"I've had a busy one. And this afternoon I have two men coming in I hope are in a better place than the last time I saw them. Hey! Do you think we have time to catch a bite at Frank's Deli? Let's check with Mary Beth. We may just have enough time before the next patient is scheduled."

෬෧

The diner was crowded and there was a mixture of aromas in the air of homemade chili and freshly baked apple pie. An odd combination, but that was exactly what I was having. We found a booth at the back of the diner and sat down. Paula, the waitress, knew us by name, unfortunately, which meant we'd eaten here too often. We both ordered and leaned back against the seat to take a breath.

"I've never told you about Jessica Reeves, have I?"

"No, I don't recall you ever mentioning her name."

"She's a patient of mine. During her first exam, she opened up and shared with me that her only daughter Charlotte was kidnapped eighteen years ago. And no trace of her has ever been found. She's really given her up for dead, but is still mourning her loss. She hasn't touched the daughter's room, and by looking at her you can tell it's slowly killing her."

"What an interesting story. So the police never found a clue? Nothing?"

"Nope. I read on the Internet all I could get my hands on about the kidnapping. All the articles were pretty much the same; no one saw anything. It seems so weird to me in this town where everyone knows everybody else. I'm trying to dig up something, even though it's probably futile. Since we lost our daughter, I really have empathy for Mrs. Reeves. Do you think it's possible that the girl could be alive after all these years?"

"Well, that's difficult to say, Mike. So many factors are in play here. She could be alive, all right, but the odds are against it. If I was a bettin' man I'd say she was gone. But that doesn't mean it's not worth looking into. I don't want to discourage you or anything. Stranger things have happened. In fact, I remember a story on television years ago where a young girl was kidnapped while her parents were sleeping and they found her about twelve years later. She had adjusted to her kidnapper and lived a very sick controlled life with him. That could very well be the case here, but how does one go about checking into something like this? How would you find clues that the police overlooked?"

"That's the question of the century, isn't it? I don't know. But my gut tells me that she may be alive."

The waitress brought our food and we swallowed the chili whole so we could get to the apple pie before it was time to head back to the office. "There's another patient of mine who is a weird sort. He's sickly, I don't think he bathes regularly, and has never seen a dentist. He got squirmy when I asked for his phone number so I could check up on him. Normally I'd feel sorry for a patient in that shape, but he gives me the creeps. He lives on the same street as Peter Darby and even Peter feels weird walking by his run-down house. I don't feel good about him, but nothing he's said would really make me feel uneasy—it's the way he looks at me. I may be crazy, but I want to find out more about him, Greg. And to top it off, another patient called me and said he'd done some work at her house, painting or something, and he wouldn't take a check. He wanted cash. She asked if she could bring it to his house the next day and he refused to let her come to his home. He wanted to meet her somewhere else. The whole thing doesn't add up, you know?"

"Sounds pretty fishy to me, but what're you going to say to him, if he lets you in?"

"Well, he was supposed to come back and see me because he has pneumonia and really needs to have some tests run at the hospital. I told him if I didn't hear from him I was going to drop by. He was pretty sick the last time I saw him. So I sort of have an excuse."

"Well, be careful, Mike. You don't know this guy very well and you already don't trust him. I don't know if it's smart to just show up at his house unannounced. That could set him off if he's not balanced emotionally. You seem to think he isn't, right?"

"No, I don't think anything about him is balanced. But because of how I feel, and I can't explain it, I'm going over there. I thought someone should know, in case something happens."

"You want me to go with you, Mike? I'd be more than happy to. I could wait in the car. How's that sound?"

"Well, I'll give that some thought. That might not be a bad idea. It's going to unnerve him for me to show up, that's for sure. I'll talk to you before the day's over, and let you know if I need a back up."

"Sounds like a caper to me! We'd best be heading back to the office. Mary Beth will be standing on her nose trying to keep those patients happy."

Just for a moment it felt like I was with Case again. Just the idea of planning something like this brought back memories when we were young. Case would be all over this guy Lucas.

CHAPTER 33

Lucas had decided to stay home all day because Charlotte was scaring him. He was losing ground with her and he didn't like it one bit. Somehow he had to maintain the upper hand, or she'd find a way out. He could sense a new strength in her. He wondered how much longer this could go on without someone finding out. It'd already gone on longer than he ever thought it would, but he was very attached to her and knew he would be in for life if he got caught. He just hadn't thought out things carefully enough. Leaving her in the cellar had turned out to be a bad idea.

He fixed her supper early in the afternoon and brought it to the door. She was sitting on the sofa reading and never looked up. He slammed the door and locked it, got his own meal and sat down and turned on the television. He heard something in the front yard and got up to look out of the window. What he saw caused his heart to race in his chest. He grabbed his gun and pulled the blinds slightly apart so he could see who it was. A man who looked like Dr. Lankford got out of his car and was walking towards the house. *What in the world would he be coming to my house for? Does he know something?* Lucas broke out in a sweat and thought a moment; his last visit with the doctor. *He did tell me he would come by here if I didn't show back up for a checkup. Now look what he's done.*

He squinted and thought he saw another man sitting in the car but he had no idea who he was. Dr. Lankford stepped up on the porch and rang the bell. Lucas didn't know whether to answer it or not. He decided to wait and see what happened next.

Michael was standing in front of the door and began to yell at Lucas. "Hey, Lucas! It's Dr. Lankford! I've kept to my word and come by to check on you. I want to know how you're feeling now. Lucas? Are you home?"

Lucas didn't know what to do. He felt trapped. It wasn't a good feeling and he'd avoided this type of situation like the plague. *If I don't answer, I'm not sure what he'll do. I sure can't bring him in the house. What if Charlotte yelled out? Anything could happen.* He was sweating profusely now, and his mind was going blank. He was freezing up. He decided to wait it out and kept still by the window.

Eventually Michael stepped off the porch but he didn't go straight to the car. He walked around the side of the house calling Lucas's name. *What would the neighbors think?* This was going to attract unwanted attention to him and that's just what he was trying to avoid.

Finally there was a knock at the back door. Lucas stayed against the walls and moved slowly to the back of the house. He could see him standing on the porch. He was afraid to move or he'd be seen.

෨෨

I knew Lucas was in the house. I could feel him watching me. I didn't know why he was afraid to answer the door but I wasn't going away that easily. I ran around the back of the house and stood on the back porch. I could see straight into his house. For a moment I thought I saw movement, but couldn't be sure. I didn't want the neighbors to think I was snooping, so I kept knocking on the door.

Greg came running around the corner of the house. "Mike! I felt like I better check on you, because I couldn't see what was going on. You okay?"

I laughed quietly. "Yeah, I'm good. He's not going to let me in. I know he's in there but I just don't know what to do next. Should I push it, or just let him be?"

"Well, that depends on how bad you want to talk to him. If you push too hard you'll never see him again as your patient. He did trust you enough to come to the office. Now he may feel uneasy and not show up for another appointment."

"I didn't think of that. I was so eager to get over here that I was oblivious to the consequences of my barging in like this. Maybe I should go home and leave the poor guy alone. I wish I could shake these feelings I have, Greg."

We walked back to the car, but when we got to the front of the house I noticed a small window low to the ground. I knelt down and tried to peek in but the glass was dirty and it was so dark inside I could barely see in. It looked like a cellar but I couldn't see much of anything in the room. I got up and brushed my pants off and headed for the car. I turned and looked back at the house and noticed an old blue pickup in the driveway. I made a mental note to remember that so I'd know if he was home the next time I came for an unexpected visit. Greg had already started the car and pulled up into the driveway to get me.

"Oh well, so much for that caper! I guess I better have plan B if I want to find out about Lucas. I hope he doesn't get spooked and drop me as his doctor. If that happens, I'll still find a way to talk to him."

"Better be careful, Mike. This guy could be a live wire. We just don't know. He definitely is a recluse and usually that type of person doesn't want to be cornered."

"You're probably right, Greg. I'll back off a bit and think of another way. Thanks for going, though. At least we tried."

"Yeah, it was fun. But I got a little nervous when you headed for the back. He could've had a gun in there and you would've been a sittin' duck."

We both had a good laugh but we also knew there was truth to what he'd said.

∽

Lucas peeked out of the front of the house and saw the car pull away. He felt relieved and sat back down in his chair, but his body was shaking like a leaf. His cover was almost exposed. He better watch himself now, for sure. And even though he would prefer to never set foot again in Lankford's office, he knew that might cause more curiosity and Dr. Lankford might try to visit him again. Best stay like things are normal and not act any different towards the doctor.

He went to the door of the cellar and listened. All he could hear was the slight noise of the television. He slid down against the doorway and sat on the floor with his back to the door. Here he was with a woman in the house, locked up. And all he wanted was a family. Someone to care about him. Someone for him to love. He'd done it all wrong. She wasn't family after all these years. She was a prisoner. He finally broke down and cried as hard as he'd ever cried in his life. He gave out a scream that came from his guts and beat on the door. "All I wanted was for you to be family. And now you hate me. I might as well kill you like I killed my own father. What difference does it make now?"

Charlotte listened in fear. She was petrified now that she'd set him off and he might very well kill her to stop this roller coaster of emotions he was feeling. *So he shot his own father? I wonder why? Maybe that's what has messed him up in his head. It would mess anyone up to have to kill a parent.*

It got quiet in the house and she relaxed a little. She put her tray up at the top of the stairs, like always, and climbed back down the stairway. This was going to be a long night, because she wasn't going to sleep with him being so upset. In the darkness of the cellar, with a single dim light on, she found herself feeling sorry for Lucas. All these years with him, she'd adjusted being there, and she realized she had developed a sick kind of attachment to him. Guessing this was normal, she still was confused about how she felt about him now. He was obviously tormented, but he'd admittedly committed a crime by kidnapping her. He knew it was wrong, and now she also knew he'd killed his own father. And she was a target now simply because she'd stood up to him. She decided to lay low for the next few days and not bother him. Until something changed, or she found a way out, she was stuck living in the same house with Lucas. And it probably was smart to treat him nice so that his temper would remain in check. There was a loaded gun in the house, and now more than ever, he might choose to kill her rather than risk being found out.

CHAPTER 34

Jill and Olivia had been spending a lot of girl time together and it was obvious to Michael that Jill was really enjoying her friend. They'd decided today that they would make the trip to the cemetery, and Jill was already getting butterflies in her stomach. She pushed her breakfast plate away and sipped the hot coffee. It was cold outside so they both had dressed for the weather. When they walked out the door Olivia faced Jill and hugged her. "You know without saying that if this gets to be too much to you, just say the word and we'll leave. No questions asked. Okay?"

"I know, honey. I'm trying to prepare myself for what I'm going to see, but there's really nothing that's going to make this any easier. I want to be able to go there sometimes just to sit and think. But that's going to take longer than I thought it would. I still feel pretty fragile and even a little angry about it all. She was too young to die, and obviously didn't think about how it would affect all of us. Or maybe that just didn't matter at the time."

"I don't think the person who's committing suicide is capable of sorting through all of those emotions and feelings. They're focused on one thing and one thing only; to get out of the situation that's making them feel so bad. They're drowning in a situation and don't know another way out. I'm sure she must've felt like nobody understood how she felt. It's so sad that she didn't talk to you or Mike about it."

"That fact will haunt the both of us for a long time. I thought we were watching her closely. But now I see how easy it is to miss the signs of depression."

Both women were quiet on the ride over to the cemetery, lost in their own thoughts and feelings. When Jill pulled up to the parking lot, they got out and began the trek up the hill to the huge oak tree. Like Michael, Jill was overwhelmed with the sight of the tree stretching out across the graves. She was glad Anna had this spot on the hill; it was peaceful and the tree seemed to give shelter from the weather. She walked right up to the grave and looked down. The sight of Anna's name on the ground overwhelmed Jill and she fell to the ground and was overcome with grief. Olivia knelt down and put her arms around Jill and they both cried for a few moments. Both knew it was good for Jill to let out her emotions, and after a several minutes she was able to speak.

"I knew this was going to be hard, but I didn't realize it would hit me so hard to see her name here. The day of the funeral was a blur, so I feel like this is the first time I've really seen her grave. My child is in the ground, Liv. I wasn't ready to give her up. She was so young and had her whole life to live."

"I know, honey. Take some time to sit here and I'm going to go over to that bench right across the way, so you can have time to yourself with her."

Jill spoke quietly into the air. "Anna, my sweet girl. I still can't believe you're gone. It plagues me about why you did this thing, Anna. Why would you take your own life? I want you to know how much I love you and miss you. I feel close to you sitting here, but at the same time I feel you're a million miles away. I don't know how I'll physically and emotionally make it the rest of my life without you being here, but I have to try. I have your father to go through this with me, but it's going to be tough on both of us. You were the light of our lives and now that light is gone. I don't know quite what to do next, Anna . . ." Jill laid her hand on the grave marker and tears ran down her face. She looked out across the hillside at all the graves and shook her head. *So many people who had lived and died, and life goes on like they'd never lived. That's the strange thing about death; a person who was once so vital to our lives dies and it's not long before we forget them. Days go by and we don't think about them. Days that turn into years.*

"Anna, I won't come often to your grave. It's too painful and I want to remember you the way you were, so alive and happy. The last time I saw you, you were smiling and talking to us about all your hopes and dreams. One day I'll see you again, honey."

Jill slowly lay down on top of the grave and kissed the ground. *God help me walk away from this grave and feel some sort of peace knowing she's with You.*

She got up and motioned to Olivia that it was time to go. She turned back one time to look at the grave and then got into the car. The ride home was quiet but Jill felt calmer than she had in weeks.

"It was a good thing that we came here today, Liv. It really helped me, as difficult as it was to see her name on the ground. I think that was the toughest thing. Just to see that name. Thanks so much for coming with me. I couldn't have made it alone, and I don't think Mike and I are ready to come together; I think that would be hard on both of us."

"I came because I wanted to, and you were there for me when Case died. He didn't allow you to be there at his death, but you came as soon as you could. And that meant the world to me, Jill."

"Let's go get some lunch, and laugh a little. That would help me more than anything right now.

CHAPTER 35

I was sitting at my desk getting ready for my next appointment and Mary Beth buzzed me on the intercom. "Dr. Lankford, can you take a call from a Mr. Darby?"

"Yes, I'll talk to him. Thanks, Mary Beth."

"Hello. Peter? How you doin' buddy?"

"I'm feelin' pretty good today, Doc. Say, I know you're busy and all, but I wanted to see if you might come by Sunday again for a visit?"

"Sure, Peter. How about two o'clock? Does that sound like a plan?"

"Sounds good to me, Doc. See you then. Don't mean to interrupt your day."

"No problem. See you on Sunday!" I kinda liked talking to Peter and was tickled that he wanted me back so soon. Our visits were becoming more frequent and that suited me just fine.

Jeff Windsor was sitting in the first exam room waiting on his test results for his MRI. I walked in and shook his hand and checked his file. The nurse had taken his vitals and they were normal. "Good afternoon, Jeff! How's your back been feeling?"

"It's been acting up a lot since we last talked, Doc. I'm anxious to find out what the test results are. Is my back in a mess, Doc? What's going on?"

"Oh, it's not so bad, Jeff. But there are a few issues." I pulled out the report and pulled the film up on the computer. "You see here, Jeff, where the two vertebrae come together? You have a bulging disc with a slight tear. That's what's giving you so much trouble. The bulge is slight so surgery isn't warranted. But you do need to get on some physical therapy to strengthen the muscles in your abs, your core, and your back. I can give you some pain meds that'll help you get through the healing time. You'll always have to watch this area of your back, Jeff. It'll be the weaker area of your body now, and all the stress you go through will cause that lower back to flare up. I know that's not what you want to hear, but we all have back issues as we age. Yours is just showin' up a little early, is all."

"Sounds pretty wicked, Doc. How long do I need to do these exercises?"

"For the rest of your life, Jeff!" We both laughed and I put my hand on his shoulder.

"It's not so bad, Jeff. We need to exercise, anyway. Do you walk much? Or ride your bike? You need to be doing something on a regular basis to keep your back and core strong."

"I'll get back on my bike as soon as I feel better in my back. So is that all, Doc? Anything else I need to know?"

"Well, there was one thing I wanted to ask you that I forgot to ask the last visit. Remember when we were talking about Charlotte Reeves the other day?"

"Yeah, I remember, Doc."

"Well, I wanted to know if you've ever heard the name Lucas Cunningham?"

"Lucas Cunningham? Let me see. How would I know him, Doc.? He lives here in town?"

"Yeah, he does. Been here for some time now. Does that name ring a bell? I happen to know he drives an old blue pickup around town—"

"An old blue pickup? Is that what you said?"

"Yep. Just saw it the other day in his driveway."

"Well . . . I did see a blue pickup the other day when I was pulling up to a red light. It sort of bothered me because I felt like I'd seen that truck before. But I couldn't for the life of me remember when."

"It had to be his, Jeff. How many of those trucks would still be around in Crosgrove?"

"You're probably right. I wish I could remember where I saw it last. I had to make myself stop thinking about it or I was going to go nuts. Since you brought up Charlotte Reeves to me, I've had a lot of time to think about her and just can't put my finger on the last time I saw her. If it comes to me, I'll give you a call. But it's interesting that the pickup truck that I saw and somehow remembered from some time ago belongs to Lucas Cunningham."

"Well, think about it. If something comes to mind, let me know. Now, about your back. I'll set you up with some physical therapy or decompression with a chiropractor and after about six to ten weeks, I want you back in here so we can reevaluate how you're doing. In the interim, let me know if you're having any problems. Sound good?"

"Sounds good, Doc. I just hope it works. 'Cause I'm gettin' tired of the pain."

"You'll get better pretty fast, Jeff. You're young and your body will heal quickly given the right environment."

"Thanks Doc. I'll give you a call soon and I hope something comes to mind about that pickup truck!"

∽

I sat in my office after Jeff left and had some time to think. I almost felt like things were coming together in the universe and I was about to figure this whole thing out. I needed to be patient and not blow the whole thing, which was difficult because I already felt like I knew what was going to happen. I needed proof. Tangible proof. This had been a busy week and I was worn out. I know Gregory had to be exhausted. We were each seeing about twenty patients a day and after a full week of that, we both were feeling pretty rough. Mainly because we weren't getting any younger, and this routine was ruthless even for a younger man. I thought it would be a slower pace in Crosgrove, but evidently we were getting pretty popular around town.

I was back into my routine of studying my medical journals and any publications I had coming in the mail or on the Internet. That was my love and I wasn't able to spend as much time researching as I really wanted to. But my patients were hugely important to me and I was developing good relationships with them. That's what every doctor wants, but it also meant that those patients were going to refer others to us. Family members, friends; it built and built until we almost needed a third doctor; yet in spite of that I was determined to keep this practice small. Containable. Yet I wasn't sure exactly how you turn people away. That was the dilemma of it all.

When I opened this practice, I wanted to have time to really get to know the patients and use this sense of understanding that I'd been given. It had been developing for years, even when I was with Case. But it had heightened since I moved to Crosgrove. It was hard to contain what I sensed about someone when they were in my exam room and I was pretty certain I was right about what I was feeling. I've held back because I'm not sure of myself yet. But with Lucas Cunningham, I'm afraid I'm dead on. I'm looking forward to my next visit with Peter; more information may come out, I just don't know. He walks by that house every single day. He's bound to see something if he stays with it long enough. If I'm wrong, I'm wrong, but I sense something is amiss with that guy and I want to find out what. I still hadn't shared anything with Jill, because I didn't want her to worry. And she would worry, after Anna's death. All we have is each other, and I need to remember that when I go on a manhunt like I did the other day with Gregory. I have to realize that I could get shot going on someone's private property unannounced.

My life is going by at the speed of light. I've had this practice over a year and it seems like yesterday that I moved there. I want to make every day count but they are flying by and I don't feel like I am able to take enough time to think things through. The whole world is speeding up and I wish I knew where we are headed. People claim that Crosgrove is crime free but I've seen cases of abuse that have been hidden for years. There is some theft going on, but nothing serious that I can tell. The police are busy giving speeding tickets, so that says a lot right there. *I just want to make a difference. I want to be remembered for trying, for helping mankind. And I want to find Charlotte Reeves.*

CHAPTER 36

Sunday came around like an unexpected gift. It was cold outside, but there was the tiniest hint of rain in the air. The trees were bare, and there were still piles of leaves gathering in the gutters along the street. The sky was a lovely shade of blue and it felt good to inhale the fresh air into my lungs. I had a wonderful late breakfast with Jill and made sure our cars were ready for winter. I had covered some of the plants in the yard to protect them from the freezing weather. At about 1:45 I said goodbye to Jill and headed on over to Peter's for the afternoon. I looked forward to seeing him more than I'd realized. He'd become a good friend to me and I really admired him for what he'd come through in his life. But what meant so much was that he cared enough to listen to me, too. He was there for me a hundred percent, which was something he hadn't experienced in his own childhood. I pulled up in his driveway but this time he wasn't waiting for me on the porch. It was chilly so I figured he was in the house staying warm. His skin was thin and he didn't have much fat on him to insulate him from the cold. I stepped up on the porch and rang the bell. It took him a few minutes to get to the door, but he asked me to come in and shut the door quickly to keep the cold air out.

"Hey, Doc! Good to see you. I've been lookin' forward to seein' you all week long. Thanks for takin' the time to come over again. How was your week?"

"I've been busier than a beaver building a dam to hold back Niagara Falls! How are you feeling, man?"

"Sit down, Doc. Take a load off. I've got us tea and some cookies a neighbor brought over. They're still warm from the oven. I'm glad you're here today because I'd make myself sick eatin' these things." He looked pretty weak but it was hard to tell how he was doing.

"You feeling okay, Peter? Are you feeling as tired as you were the last time I saw you?" I took a big bite out of a cookie. They were pretty deadly.

"Nope. I'm much stronger. I mean, I have my moments where I can't stand to put on my pants. But hey, it happens to the best of us. Other days I enjoy my walk and go to bed after the late show."

"Well, I hadn't heard any complaints from you, so I gathered you were doing some better."

Peter walked over to the bookshelf and picked up a photo album. "I wanted you to see these pictures. Just a few shots of my family, what little I had. They don't mean anything to anyone but me, but I knew you might be interested in seein' them."

"I'd love to see anything you have about your past." I made room for him on the sofa, curious about what photos he'd managed to save from his childhood.

He opened up the cracked and worn album and turned to the first page. The first photo was of his house he grew up in. The picture was faded so I couldn't see much about the house. There were pictures of an old truck, a tire swing in the yard, but oddly, no family members. Because he lost his twin brothers and his parents so early in his life, he had lost the memories of their faces. "I know that's frustrating, Peter. It's hard for me to remember faces from my childhood, so I can imagine how difficult it is for you to remember the faces of your parents and brothers. I wish there'd been more photos taken when you were younger."

"Well, oddly, there's only one photo here of me when I was a little boy. It saddens me because I yearn now more than ever to see the faces of my brothers. But I look at these few photos often, hoping it'll trigger some kind of memory that's tucked back in this old brain of mine." He sipped some tea and took a bite of a cookie on his plate. "You know, Mike, sometimes I'll be dreaming and a face will pop up that I don't recognize. I wake up wondering if that was my mother or father. I mean, can you dream faces that you've never seen before? Is that even possible?"

"That's a good question, but my gut feeling is that we can't dream faces that we aren't familiar with. A lot of my dreams have people with their backs turned or I never see their face. But I don't recall ever seeing a face that I didn't recognize. Even if I dream a bank is being held up, I can't ever see the faces of the robbers."

"So that means probably they are my family, and it makes me wish I could take a picture of that dream so I could see those faces the next day. They're so clear in my dreams."

As usual, time flew by when I was with Peter Darby, because we talked about so many different things when we were together. I was always shocked when I looked at my watch and saw what time it was.

"Your business goin' well, Doc? You stayin' busy?"

"We're swamped! I was just talking to Gregory about how busy we've been. I was trying to keep this practice down so we could give more attention to our patients. But it's snowballed on us. That's telling me we're doing a good job, but we may have to tell people we aren't taking new patients at this time. I've only been in practice for a year, and I'm amazed how fast this happened."

"I been runnin' my mouth to people about how good you are. Maybe I should shut up, Doc!" He laughed and made my day.

"Say, Peter, I wanted to talk to you about something before I go. You know we spoke about Lucas Cunningham on one of my visits with you, remember?"

"Yeah, he's in that house down the street here."

"Right. Well, I went by to see him the other day and I know he was home; his truck was there. But he wouldn't answer the door. I was wondering if you ever see anything when you walk by the house. You must've walked by that house hundreds of times, and I was thinking that surely you've seen something in all these years."

"You know, Doc, I agree with you. You'd think I would've seen him out in the yard or someone comin' in or goin' out. But to be honest, it's like the house is abandoned. I never see anyone there. One evening I thought I saw a light in the cellar. But my eyes aren't too good anymore and I couldn't see that well at dusk. In fact I've seen lights on in the house and thought I saw him at the front window once, but I've never seen Lucas walkin' outside. He's a recluse, Doc."

"Any neighbors ever say anything to you about him?"

"Only that they don't know anything about him. We all think he's peculiar. He doesn't talk to anyone so we don't know where he came from or what he does for a living. His old blue truck is parked there most nights, but I've noticed that he does leave for a while during the day. Maybe he's doing odd jobs to earn money. I know I feel uneasy when I walk by the house, but I don't have any real reason to tell you why."

"Well, I felt it when I was at his house. I took a risk and walked around the back of his house; I could see straight into the kitchen and hallway, but I never saw him. There was some movement for a second, but he never came to the door. The truck was there, so I know he was home. I went there to check on his health, because he never came back for a checkup and he was pretty sick."

"Better be careful, Doc. Someone like that could be trouble. Don't set yourself up for getting' shot."

"Yeah, Gregory said the same thing. I wasn't really thinking about the fact that he might have a gun in his possession. So next time I need to be more careful." I paused and took my last bite of cookie. "You remember we talked about Charlotte Reeves, the girl who was kidnapped?"

"Yeah. You find anything more about that case?"

"No, and I spent a lot of time on the Internet and in newspaper articles reading all I could get my hands on. Nothing. I mean, it looks like they dropped the case pretty quickly. It's been so long now that it would be hard to find any clues."

"I know you've been doin' a lot of thinking about Jessica Reeves and her daughter. Doc, take it easy. You need to give yourself time to get over your own daughter's death. That hit you pretty hard; it was so unexpected. I'm worried you're tuckin' your emotions down and stayin' so busy focusin' on Charlotte Reeves that you aren't allowin' yourself to grieve about your own daughter's death."

"Well, you may be right, buddy. But I know I'll grieve over Anna's death for many years. Maybe forever. I'm just so aware of how Jessica Reeves must feel, knowing her daughter could be alive. The odds are slim, but I wouldn't be able to stop looking until I'd turned over every stone."

"Well just make sure you don't dig your own grave while you're looking for that stone."

"I want you to be aware of the pickup truck and see if you ever notice it around town. I'd love to be able to talk to Lucas outside the office. I want that guy to open up to me and let me in. It's a long shot, but that's my goal for now."

"I'll do what I can, Doc. If I see anything at the house unusual, I'll let you know. Maybe since I'm in my eighties, it'd be safer for me to go knock on the door instead of you."

I started laughing so hard I could barely breathe. "No way. You stay off that porch! But keep in touch with me. And I'll get the results of your tests this week. I'll give you a call, and we can discuss all the results. See you next Sunday?"

"Sounds good to me, Doc. Have a good week."

CHAPTER 37

November had finally pushed its way into our lives, bringing with it the smell of pumpkin pie and the colors of fall. Kids were piling up leaves in their yards and diving into them. It made me smile every time I saw that, because I could remember doing it myself. It was much colder now and everyone was bundled up in jackets and catching their hats in the gusty winds of winter. I'd been meeting Peter for months now on Sunday afternoons. That was our day and I wouldn't change it for the world. Jill had been a real trooper about my being gone on Sunday afternoons, but somehow she understood how much I cherished my relationship with Peter. I also stopped by the cemetery and visited with Anna on my way to Peter's, and that visit with her rolled the stress of the week right off my back. Like Olivia shared with us, the sadness of the cemetery had lifted a little and I sort of looked forward each week to my time there. I tried hard not to dwell on the whys, and if I hadn't been able to settle that in my mind, I would've been one miserable man for the rest of my life. Jill was feeling much the same, although it was still difficult for us to talk about Anna when we were home alone. Somehow the walls were too close for us. Around other people we could laugh and remember good things about our time with Anna. But alone, it was a bit close and too raw.

Peter had taken ill and after a short hospital stay he was back home. I'd committed to seeing him each day in the late afternoon, until he was stabilized. I was worried that I was going to lose him when he was in the hospital, but he rallied and was doing much better. His body was about to give out and I wanted to spend as much time with him as I could. We had become like father and son in a neat sort of way and I had learned so much in this time together. We had talks everyday about whatever came to our mind, and we'd reached a treasured place in our friendship where we could talk about anything even if we disagree. I thought about how I'd handle his passing, because he was so much a part of my life. I had lost Case almost a year ago and Anna Grace not many weeks before and now after letting someone else in, I was facing another loss before too long. His spirit was unbending; he absolutely would not allow self pity in the door. As I walked up the steps to his house I couldn't wait again to hear what he had to say to me.

The screen door opened with a loud creak and I walked into the warm, cozy house. "Peter! It's me. Just didn't want to catch you off guard. How're you feelin' this afternoon? Any change?"

"So it's you creepin' into my room again! Did you bring me a milkshake like you promised?"

I laughed and placed a sack on his bedside table. "Yeah, yeah. I wouldn't forget that milkshake for anything in the world. Let me look at you. You still feel achy?"

"Nope. Feelin' pretty good, actually. Thinkin' about getting' out of bed for a change. What say I try to walk around the house this afternoon? You think I'm ready, Doc?"

"Well, that might be pushing it a bit, but we can see how you do. First let's drink some of this shake, and I'd love to see you take a big bite out of the hamburger I brought you. Can we do that?"

"I'll eat the whole darn thing if I can get up and walk around. My bones are too familiar with this bed and I'm so tired of layin' down I don't know what to do. This bein' sickly is for the birds. I ain't never been sick in my life, and suddenly I feel like I'm goin' down so fast. It ain't right, Doc. You doin' your job around here? Or are you slackin' where my health is concerned?"

I slapped my leg and roared with laughter. "You ornery old man you! I wait on you hand and foot every single day and you're gonna to tell me I'm slackin' when it comes to taking care of you? Why, I think your mind's goin', right along with your body!"

"It'll be a cold day in hell before my mind goes, and you know it."

We both laughed and he began to eat his meal with much effort. I could tell he was hungry, which was a good sign. He hadn't eaten much lately. "Peter, guess who's comin' into my office next week? You'll never guess."

"I have no idea, Doc. Is it Santa Claus?"

"Oh, aren't we feeling better! No, it's not Santa Claus. It's Lucas Cunningham. He finally made an appointment with me after all this time. So I'll be able to check him over and see how he is. I'm thinkin' I just might ask him why he didn't answer the door a while back when I came to see him. What'd you think?"

"I think you should keep your mouth shut about that until you find out more about him. Your gonna get yourself killed, Doc. Somethin' 's not right with Lucas. I know it for sure."

"You're spot on, buddy. But I just don't know why we feel that way. I've got to find out, though, or it'll drive me crazy thinkin' about it. And I'm worried about ever finding Charlotte alive."

You know, Doc, if I was Charlotte Reeves and I was still alive, I would've given up by now ever hopin' to see my family again. I would know there was no one looking for me anymore."

"Yep. That's how she probably feels if she's still alive. Can't say either way, Doc. It's been so long now that her own mother wouldn't know her if she walked right up to her."

"True. But I'm on a mission and I want to know where she is."

Peter dusted off his sheets and took the last sip of his milkshake. "Okay, Doc. Enough of this chatter. Let's get my scrawny body up off this bed and see if I can walk a little. You think we can do that?"

I pulled his legs over the side of the bed and let him sit up for a moment. When he felt steady enough I put my arm underneath his and wrapped it around his waist. He slowly stood up and swayed a minute, and then sat back down on the edge of the bed. "Whoa, Doc. Goin' too fast there. We're gonna have to go slower than that. The room was movin' on me."

"Well, you've been lying around so much that your blood pressure is a little low. Give your body time to adjust to sitting up, and then we can stand you up and walk around the room."

We worked on his walking for an hour and then he was ready to lie back down and take a short nap. I cleaned up the mess he'd made eating his supper and sat down to watch him sleep for a few minutes. I hoped to see him up and around in a few days, getting back to some sort of routine like he was before he got so ill. If he continued to be so weak and remained in bed, he might never get up again. Watching him sleep I thought about all the stories he'd shared with me about his youth. How alone he was. How he'd had to struggle to eat at least once a day to make it to school. *It was amazing what he got accomplished in his life on such little money.* And now, even though he has money, he lives like a pauper because that's all he knows.

I must've sat there an hour when he suddenly opened his eyes. Without any hesitation he started talking. "Doc, get a pen. I want you to write this down. I made a will years ago but we're about to change all that. You got a pen?"

I scrambled around to find paper and pen and sat back down on the hard wooden chair beside his bed. "Yep. Got a pen. What in the world do you want me to write down?"

"I'm addin' somethin' to my will. We been talkin' about Charlotte Reeves and all. Well, I just got a great idea. When you find her, and you will, I want to leave money for her. She'll have nothing to live on, Doc. She'll have nowhere to go. I'd take her in here in a New York minute, but I guess if her mother's alive she'll want Charlotte to live with her." He took a breath and kept on talking. "The least I can do is leave her some money so that she can buy a car or whatever she needs."

I was shocked at this revelation. I didn't know how much money Peter had, but for him to say he wanted to leave it to a younger woman he possibly had never met just blew me away. "You sure, Peter? That's stepping out pretty far on a limb here. Do we need to talk about this or is your mind made up?"

"I'd say it's made up, but what's on your mind, Doc?"

"Well, we don't even know if she's alive, right? And let's say she is alive; we don't know how friendly she'll be to us or how she'll take to us meddling in her life. I guess we could wait to tell her about the money until she's adjusted to the real world again. That may take some time; it all depends on Charlotte and how she's handled being locked up all these years. If she's even alive."

"I'd say we're thinking way too long about this. I'm not sayin' I'll leave her all my money. I just want to set up a —what's it called? A trust fund. Yeah. A trust fund for you so you can give her the money if she's ever found. I bet her mother ain't loaded with money, either, am I right?"

"I'd say you were reading that pretty well, Peter. We'll need an estate plan-ner for this; I can't just write this up on a napkin and have it stand up in court, you know."

I got a raised eyebrow on that statement. "I realize that, Dr. Lankford! But I want you to write all this down and I can sign the paper in case I die tonight, God forbid. And if for some reason she's never found, then I would trust you to distribute this money to someone in the town who needs it. We're talkin' like we know she's alive. We don't know anything right now about Charlotte Reeves. We're dreamin', is all."

I left that afternoon with a new understanding of who Peter Darby was. I thought I knew all I could know about him, but today he had just shown me another side of himself. Giving 101. And he was much smarter than he looked..

CHAPTER 38

My behavior concerning Jessica Reeves and her daughter Charlotte might have been considered strange to some; I wasn't even certain if Jill understood it completely. At first I had a normal curiosity about Charlotte after Jessica opened up to me about her kidnapping. The more I saw Jessica the more it occurred to me how difficult her life was as she tried to adjust to the fact that her daughter was not ever coming home. I had the normal amount of sympathy for Jessica, just as anyone would after hearing about her loss. But after Anna Grace died and I had to experience losing my own daughter, the feelings I had about Charlotte Reeves and the slight possibility that she may still be alive increased tremendously. I tried hard not to talk about it with Jill; she was still dealing with her own emotional roller coaster and we both were missing Anna more and more every day. I was told that it would get easier, but so far, it hadn't.

I had shared with Peter and then with Gregory about my interest in finding Charlotte. I was aware that it might be a dead end street and I didn't want to give Jessica false hopes about having her daughter back. I really didn't want to tell anyone else about how hard I was digging to find out information about the day she was kidnapped. I was able to contact her best friend Lacy Milner after asking Jessica some questions, and she remembered well the last time she saw Charlotte. The police had spoken with her many times after Charlotte's disappearance but she had nothing to share that would help the case, so they eventually left her alone. It took her years to stop having nightmares about the kidnapping, and even now, occasionally she said she thinks back on that day and tears well up in her eyes. After our conversation, I knew that the time of day Charlotte walked home was around 3:00 in the afternoon on October 19˙. Her normal route was down the street where Jeff Windsor lived and still resided. So in my mind, there was a slight chance that Jeff saw her that afternoon if he happened to be outside. I wished I could recreate that day in his mind to nudge his memory of that afternoon. Even if he did see her, that wouldn't help me in discovering who snatched her off the street. I decided to visit some of the stores on a corner near Jeff Windsor's house. I knew it was a long shot, but I'd feel much better if I could narrow down the options.

I parked and took a short walk down Middleton Avenue. It had great oaks with boughs that were leaning out over the street. The shop fronts were newly painted and there were potted plants in front of every store. The area had been renovated recently and it looked new. One of the shops that was on that corner eighteen years ago no longer existed. It was J & J's Hardware Store. It had been closed for ten years, so that eliminated one of the shops Charlotte saw that day. Next to that space was The Apothecary, a pharmacy and drug store. I walked in and looked around. It had obviously been redecorated years ago, so I knew I would find nothing there to help me. I left that store and moved on to Jerry's Auto Parts. When I opened one of the heavy walnut doors, I was amazed; it was like stepping back in time. Even though the shop had changed over the years, it looked like the owners had tried to keep it similar to the way it was when it first opened in the seventies. I totally lost myself in the aisles full of auto parts, tires, spray paint cans, floor mats, and everything else you could possibly want for a car. The smell pulled me in, along with the rows and rows of stained shelving that were packed with tools and things I'd never seen before. And like every man in the store, I didn't want to leave. There was a fully restored red and white '55 Chevy Bel Air that had been brought back to its original factory condition right down to the radiator clamps. Guys were hanging around the car like flies.

I spoke for a moment with the owner, Jerry Oglesby, who was one of the nicest guys you'd ever want to meet. His father had owned the shop before him and passed it down to the two sons. Jimmy, his brother, had passed away last year, so he was the sole owner. He walked me to the front counter and showed me a bulletin board of old postcards and also a wall of framed photographs from the past. I took a few moments to look over the photographs that were in color but faded. They were insignificant and seemed to be random shots of the outside of the building, and also shots of people they apparently knew, coming through the front door. I was trying to be polite and commented on some of the photos; it was fun to see the clothes people were wearing and also the cars parked in front of the store. Suddenly something caught my eye. In one of the photos someone had taken a picture standing in the store facing out. There was a red light and cars were stopped at the light when the photo was taken. On the left side of the road was a '71 Hemi Cuda convertible; obviously the reason for the photograph. On the right side of the road, across the street from the store, I could barely make out an old blue pickup truck stopped at the red light. Jerry was talking to me and I couldn't respond. I couldn't even hear what he was saying to me. All I could do was stare at the image of that truck. *Had to be Lucas Cunningham. Had to be. No one else could possibly have had a truck like that, no matter what year it was.*

Jerry was talking to me and I suddenly snapped out of my daze. "Dr. Lankford, what brings you here this afternoon? You lookin' for a part or something?"

"Uh, actually no. I was just checking out the shops here on the corner. I moved here a while ago and just hadn't made it to this part of town yet. I had some extra time today and took a drive out your way; love the store, Jerry, absolutely love it."

"Don't be a stranger, Doc. We'd love to have you back."

"Say Jerry, I was noticing these photos here; one in particular. You wouldn't know what date is on this photo, would you?"

"What, the one with the '71 Hemi Cuda in it?" He laughed and slapped me on the back. "Who wouldn't want that car, huh, Doc?"

"One of a kind, man, one of a kind. Is there any way for you to know when this was taken? Like on the back of the photo or something?"

Jerry pulled the photograph off the wall and turned the frame over. We couldn't see anything because the back of the frame was covered with old brown paper. "I'd have to take the frame apart to tell, Doc. Why do you want to know? Is it that important? Because if it is, I'll get to it quick as I can. I got people in here right now."

"I'm just curious about the old pickup in the distance. It sure would help me out if you could find out the date on that photograph. At your convenience, of course, Jerry. There's no big hurry, but here's my card. If you find out the date, give me a call, will you? This has been a real treat for me. It's my first time in here, but definitely not my last!"

"Anytime, Doc. And I'll give you call on your cell as soon as I find out the date on this photo. Have a great afternoon."

I couldn't get out of that store fast enough. My heart was racing and thoughts were flying through my mind. *What if that was Lucas's truck? It would be too good to be true. I should've asked for a magnifying glass so that I could check out the driver of the truck. Although it might be difficult to tell if it was Lucas or not, because it was eighteen years ago. If it was him, that still doesn't place him at the scene of a crime, but I can hope. What a fantastic store that was! I'll have to take Gregory there soon; he'll go nuts in there.*

On my way home, on a whim, I decided to stop in and say hello to Peter. Our normal day to visit was Sunday, but I didn't think he'd care. I knocked on the door and waited for what seemed like five minutes. He finally came to the door, tapping that cane on the hardwood floor. "Hey, Doc! I hope nothin' 's wrong! What are ya doin' here on Saturday afternoon?"

"Didn't mean to surprise you, Peter. Just wanted to talk to you about what I did today. You got a minute?"

Peter shook his head and smiled. "Are you kiddin'? I always got time for you, Doc. Come on in and take a load off. I'll get us somethin' to drink."

I sat down smiling. He was getting stronger and back to the Peter I had seen when I first met him. But I knew how fragile his health was. I had backed off coming every day, but I was still keeping a close eye on him. I couldn't wait to tell him about the photo. It felt good to just relax a minute and not think about anything.

"Here you go, Doc." He handed me my tea and sat down in a chair next to me. "So what's on your mind? You look like you're gonna' bust."

I laid my head back on the sofa and laughed. The tension eased up a little and my neck loosened up. I just realized I had a splitting headache. "Well, I've had an interesting afternoon, Peter. Wish you'd been with me. I took a short drive to a part of town I'd never been before. Over on Middleton Avenue. You know the area?"

"Sure do. They've done some neat renovatin' but it's been a while since I've been to the stores. Did you enjoy yourself?"

"I especially enjoyed Jerry's Auto Parts Store. You seen the work he's done in there? Peter! It looks like you've stepped back in time when you come through those big double walnut doors. I could've stayed in there all afternoon. Guys were hovering around this fully restored '55 Chevy Bel Air hardtop; I had one of those cars when I was young. It was the first year they had an overhead valve V-8 engine in it. Man, did that car move!"

"Sounds like you were pretty hyped up over it, Doc. I haven't seen you this excited since I've known ya!"

"Well, that's not the best part, Peter. The owner, Jerry Oglesby, came up and talked to me. Nice guy. He showed me around and then we headed up front to the counter where they had old post cards on a bulletin board and some framed photographs taken years ago. I was just being polite checking out the photos when suddenly something caught my eye in one of the photos. You'll never guess what it was!"

A twinkle jumped into Peter's eyes with both feet. He grinned and sat on the edge of the chair looking at me. "Now don't make me guess, Doc. I'm too old for games. What in the heck did you see, anyway?"

"Take it easy, Peter. I was looking at one of the photos that was taken from the inside of the shop looking out at the street. There's a traffic light at the corner and sitting at the light on the left side was a '71 Hemi Cuda convertible. That alone was enough to catch my attention. But as I studied the photo, I got a glimpse of an old blue pickup truck sitting on the right side of the street. I nearly fainted when I saw that, Doc. You know who drives that kind of truck around here?"

Peter grinned. "I only look at it every single day of my life on my walk. Lucas Cunningham. You think it was him? In that photo?"

"I'm hoping it is, buddy. I'd almost bet the farm on it. But I asked Jerry to remove the back of the frame and call me with the date on that photo. That's all I need right now; the date on the photo. And it probably wouldn't hurt to get a magnifying glass to check out the driver of that pickup. Can you believe my luck today?"

"I know you been lookin' hard for clues about that Charlotte Reeves. I never seen anyone so devoted to findin' that girl as you are, Doc."

"Some people would say I'm crazy. But for some reason, I just can't stop wondering if she's alive." I took a long drink of the tea and wiped my mouth on my sleeve. "Anyway, we have to wait for that call from Jerry with the date. Then I don't know what I'll do with that information. But it's a start, Peter. It's a start."

"I'd say it was. That guy's been given' both of us the creeps for months now. I hope we do find out somethin' about him so we can quit thinkin' about it. You're pretty much driven' yourself crazy worrying about Charlotte Reeves, Doc. And we still don't know if she's alive or not. You need to remember that, above all else. She just might not be alive anymore."

I shook my head and rubbed my neck. "I know. It may be too late. It's been eighteen years, for God's sake. And most people wouldn't be able to last long under that kind of stress and abuse. That is, if she was even kidnapped in the first place. Nothing was ever found to prove that. She could have easily run off, but even her girl friend didn't think that was a good possibility."

"Oh, so you talked to an old girl friend of hers? How'd you manage that?"

"Jessica Reeves told me the name of Charlotte's best friend. I called her and she agreed to talk to me. I didn't get much useful information out of her, but it was good to meet her and go over that day that Charlotte disappeared."

"I sure hope you turn up with somethin' after all this work you've done. I'll help anyway I can, Doc. You know that."

I stood up and shook his hand. "Thanks for the tea and the visit. Always good to see you. You seem stronger, Peter. Take it easy, though. Don't overdo it and have a relapse. I may pass on our meeting tomorrow, if that's okay with you. That is, unless I hear from Jerry on that date. I'll keep you in the loop. Have a good night."

≈

Peter started out the door after Michael left, ready to take his walk. He was walking slower but he enjoyed the fresh air. As he approached Lucas's house, he slowed way down and checked out the house and yard. The pickup truck was there. He walked past the house and kept on going to the next block and then headed back home. He didn't want to push it too hard. He was tired and wanted to sit and think about what Doc had said about the photo.

He was unaware that Charlotte was standing on the chair looking out the window of the cellar. She saw Peter walking by and tears streamed down her face. She was daydreaming about the day she would be able to meet him face to face and thank him for giving her hope. The glass was distorted just enough to where she couldn't see his face clearly. But she saw enough to burn that image into her mind. She waited to see if she could see him walking back, but he didn't pass the house again. She climbed down from the chair and moved everything back. Lucas didn't come to the door so he must have been asleep.

A thick pane of glass separated her from freedom. From going home. And from meeting the men who were trying so hard to save her life. She sat on her bed and cried again for the thousandth time, wanting so much to believe she would someday escape this nightmare. Just seeing this man again gave her a tiny seed of hope, and the tears she shed watered that seed.

CHAPTER 39

Jill and I spent the morning thinking about the holidays coming up. It seemed like the distance between Thanksgiving and Christmas got shorter every year. Jill had gotten involved recently with a homeless shelter for women and was spending more and more time there, working as a counselor for the girls and also raising money for the shelter. I was thrilled that she'd found something she could sink her teeth into, but between the shelter and my office, we weren't doing much with each other. I stared across the kitchen table at her, watching her smile, looking at her hands, and loving the spark in her eyes when she shared about the shelter. She was a lovely woman and I still loved her as much as I did the day we got married. Anna's death cemented us in a new way and it felt good to be able to be open and honest now about losing our daughter.

"Jill, I've been thinking."

"Well, I've never wanted to stand in the way of that!" She laughed and tossed me the morning paper.

"All right, Miss wise guy! Seriously. I've been thinking about us going back to St. Martins for Christmas. I know Olivia would love it if we filled her bedrooms up and just enjoyed the holidays with her and her family."

"It sounds enticing and it would keep us from getting too melancholy about having a Christmas without Anna. Would you like me to talk to Olivia about your idea? I'd be glad to give her a call and see what her calendar looks like.

I want to make sure she hasn't already made plans for the holidays. It just might be the perfect answer for all of us."

"Yes, I want you to call her. But I was also thinking about asking Gregory if he wanted to tag along with us for the trip. He does have kids but I heard him say they were both going skiing this year with friends. I don't know, I just didn't want him to be sitting here alone while we're in St. Martins."

Jill thought about it for a moment and looked at me. "There's no ulterior motive there, Mike?"

"Oh, you mean because he's single? Heavens no, Jill. I realize Olivia's still healing over Case's death. I just thought we'd all have a great time together, is all. Why? Don't you think it's a good idea?"

"It sounds okay, but I want to shoot it past Olivia first. See how she feels about having a stranger in her house over the holidays. I don't want her to get the idea that we're introducing her to a potential future husband, you know?"

"That couldn't be farther from the truth, and you know it. Gregory's a nice looking man and I love him to death, but I'm not playing matchmaker with him or Olivia. Give her a call and let me know what she says. I'll hold off saying anything to Gregory until you give me the word."

Jill shook her head and smiled, even though Michael had already walked out of the room. *I wonder what he's up to? Maybe it's innocent, but I just hope Olivia sees it that way. It might be nice to have Gregory around. He's funny and easy to talk to. We all could use that."*

∽

We were slammed when I walked in Monday morning so I hurried back to my office. Gregory was already with a patient and I had one waiting in the exam room. I took the file from the pocket in the door and noticed it was Lucas Cunningham. The hair stood on my arm but I had learned to ignore some of my body's reactions to Lucas. I walked in and had a smile on my face, but when I looked around the corner he was sitting on the table rubbing his leg. "Hey, Doc. Thought you were never goin' to get here this mornin'. I'm really hurtin' here, Doc."

I paused and acted like I was reading his chart. For some reason I was feeling nauseous and I excused myself and got some cold water and took a long drink.

I headed back into the room and walkedover to Lucas. "So what's going on with your leg, Lucas? Did you injure it?"

I fell down some stairs last night and I'm not sure if I cracked a bone or what. But it's hurtin' like hell and knew I'd better come in and see you today."

"Well, let me check this out. Show me where it hurts, Lucas. Right on the shinbone?"

"Yep. And all the way down my shin to my ankle. I can hardly walk, Doc."

"Let's get an X-ray of that leg. I don't want to move it around too much until we know what's going on. I'll get Mary Beth to call the hospital and see if they can take you in now for that X-ray. Hold on a sec,, Lucas."

I walked out of the room feeling like I was going to lose my breakfast. I hadn't felt sick until I saw Lucas. What in the world was going on? "Mary Beth, would you phone the hospital and see if X-ray can take Lucas immediately? He may have cracked a bone during a recent fall. I'll keep him here in the room until you get an answer."

I moved to the next room where the nurse was taking vitals on a young boy sitting on the table with his mother. "Good morning, Leslie. What's going on with Jack this morning? Not feeling too good today?"

Jack was looking down and not saying anything. "Yes, he got up this morning and said he felt hot. I took his temperature and it was 102. He can't miss school without a doctor's note, so I thought I'd better bring him in."

I looked at the thermometer that the nurse handed me and it read 101. I checked his throat and it was inflamed and his right ear had a swollen ear drum." I'll write a prescription for an antibiotic and also a decongestant. Use these drops in his right ear twice a day, as directed and let me know if he doesn't improve in about four or five days. I'll leave a note at the desk for the school. I hope you feel better, Jack."

I checked back with Mary Beth and X-ray was going to take Lucas right in. I headed back into his room and he was sitting on the table holding his leg. "Lucas, the hospital will take you right in for that X-ray. Head down to ER and they'll take you to X-ray. If it's broken they'll set the bone and put a cast on you. The orthopedic surgeon will probably want to set up an appointment in six or eight weeks to see you and check on your leg."

"I ain't goin' to no orthopedic doctor, and that's the end of it. You know how I feel about hospitals, Doc. Can't you take care of me after I get the cast?"

"Let's take one thing at a time, Lucas. Go get that X-ray and we'll deal with the follow up appointment later."

As soon as Lucas left the office, I slipped into the bathroom and threw up my breakfast. I was sweating and felt edgy. I walked back to my office and sat down at my desk and wiped my face with a wet paper towel. Thoughts were racing through my head. *What if that was Lucas' truck in that photo? And what if he was the one who kidnapped Charlotte? I'm almost dead positive that he was at that intersection and I wish Jerry would call and give me the date on that photo. I should go over to Lucas' house right now while he's at the hospital. He'd never know I was there, and I'd have plenty of time because he's going to be tied up for a couple of hours at least.*

I knew it was risky and against the law to enter someone else's property without their permission. I also knew it was a long shot and I was probably wasting my time. I caught Gregory as he was coming out of an exam room. "Greg. I got something I need to talk to you about for a second. Step into my office for a minute, if you don't mind."

We turned the corner and walked in my office. I sat down on the sofa and he sat down beside me. "Gregory, I know full well this is going to sound ridiculous. Just bear with me, will you?"

"Without you saying any more, this has got to have something to do with that Lucas guy, am I right?"

"Yep, it does. He just left my office headed to the ER to get an X-ray on his leg. He claimed he fell down his stairway and cracked his shin on the steps. The whole time I was around him I felt like I was going to throw up. I couldn't shake the nausea and when he left I ran to the bathroom and threw up my breakfast. I can feel it, Greg. Something's going on and I want to head over to his house right now while he's tied up at the hospital."

Greg started to say something but I wouldn't let him get started. "I know, I know. It's against the law. I'm aware of that. But what if I'm right? What if she's there? I know it's a long shot, but help me out here. Could we run over there right now? It's lunch time and the waiting room has emptied out. It's now or never. He won't be back home for hours. What do you say, Greg. Are you in or out?"

Greg smiled. "Now don't put it that way, Michael. Damn. This is a serious thing we're about to do. You need to think about it a minute before you go diving head first into this guy's house. We know absolutely nothing about Lucas

Cunningham. He may just be a weird guy that gives you the creeps. He may be innocent as all get out, but we have no way of finding anything out about him. I don't want you going over there alone, that's for sure."

"All I want to do is check out the house real quick. We could be in and out in less than twenty minutes. Less than that. If we're careful, and pay attention to the neighbors' houses and any activity going on when we pull up in his driveway, we possibly could get in there without being seen. At this point, I personally believe it's worth taking the risk."

"I'm thinking, Mike. Give me a minute. You've popped this thing on me all of a sudden and thrown me for a loop. Of course, it doesn't surprise me at all. You've been so wrapped up in this guy and trying to figure out what happened to Charlotte Reeves that you're capable of anything. Did you ever find out about that photo you told me about? The one with the old blue pickup in it?"

"I'm still waiting to hear from the owner of the auto parts store. Jerry Oglesby. He promised he'd get back to me, and I trust him. Just wish it was now."

"Mike, have you thought about what you would do if she's there? What in the heck would you say to her and what would you do with her? Take her to the police? To her mother? What's the right thing to do? You'd have to call the police if she was kidnapped by Lucas. They'd have to arrest him immediately, even if he was at the hospital. In fact, that might be better if he was there. Then he couldn't run as easily."

"My thoughts exactly." I stopped and looked right at Gregory. "I don't know what I'll do if she's in that house. I'll freak out, and so will she. I'll have to think of how to approach her without scaring her to death. Listen, Greg. Two things: we don't even know if she's alive, and second; if she's alive, we can't be certain that she's in that house. I just have this gut feeling that's so strong that it made me sick this morning. I'm willing to take the risk. I want to stop by Peter's house and pick him up. He'll want to be a part of this, too; after all, he walks by that house nearly every day and has for years. He's felt uneasy about Lucas, just like I have. What do you say, Greg?"

"I guess I'm in, Mike. But this is the craziest thing I've ever done in my life. I just hope we don't regret this. We could be sitting in a jail discussing the mistake we just made if we aren't very careful. And I sure don't want to spend Christmas vacation sitting in a jail because of your buddy Lucas."

"I realize the risk. I don't want to drag you into something you don't feel good about. Maybe it would be better if you stayed here so that I can contact you by phone and let you know what's going on. I'm nervous as a cat, but this is something I feel I have to do, Greg."

I stood up and looked at Greg. "You with me or not?"

He smiled and stood up. "Look, you aren't going to have all the fun here, Doc. If you're determined to do this, then I'm going with you. But let's have a plan ready just in case you run into something when you get in that house. Are we calling the cops or not? We almost have to, because the whole town will know if we find her. Lucas is going in for life, you realize that, don't you, Doc?"

"I can't even think about what'll happen to Lucas. That sounds sick, but all I can think about is Jessica Reeves getting her daughter back. Let's go see Peter. He's pretty wise and I want to hear what he has to say. I'll tell Mary Beth we're going out for lunch. Meet me at my car in ten minutes."

∽

Charlotte was pacing the floor, trying to figure out how she could get out of that window or open the locked door. It was a bolt lock so it was nearly impossible to crack open. And the door was solid wood; Lucas had seen to that after the first year she was there. She had tried to knock a hole in the door and had nearly succeeded. He had immediately hung a new door that was solid wood and put the bolt lock on. Right from the beginning he had been determined to keep her no matter what. She had soon given up trying to find a way out, but now that she had seen the outside again, she was determined more than ever to escape.

She pushed the sofa up against the wall and pulled the chair over. She had the books ready to go underneath the legs of the chair and climbed up on the seat. She then took the books from underneath her arms and placed them on the seat of the chair and stood up. It was a little wobbly, but she was used to it by now. She looked through the window, using her elbow to clear the haze off. It was another sunny day but cold. She loved to put her nose on the window to feel the cold air. Maybe it would snow this year and she would be able to see it for the first time in a long time. She must have stood there for an hour and suddenly realized how much time had passed. She climbed down and decided to wait to move the sofa until she heard his truck pull up in the driveway. His leg must've hurt pretty badly if he had to go to the doctor. But he did take a bad fall on the stairs.

She'd hidden some fruit and decided to sit and eat an apple and read for a while. She took turns reading and looking out the window. It was a nice way to spend the afternoon. The house was quiet . . .the calm before the storm.

CHAPTER 40

I pulled up in Peter's driveway and turned off the engine. Gregory let out a huge sigh and shook his head. "What in the world are we gettin' ourselves into, Mike? Are we nuts? No one would ever believe in a million years that we'd get ourselves involved so deeply into the case of the missing Charlotte Reeves that we would risk our reputation and careers to sneak into Lucas Cunningham's house. I know you feel strongly about it, and I'm here to back you up, but this is one time I hope your intuition is right. Now what are you going to tell Peter? That you want him to come along? Is that wise, as ill as he's been?"

"It might not be the best thing, but I'm gonna to leave it up to him. He may just want to stay home and let me tell him about it when it's all over with. If that's the case, then we'll meet back here after we're done."

"So you and I are going to go traipsing around this guy's house, is that correct?"

"Look, Greg. I'm no more accustomed to breaking into a house than you are. But we can go in different directions and meet back at in the kitchen. It'll only take a minute or two. Either way, it can't take that long to check out the house; it's not any bigger than a cracker box."

"You're right. Okay, let's get this over with. You're the boss!"

We both fell out laughing but that did nothing to calm our nerves. I knocked on Peter's door and heard him walking with his cane on the wood floor. "Well, this is becoming a habit, I'd say! You keep surprising me with a visit. And this time you brought your cohort Gregory. Come on in, both of you. Sit down and tell me what's goin' on?"

I looked at Gregory and took a deep breath. "Peter, this is a different kind of visit today. You and I've had some pretty poignant conversations about Charlotte Reeves, right? Well, today I've decided to check out Lucas Cunningham's house while he's at the hospital getting an X-ray on his leg. It's a perfect time to see what's going on in that house and Gregory has agreed to go along for the ride. I wanted to let you know what we were up to, so we stopped by on our way to his house."

Peter rubbed his chin a moment and I could tell he was thinking. "Are you certain this is what you want to do, Michael? We need to think about the repercussions if he finds out you've been in his home. He'll never trust you again. Of course, he might not be able to find out who it was that broke into his home, if no one sees you entering. It's such a small neighborhood that it would be a miracle if you got in there without being seen. I'm not trying to be a party pooper here, but you need to cover your bases. I know you've thought this out, Doc. What's going through your mind?"

"There's no way to plan for this, Peter. I have a feeling we're gonna find something. I don't know if it's going to be Charlotte or just some type of clue about her death. But I just have to look while I have the chance. I wanted you to know I was doing this, because I know how you feel about Charlotte."

"I'm weaker today or I'd ask to go with you. But I'm here if you need anything, Doc. All I can say is be careful and be aware of who's around you. Let me know immediately if you find something. This whole damn town will go nuts if you find that girl. It'll never be the same around here; you might even have to move away to get some peace and quiet. But I'm getting the cart before the horse here. You guys be careful. Now go while you have the chance. I wish I wasn't so darn weak or I'd go with you in a heartbeat."

"We're out the door, Peter. Wish us luck. And say a prayer or two; we could use it.

"You got it, Doc. Now go."

"I know you're wondering, Greg, why I didn't push Peter into going with us. He didn't look too good when I came through the door so I just decided to let it go. He could fall and then where would we be?"

"I agree totally. As it turned out, he made the decision for you. Now, are we pulling in the driveway or parking down the street somewhere?"

"We're leaving the car here at Peter's. It's not that far to walk and that way nobody will see an odd car anywhere near his house. When we get close to the house, let's split up and go around both sides of the house to the back door. I've got a credit card in my pocket and I'm going to try to unlock his back door without having to break the glass. I was back there once, remember? I don't think there's a deadbolt on the door."

I was so nervous and excited that I could hardly think. I wanted to be sure I had thought of everything and I was counting on Gregory to keep me straight. I walked around the left side of the house and he headed for the right side. We met at the back door and looked around the yard to see if anyone was outside. It was pretty quiet in the yards on both sides of his house. From where I stood, it looked like we were going to make it inside the house without being seen. Suddenly my cell rang and I grabbed it on the first ring. "Hello?" I answered in a low voice.

"Dr. Lankford, this is Jerry Oglesby, from the auto parts store. I promised you I'd check the date on that photo for you and I've finally taken the back off the photo. I have the date, Dr. Lankford. It says October 19. I hope that helps you out."

I was almost speechless. "Thanks, Jerry. You've been so kind to go to all that trouble to take the frame apart to find out that date. I appreciate it so much. Say, I'll stop in soon and we can have a chat. Thanks again for calling me about with that information!"

I looked at Gregory and grinned. We both blew out a deep breath and I shook my head. "I can't believe the date was October 19. It had to be Lucas at the red light in that old blue pickup truck. Now, more than ever, I'm convinced we'll find something in this house to solve this mystery."

I took the credit card out and tried to maneuver the lock and suddenly it gave way and the door opened. The smell in the house nearly made me want to turn around and leave. I whispered to Gregory. "Try to check out the rooms on the left. I'll go to the right side of the house. Let me know if you see anything pertaining to Charlotte or something you think I might want to check out. I don't even know what we're looking for, but we only have a few minutes to get this done, so let's get going."

Gregory nodded and took off towards the living room and bedroom to the left of the kitchen. I stood and looked around the kitchen and tried to get a feel for the house. It was eerie being in his house and I sure didn't want him to come home and find us here. I went into the living room and took my time looking around. I saw a gun lying beside what appeared to be his chair. I looked around the cluttered room and spotted a desk on the short wall between the front door and the end of the living room wall.

∽

Charlotte thought she heard something and climbed the stairway. She strained to hear Lucas but couldn't tell what he was doing. She heard a book drop and was puzzled as to why he wasn't saying anything to her. Usually he yelled down to her that he was home. Her heart was beating hard, and her thoughts were racing. *What if someone has broken into the house? Should I scream out? What if they have a gun? I don't know what to do. I wish I could open the door, but there's no way.* She listened hard but the house seemed quiet again. Maybe she'd been mistaken and it was only something outside that she'd heard. She started to move down the stairs again and she heard footsteps near the door. It startled her and she yelled out.

"Lucas is that you? Lucas?"

∽

My hand was on the door that I thought led to the cellar. I accidently kicked the door and heard a muffled voice. The hair stood on the back of my neck and I yelled out for Gregory. "Gregory! Come out here, man. I think I heard something in the cellar!"

Gregory came running around the corner into the living room and saw me standing by the cellar door. "What? You heard something? Can you open the door?"

"I don't know. I'm almost afraid to try." We were talking low because we didn't want the neighbors to hear anything.

Charlotte could tell it wasn't Lucas. She was so scared she was afraid to breathe. She wanted to call out, but was afraid of who might be on the other side. *What if Lucas was playing a game with her? Tricking her?* She saw the handle of the door turning and she screamed. "No! Don't come in here. Lucas, is that you? Who is it?" She moved back down the stairs and hid near the sofa.

I couldn't get the door open fast enough. I yelled out. "Who's down in the cellar? This is Dr. Michael Lankford. I'm looking for Charlotte Reeves!" I kept struggling to get the dead bolt unlocked and suddenly it gave way and I opened the door.

My eyes had to adjust to the darkness of the cellar. I couldn't see anything for a few minutes and then I found a light switch at the top of a stairway. I turned on the light and stepped down to the first step. "Is anyone down here? I heard your voice. Don't be afraid. I'm just looking for Charlotte Reeves. Are you Charlotte?"

"It's me. I'm Charlotte Reeves. Have you come to help me?" Her voice was shaky.

I nearly fainted and my legs were shaking. *Don't tell me I've walked up on Charlotte Reeves after months of wondering if she's dead or alive! How could he keep her in this cellar for so many years without anyone ever knowing?* I squatted down on the second step and looked down into the cellar.

"Can I come down the steps, Charlotte? I'm not going to hurt you, I promise."

"I'm afraid. I've been here so long. . . .Oh, God, I want out of here. Are you here to get me out? Oh, God. . ."

"Charlotte, I've been looking for you for quite a few months. I'm coming down the steps and I don't want you to be afraid. I'm a doctor, Charlotte. Your mother is one of my patients. She told me about your disappearance. I want you to know your mother loves you so much and has never given up hope that you would be found."

Charlotte came out of the shadows and walked slowly towards me. I reached out to her and she fell into my arms, sobbing. "My mother? My mother?" She grabbed my shirt and fell to her knees crying. "My mother hasn't forgotten me? My mother . . ." She looked up at me and for the first time the light was shining in enough from the window that I could see her face. Even though her brown hair was a mess, her clothes were baggy and wrinkled and her skin was sallow, I could still see she was a beautiful young woman and her dark brown eyes looked right through me. I had to stare at her for a few minutes because I'd thought about her for so long and it was weird to see her face to face. *Good gosh, it was hard to grasp that she was alive! I had to get her out of there.*

I grabbed her shoulders and pulled her up so she could see my face. "Charlotte, this is a miracle that we've found you today! Nothing short of a miracle, do you get that? The whole town looked for you but they found no clues. And you were right here all the time!" She was staring at me but her eyes weren't focusing on my face. "Listen, Charlotte. We have to get out of here! Where is something we can put your clothes in? Do you want to take anything with you?" I grabbed my cell and dialed 911.

"Officer, this is Dr. Michael Lankford. I'm at 1325 Elmore Street at the home of Lucas Cunningham. Dr. Gregory Hinson is with me and we've found Charlotte Reeves. She's been in Lucas's cellar for eighteen years! Right under our noses."

The officer interrupted Michael. "What do you mean, you've found Charlotte Reeves? That girl's been missing as long as I've been on the force! Is Lucas there? We'll send a S.W.A.T team over there immediately."

"Officer, we don't have time to answer a lot of questions. Lucas may come home any moment and discover Charlotte's gone. I 'm gonna assume he's a dangerous man, and he's not going to be too happy to find out she's gone. He does have a gun in the house."

"We're two minutes away, Dr. Lankford. Get out of the house and we'll take care of Mr. Cunningham."

"Michael!" It was Gregory yelling from the stairway door. "A blue pickup has pulled into the driveway. It looks like Lucas is home!"

I froze for a second and then grabbed Charlotte. "Honey, we've got to get out of here now! Be very quiet. We're going out the back door." I dragged her behind me up the stairs and Gregory and I halfway carried her out the back door. Adrenalin was rushing through my body and I probably could've lifted a refrigerator off the floor at that point. Nothing was going to stand in the way of my taking Charlotte out of this house. Lucas came in the front door just about a minute after we ran out the back door. We headed across two yards and ran the rest of the way to Peter's house. I was debating whether to take us all up Peter's steps and into his house, or jump into my car and race the heck out of here. I decided to head in to Peter's house and called the police to let them know where we were.

"Peter? It's Michael. We're coming through your door! I've found Charlotte! She's alive, Peter!"

Peter came walking into the living room with his cane tapping on the floor and stopped when he saw Charlotte standing there. He was surprised, to put it mildly. He walked up to her slowly and looked into her eyes. Charlotte started crying and went to her knees; she had seen the cane. I bent down to see if she was okay and pulled her to her feet. I led her to the sofa and she sat down, putting her face in her hands. It was all too overwhelming for her.

"Dear child, I'm Peter Darby. You don't know how happy I am that you've been found! Michael worried about you for so long and now you're free! I can't imagine what you're feelin' inside right now, but don't worry about anything. It's goin' to be all right now, Charlotte. You'll see."

Peter put his hand on her head and smiled. He had tears running down his face and wiped his face on his sleeve. "I just can't believe you found her, Michael. It's nothin' short of a miracle. I'll get her something to drink."

Charlotte looked up and finally was able to speak. "I don't know who you all are and how you were able to find me but I'm so thankful you did. . . .I guess I'm in shock. Peter, if I may call you that . . . are you the one who walked by my house everyday with a cane?

"Yes, sweet child. That was me."

"I've waited for so long to finally meet the person who walked with a cane by my window. You have no idea the effect you've had on me. I daydreamed about how you were goin' to rescue me from bein' in that cellar. I waited every single day for the time you would walk by; it was my one connection to the outside. You can't imagine the days and nights that I spent in that cellar alone wonderin' if anyone in the town every thought about me or wondered if I was still alive. And to think I'm sitting here in your house, well . . . it's just too much for me to comprehend."

Charlotte got up and walked over to Peter and put her arms around him. He hugged her and told her he was honored to have her in his home. "Now you sit down, child, and we'll get you something to drink. Are you hungry? Do you need anything?"

Charlotte thought for a moment and then spoke quietly. "Do you men know how strange it is for me to be sittin' here talking to you? I've lived alone for years and years in that cellar, occasionally talkin' to Lucas. I have no idea what the world is like now. I feel like I'm in a dream." She paused for a moment and wiped her eyes. Her hands were visibly shaking. "I think I'd like to call my mother, if that's possible. I haven't heard her voice for eighteen years and it's goin' to be a shock for her to hear mine. We won't even recognize each other's voices. That's pretty sad, Peter."

She looked at me and took my hand. "You're my hero, Michael. You said you've wanted to find me for months. What made you break into Lucas's house? Did you hear something, or did he say something to give you a clue that I was there?" Her hand were shaking.

I scratched my head and answered her the best I knew how. "Charlotte, some things just can't be explained. I knew in my heart that somethin' was goin' on in that house, but I wasn't sure what. Your mother really started this by sharing with me about your disappearance. I couldn't get you off my mind. But Lucas was also a patient of mine and he was a seedy character; somethin' just felt wrong about him. I checked around town and found a photograph in Jerry's Auto Parts Store that had the truck Lucas drives in the photo, and the date on the photo was the same date as the day you were abducted. October 19th. That was too much of a coincidence. There was a million to one chance that anyone would see that photograph and put two and two together. I'm going to get a magnifying glass and see if you're in that truck. Don't know why I didn't do that in the first place!"

"I was in that truck, Michael! I know you'll see me in that front seat if you look carefully. I would love to see that picture sometime. That's amazing that somebody took a picture of that intersection at just the right moment when we were stopped for a red light. I can't believe you found the photograph in that auto parts store. Nothing makes sense to me."

I held her hand and patted her shoulder. "It will take time for all of us to sort through all these events, Charlotte. Give yourself time. I'm still in shock too, about findin' you in that house. Now, you can call your mother but it's goin' to be quite a shock to her, and to you, too. Are you ready for that, Charlotte? Things have changed since you were kidnapped. Does the world look different to you? That's an awful long time to be hidden away from the world with all its technology, not to mention your family and friends. You have a lot of catching up to do."

"It feels very odd, but I'm more than ready to catch up with the world. I need to see my mother before anything else happens. She's all I have, and through all of this I prayed she wouldn't stop lookin' for me. Or hopin' that I was alive."

I took my cell phone out and dialed Jessica Reeves' number. She answered on the third ring and was surprised to hear my voice. "Jessica, this is Dr. Lankford. I know you're surprised that I'm callin' you like this, but I have some good news for you! There's someone here who'd like to talk to you, Jessica. Are you sittin' down?"

"Yeah, yeah, I'm sittin' down all right. Now who in the world would want to be talkin' to me, Dr. Lankford?"

"Hello, Momma? Momma, is that you?" Charlotte burst out crying and handed the phone back to Michael. She was shaking uncontrollably. He hugged her and gave her back the phone.

"Who—who is this? What do you mean callin' me 'Momma'? I have a daughter I ain't heard from for eighteen years. She's the only one who can call me 'Momma.'"

"This is your daughter, Momma. Dr. Lankford has rescued me! I was here in town all along, Momma. They've found me! Momma . . . I want to come home. Are you there, Momma?" Charlotte was almost screaming through her tears.

Silence on the other end of the phone. I took the phone from Charlotte and spoke to Jessica. "Now, Jesse. I know you're in shock, but it's true. Dr. Gregory and I broke into Lucas Cunningham's home this afternoon and found your daughter in the cellar of his house. She's okay, Jesse. A little ragged, but amazingly well after all this time."

Silence. Jesse was in total shock and crying hard on the other end of the phone. "My daughter? Are you tellin' me you've found my daughter? Oh, my Lord! This ain't no time for jokin', Dr. Lankford. Is that really my daughter?"

"I'm very serious, Jesse. Talk to her for a minute and we'll bring her to you in a few minutes." I handed the phone to Charlotte and she sat there with it in her hand. Tears were streaming down her face. I looked at Gregory and he had tears in his eyes, and Peter was crying too. What a fantastic thing to witness! I knew Jesse was in shock; the last thing she thought she'd hear was her daughter's voice on the other end of the line...

Charlotte talked a few more minutes and handed me the phone. "Why don't we head over to Jesse's now and I can let the police know where we are. I'm sure they have their hands full with Lucas right now, and it really doesn't matter where we take Charlotte as long as we keep in touch with them." Michael stood up and grabbed Charlotte's hand.

They hugged Peter goodbye and headed out the door. On the way over to Jessica's, Charlotte was nervous and talkative. "How am I goin' to know her anymore? I haven't seen her in so long I don't even feel like I know her. And she doesn't know me, either. I want to see her so bad, but I'm scared it won't be the same."

"I want you to calm down and just enjoy this trip over to your mother's house. Do you recognize anything, Charlotte? I imagine all the landscape has changed so much you don't even know where you are."

"Nothin' looks the same, Dr. Lankford. It will take me some time to get my bearings again. So much has been built up that I don't recognize anything. It doesn't look like the same Crosgrove I remember."

We parked and got out of the car. Jesse was already standing at the door crying and waving her hands. "Charlotte? Oh my Lord . . . my child. My child. I can't believe they found you!"

"Momma? Oh, Momma." Charlotte ran to her mother and they fell into each other's arms. Gregory and I hung back as the two women saw each other for the first time in eighteen years. What a reunion! It was more than either one of us could take.

"Lawd, let's go into the house. I feel weak and need to sit for a moment. Charlotte? You hungry, child? Can Momma get you anythin'?"

"No, Momma. I'm fine. I just want to sit with you. I'm still in shock about bein' free. It feels so weird to be able to walk around outside like this. To see houses and trees and grass. To hear birds singing. It almost feels loud to me, because the cellar was so quiet. It was my world."

"I know we don't understand what you've been through, Charlotte. But we want to hear all about it when you're ready to talk. I'm sure the police will ask you hundreds of questions and I don't want to wear you out before they even get to you." I smiled at her, still in disbelief that she was really here.

"I love hearin' your voices and I'll never get tired of talkin' to all of you. I've been alone for so many years and I've had nobody to talk to. Nobody to share what I was feeling. It's been a nightmare." She put her hands over her eyes.

"Well, that nightmare is over now, honey. Momma's not gonna to let you out of her sight for a long time. I want you to have plenty of time to recover from this, Charlotte. You may even need counselin'. Just for now, Dr. Lankford might can give you somethin' to help you sleep. I know I may need that, too. This is too much for me to grasp. I feel like I'm gonna wake up from a dream, you know?"

"I feel the same way, Momma. Thank you so much, Dr. Lankford. I don't know how to thank you enough for riskin' your life to save me. Dr. Gregory, you were so brave to help him. Thank God Lucas wasn't home when you came through that door! There would have been some shootin', I guarantee you that."

Charlotte sat down on the sofa and put her head in her hands. She looked up at all of us with a serious face. "I've got some adjusting to do. I prayed and prayed to get out and now that I am, I don't know what to do. What to think. I feel misplaced, sort of; guess that's normal. I just want to sit here and give myself time to let this sink in, if it's okay with you guys."

I got up and motioned to Gregory. "Hey, we're headin' out, Charlotte. You and your mother need time alone. I want to spend some time with you and your mother when you feel more like talkin'. Right now I want to see what the police are doin' about Lucas. I'll give you a call in a few days, Charlotte. I tell you what! I'm so excited I bet I don't sleep a wink tonight. This is the greatest day for Crosgrove! It'll be on the front page of the paper in the mornin' I assure you! The whole town won't believe we've found you, girl. I'm sure you're gonna get some news reporters comin' to your door wantin' interviews. You'll have to decide who you want to talk to and who you don't. If you ever need any help with that, just call me. I'll put my card on the counter here; I'm always available to you."

I walked over and kissed Jessica's forehead and hugged Charlotte. Gregory shook their hands and we both walked to the door. I turned around one last time to look at Charlotte and just shook my head. It was hard to believe. It had all happened so fast.

෬෧

The S.W.A.T. team arrived at Lucas's house four minutes after we left. Lucas had already discovered that Charlotte was gone. He had come into the house yelling at her to let her know he was home. When she didn't answer he went to the door and noticed the dead bolt was open. He started shaking and opened the door. She was gone. He looked all around the house and then went to the back door. It was unlocked, too. He heard two cars pulling into his driveway and looked out the window. It was the police, and he knew exactly what they were going to do. He grabbed his revolver and sat down in his chair. He could hear doors slamming and people running around the house, and his heart was racing.

His whole life flashed before him; his mother being beaten up by his father; her face when he hit her over and over. He saw himself killing his father and dragging him out the door. He had been desperate for family all his life and the only way he knew to have one was to kidnap Charlotte. He had no idea it would turn out like this; it had worked for years with no glitches. *What in the world happened? Who found out she was here?* These were things he would never know, because he wasn't going to let the cops take him in. There was no way in hell he was going to spend the rest of his life behind bars. He'd rather be dead than go through that. His mind was racing at the speed of light. Tears poured down his face as he placed the gun in his mouth. His hand was shaking and he took his left hand and placed it on the handle of the gun to steady it. *God, I don't want to do this, but I have no choice. All I ever wanted was a family. Damn idiots. Why did they have to mess my life up? I'm not going to let them win.*

The cops were coming through the back door when they heard a shot. Only one shot. And it came from the living room. They walked slowly forward, keeping their eyes on the living room just in case he came around the corner. They fully expected him to fire at them but what they saw caught them off guard. When they came into the living room Lucas was slumped in the chair with blood pouring down the side of the chair onto the beige carpet. There was no sound in the house but the clock ticking on the wall. The gun was on the floor and his right arm was hanging over the chair arm. One of the men had a bag and he grabbed the gun, folding the plastic over it and sealing it. They radioed the men outside the house and soon the house was full of people. An ambulance was called but before they arrived the S.W.A.T. team dusted for fingerprints and took photos of the cellar, the bed Charlotte slept in, her clothes, and the pile of books on the shelves. They took a photo of Lucas sitting his chair. And they gathered all the photographs he had taken of Charlotte that were on his desk. These would be placed in a file at the police station that had Charlotte Reeves's name on it. It now could be marked **Case Closed.**

Sheriff George Bentley walked into the house and stood at the doorway and faced the chair Lucas was sitting in. *It's a sad picture to see this tormented man slumped over dead in his chair. He must have lived a life of a recluse, keepin' Charlotte Reeves in that basement all these years. How in the world he did it is beyond me. And what kind of past did he have to bring him to this point?*

He walked out of the house as the ambulance drove up into the driveway, directing them into the living room where the body was. They carefully placed Lucas's body on the stretcher and covered it up with a rubber sheet, and then walked out of the house and placed the body into the ambulance. You could hear a pin drop in the house. Everybody had the same thoughts going through their head. All those years that the file on Charlotte Reeves was closed, she was in this house with a man who obviously was sick in his mind. Only Charlotte knew what he did to her, and even perhaps what brought Lucas to do this terrible crime in the first place. It not only cost Lucas his life, but it took eighteen years of Charlotte's life away from her that she could never get back.

George sat in his car and shook his head. He hadn't done such a good job on this one. He had totally missed what was right in front of his nose; all of the searches were done on the outskirts of town. *Maybe it's time to retire when a fairly new doctor in town solves a case that's been sittin' in my office in a file drawer for eighteen years gatherin' dust.*

∽

I walked up to Lucas's house with Gregory and found the sheriff sitting in his car. I knocked on his window and he rolled it down. "Sorry, Sheriff. Didn't mean to interrupt you. How'd it go with Lucas? Did you have trouble gettin' him to surrender to you? We've been to Jessica Reeves's house with Charlotte and everything is goin' great with them. They were both in shock when they saw each other for the first time, but it didn't take long and they were huggin' each other and crying. Can you imagine the emotions goin' through both of them after all these years? It was mind boggling."

Sheriff Bentley looked up at me with a solemn face. "It's over for Lucas, I'm afraid, Dr. Lankford. He won't have to worry about time served in prison."

"What? What do you mean it's over? Did something happen? Is anyone hurt?"

"We walked through the back door and Lucas shot himself. He had the gun in his mouth and pulled the trigger. Just like that he was gone. We didn't have a chance to talk him out of it; he was already gone when we got to the chair. I don't like the way this ended at all. Such a wonderful thing you did, Dr. Lankford, findin' Charlotte after all these years. I just didn't want anyone to get shot during the raid."

I was shocked at what I was hearing. "You mean to tell me Lucas shot himself? Good gosh, was he so overwhelmed with our finding Charlotte that he just checked out? No one knew anything about him; not even his neighbors. I would have loved to have known about his background; like what in the world happened to him to cause him to behave like this. Now we'll never know. That is, unless he shared some of his past with Charlotte."

"Yep. That's a possibility, all right. It's sad but at least she's free. He did commit a crime here, and a serious one at that. So he was going down for life with no chance of parole. And I tell you one thing, Doc, he wouldn't have lasted two months in that prison in Redford. It's hardcore and he kidnapped a fifteen year old girl; they would see him as child molester and he wouldn't last long at all. They would rip him apart, I'm telling you right now."

"I know you are tellin' me straight, Sheriff. Lucas was smart enough to realize he was better off dead than goin' to prison. I just wish I could've talked with him, is all. He was my patient and he might have listened to me. No way of knowin' that now."

I thanked the sheriff and Gregory and I walked back to Peter's to get my car. "Well, Gregory, it's been a full day, hasn't it?"

"No kiddin'. I know one thing, Mike. If I'm goin' to continue our relationship I'm gonna purchase a 357 Magnum because it appears this relationship isn't gonna be a normal one! You could've warned me when you hired me that you get obsessed sometimes with some of your patients!"

I fell out laughing. It actually felt great to laugh. "Aw, you sissy. You enjoyed every moment of this! And look what we did! We freed a young woman who probably would've died in that cellar or taken her own life from despair. That has to make you feel good, right?"

"Yeah, Doc. But I'm still gonna pack."

I walked up to the door and stuck my head in. "Peter? Are you around?" I could hear him walking my way.

"Yeah, yeah. I'm here. What's up, Doc? Did you take Charlotte to her mother's?"

"I sure did, and it brought tears to my eyes to see them reunited. I wouldn't have missed that for anything in the world. I'm about to take Gregory back to the office and head home. Jill knows nothing yet. I just wanted you to know that Lucas took his life today when the cops were comin' in the back door of his house. He decided that he wasn't going to prison for life, and ended it right then and there. The sheriff was pretty upset when I got back to Lucas's house. It was a tough way to end the day, but actually Lucas is better off dead than in that prison in Redford, according to the sheriff."

Peter shook his head. "Well, you did a bang up job, Doc. I'm proud of ya. Now what? You gonna check in on Charlotte to make sure she gets adjusted to the world again?"

"You know I will, Peter. She's a special young woman and I want her to be able to live a full life and recover from this with nothin' but a few nightmares to deal with from time to time. We'll see how she progresses. Right now there'll be a lot of press about her being found, and that's hard to deal with sometimes. I told Jessica to call me if she needs anything."

"Well, keep me posted. I still stand with my offer to help her get a car. I bet it won't be too long and she'll want to find a job and get back into life."

"See you soon. I won't see you tomorrow but next Sunday, okay?"

"Sounds good. Get some rest, Doc. You probably won't be able to because now you don't have anything to think about all night."

I walked back to the car chuckling. It did feel good to have this done. I had never dreamed in a million years that I would find Charlotte. I had hoped but it was a very dim hope. *Jill will be thrilled. We may have to celebrate tonight and go out to dinner. I'll see if Gregory wants to come along. It's going to take me a little while to calm Jill down, because she had no idea the danger I was going to face and I preferred it that way. She would have tried to talk me out of breakin' into Lucas's house, and nothin' she could have said would've stopped me. I'm even happier it was a good outcome, or she would never let me live that down.*

When I sat down in the car I realized that I had to tell Charlotte the news that Lucas was gone. I hated to have to tell her just when she was gettin' settled at home with her mother. But it would be on the ten o'clock news tonight and that was no way for her to find out. I dialed Jessica's number and waited for someone to answer.

"Hello? This is Jessica."

"Hey, Jesse. How's our girl doin'?"

"She's a little confused but is restin' right now. We've talked so much that I think she's exhausted. I put her in my room for now. She's not used to sleeping on a nice bed like I have! I think she kind of likes bein' home again."

"There's no doubt in my mind that she's happy to be home. Say, Jesse, there's somethin' I need to share with you and Charlotte. I would wait until tomorrow but it'll be on the late news tonight and that's no way for Charlotte to find this out. Lucas Cunningham shot himself when the police came into his house to arrest him. They found him sittin' in his chair with a gun on the floor by his hand. He pulled the trigger when the patrolmen were comin' in the back door. They heard the shot and came runnin' into the living room. I guess Lucas wasn't gonna allow them to take him in."

"Oh my goodness, Dr. Lankford. That's horrible! But ya know, in a way it feels good to know he's gone. He had my daughter all those years and I hate what he did to her. You understand?"

"I sure do, Jesse. And you have every right to feel that way. I just thought Charlotte might rest better knowin' he is gone. Please let her know when she wakes up and if she needs to talk to me about it or has any questions, tell her to call me no matter what time it is."

"I'll sure do that, Doc. Thanks for lettin' us know. It is a big relief for me, I'm tellin' you."

"In a way, it is for the whole town, I'm sure. You have a good night, Jesse. Perhaps the best night you've had since Charlotte disappeared!"

"I won't sleep a wink tonight, Dr. Lankford. I'm too excited to sleep. I think I'll just sit up and look at her while she's sleepin'. She's so beautiful and I'm so thankful to have her back with me. I never thought I'd see her again. I owe you my life, Doc. I owe you my life."

"Now, now. Don't go sayin' that, Jesse. I did what I could to find that girl, and that's all there is to it. I don't want any medals or attention. It's worth everything I went through just to hear how happy you are. Now get some rest because tomorrow is gonna be a busy day for the both of you."

CHAPTER 41

When I pulled the newspaper out of the plastic sleeve and wiped the water off the edges, I could see the corner edge of the headlines on the front page and without looking any further I knew it was about Charlotte Reeves coming home. I grinned from ear to ear and tossed the paper to Jill. "Can you believe it, baby? That girl is home after bein' gone for so long! The whole town is gonna go nuts over it. It'll be on everyone's mind. I bet the major question that will arise from this rescue will be why the sheriff didn't keep the search goin' longer. Here she was in her own home town, and no one was even lookin' for her."

"Well, they forget that there were no leads at all. The sheriff couldn't pull her out of thin air. I feel sorry for the guy, to tell you the truth. You come in town and you've not been here a year yet, and you walk into a man's house and unlock a door and there she is! It's rather hard to comprehend, and I live with you!"

"Oh hush, Jill. It took me diggin' and diggin' to find that girl. And it would never have happened if it weren't for Lucas bein' my patient, too. He was givin' off vibes that actually made me ill; I threw up the last time he was in my office. The sad thing is that we still didn't get to talk to him about his past. If I get a minute alone with Charlotte, I'm gonna ask her about Lucas and see what she says."

"I'm sure you will, honey. But go slow. She has a lot of bad memories in that house and we need to give her time to heal."

"By the way, did you ever talk to Olivia about us all coming to see her for Christmas?"

Jill gave me one of her rolling-eyes looks. "Of course I called her. Do you think I would forget that?" She walked over to the sink and rinsed out her coffee cup and turned to look at me. "She said she'd love for us to come but she said for you to not be playin' Cupid just yet. I knew she would take it that way, and you were so determined that Gregory go."

"I had no intentions at all in that direction and you know it! I just don't want him to be alone during the holidays with his kids out skiing and us bein' gone, too. Don't you see the logic in that?"

"Oh yes. I see it all right. She said it was fine if he came; just wants you to know she's aware of what you're up to."

I laughed and slapped the table. "We'll see who changes their tune when we all get there. Gregory is excited about goin' and I think the four of us will have a ball."

I got up from the table and looked outside the front window. The news media was all over my lawn, holding microphones and talking amongst themselves. I guess they were waitin' for me to come out of the house. "Jill, keep this door locked! Whatever you do, don't answer the door. They'll push their way into the house and we'll never get rid of them. I'm headed to the shower and then I'll have to think of a way to get the car out of the garage without bein' attacked by reporters."

Jill smiled. "I know you hate all the attention, honey, but all your hard work has paid off and now comes the fun part." I cleaned up and kissed Jill goodbye and headed out the side door that leads into the garage. I started the car, raised the garage door, and shoved the car into reverse. I revved the engine so they'd know I was comin' out, and started down the driveway. Reporters were running alongside the car trying to get me to roll my window down. It was crazy! But I managed to head down the street without killing a few of them. I thought I was safe but when I pulled into the office parking lot there were reporters waitin' for me there. I realized I was gonna have to talk to the press at some point, so it might as well be now.

A microphone was shoved into my face. "Good morning, Dr. Lankford! Will you tell us how Charlotte Reeves is doing since her rescue?"

I looked around at the crowd forming and smiled. "Charlotte is doin' as well as can be expected. You have to remember that she was locked in a cellar for eighteen years. So she has a lot of catchin' up to do. She is in remarkably good health and good spirits as well. But a little disoriented, and that's to be expected."

"How does she feel about Lucas Cunningham taking his own life? Was she relieved?"

"I haven't spoken with her personally since she found out that news, but I'm sure she's relieved that this nightmare is over. She's been a very brave woman and I'm certain that most of us wouldn't have been able to withstand what she's endured. Thank you very much."

I turned and shoved my way into the office and closed the door. *I hope this doesn't last long. I want Charlotte to get her rest and be able to adjust slowly back into a normal world. It's gonna take time and she doesn't need to do it in front of the camera.* Gregory was in his office and I stopped and sat down at the end of his desk.

"Hey, buddy. How's my favorite detective this mornin'?"

He threw his head back and laughed. "Me a detective? Who are you? Sherlock Holmes? Did you get any sleep last night?"

"Not much. I was too wound up. How about you?"

"Same here. But I feel so happy for Jessica Reeves that she has her daughter back. Can you imagine how she feels lookin' at her daughter, havin' her back in her home?"

"It's got to be the best feeling in the world, and I know for a fact the Jessica had about given up ever seein' her daughter again. I'm thrilled that it all turned out like it did. You and I could've gotten into a lot of trouble if Lucas had come home just a few minutes earlier."

"No kiddin'. Things worked out for the best. Guess our prayers worked this time."

"Say, Greg. You still thinkin' about going with Jill and me to St. Martin's for Christmas? It's comin' up sooner than you think, and I really want you to go."

"I've been thinkin' about nothing else, if you want to know the truth. It sounds like a great time and I know you mean well asking me. But is Olivia ready for a visitor; a stranger? She's had a lot on her plate and I don't want to intrude, you know?"

"For heaven's sake, Gregory. You're not intruding. She wants you to come. Jill said so this mornin'. Now just make up your mind that you're goin' and let's be done with it!"

He smiled at me and pushed away from his desk. He stood up and I was again reminded of how tall he was. "Friends don't come any better than you, Doc. I'd love to spend Christmas with you and Jill, and Olivia. That is, if she'll have me in her home."

"Great. Then it's done now. I can't wait to show you around town. There's some great restaurants and I want to take you to a very special lake. You game?"

He pulled out an unloaded gun and laid it on the desk. "I'm ready for anything, buddy."

I laughed so hard it made my stomach cramp. "You're nuts! Absolutely nuts. Where did you get that gun?"

"I had it all the time at home, but never thought I'd ever need it. I'm ready now for anything you can shove at me!"

I headed out the door and into the first exam room. This was going to be a great day, and I felt renewed after such a long night of no sleep.

∾

Jessica was sitting on the edge of the bed with her hand on Charlotte's arm. "Mother, I can't believe Lucas is dead. That he killed himself. Oh my gosh. I guess he felt overwhelmed with comin' home and findin' me gone. That was always his worst nightmare and it happened when he least expected it. I sure didn't dream someone would break into the house and help me escape. The whole thing seems like a dream now."

"I reckon it does, baby. All I know is that I'm thankful to God that you made it out of the hell hole. I know it's a shock to find out Lucas is gone. But honey, he would've had a horrible life behind bars. Those men in prison would've killed him one way or the other. He would be a child molester in their eyes. You realize that?"

"I hadn't thought about it in that light, Mother. I lived with him for eighteen years and there was a sort of love/hate relationship goin' on. He was all that I had for a long, long time. I feel sorry for him and I don't really know why. Do you think that's normal?"

"I know it's normal. Your world was very small, honey. Very small. You're doin' extremely well even now, after havin' been out only one day. I think you'll adjust to the real world pretty quickly because you wanted out so badly. If you had given up hope and let him kill your spirit, then it might be more difficult for you to adjust. You're amazin', and I'm so happy that you're back home where you oughtta' be."

Charlotte got up and stretched. *Lucas is gone. I feel sorry for him. He had to be so afraid inside when he heard the police comin' in that door. I'm sure he panicked. I just wish Michael had gotten there sooner so that he could've talked with Lucas. Maybe they'd have let him off on a lighter sentence. Who knows?* She went to the bathroom and splashed cold water on her face. *Even that felt new and weird. Listen to me tryin' to make excuses for him. He kidnapped me and took eighteen years of my life away. He deserved to die. But for some sick reason I feel sorry for him. He never had a life; at least I had memories of a good childhood to hold on to. It sounded like he had a hell of a life before he kidnapped me. He told me he shot his own father. I can't imagine the sorrow he felt and the hatred.*

"Mother, I want to go see Peter again today. Do you think we could do that?"

"I don't see why not, honey. Eat some breakfast and we'll decide what time we should go. I'm sure he'd love to see you again. From what you said, he's such a nice man. I'd kind of like to meet him myself."

Charlotte heard some noise outside and opened up the blinds on the front window. The yard was full of people with cameras and there were news reporters flashing their cameras and talking loudly. *This was what Dr. Lankford warned me about. They're dyin' to know the whole story. I'm afraid to even walk out of the house. Maybe by the time we eat breakfast and get dressed they'll be gone.* She walked back into the kitchen and her mother was crying. "Oh Mother! What is it? Are you all right?"

"I'm just . . . happy."

CHAPTER 42

A relationship was forming silently between two people who were destined to meet. Charlotte had waited for what seemed like her whole life to meet the man who walked by her window and Peter was thrilled that she enjoyed coming by to see him. The friendship developed slowly and naturally without strain. For some reason, I could tell Charlotte trusted Peter even before she met him, so it was only natural that she would feel comfortable sitting with him for hours, listening to him share about his life.

He was getting weaker by the day and walking less and less. Ever since the rescue, Peter said he had no desire to walk by Lucas's house anymore. That time was over. He loved her courage and endurance; those were the traits that had pulled him through a lonely childhood. So they had a lot in common, the old man and the young woman. She could pour her heart out to him and he understood. And he could share his loneliness with her, and his struggle to pull himself out of a dark hole to the other side. In a way, they both had been stuck in a dark place that nobody seemed to notice. It was that fact that cemented their relationship and kept Peter going in his last days. I knew this was happening; I saw it with my own eyes. It gave me great joy to see the two of them together. I'd grown to love Peter like a father and best friend, and there was a bond between Charlotte and I that was almost tangible. So two special people in my life had found each other and I loved the way things were turning out.

Christmas was sneaking up on us and it was almost time for Jill, Gregory, and I to make a short trip to St. Martins. I was looking forward to getting away for a few days and just enjoying my wife and my friends. Gregory had such a warm personality and a great sense of humor. His timing was priceless. There were so many days that he took an ordinary day and turned it into a Huckleberry Finn kind of day. We sneaked out for lunch and talked about our lives when we were kids, and laughed until our sides hurt. And just when I thought I knew him from head to toe, he showed me another side of himself. He loved doing that; and because he shared himself with me, I knew deep down Olivia was going to fall for him. It might not happen now at Christmas time, but it was goin' down. I wouldn't tell Jill this simple fact for all the tea in China, but it didn't change the fact that it was true. She guarded Olivia like a mother lion, and I knew on this trip she'd be watching Gregory like a hawk. That was okay with me, 'cause we were gonna take it nice and easy, Gregory and I. And he wasn't even aware of this yet! That's what was so great about the whole thing.

I want him to have the same kind of relationship I'd been fortunate to have with Jill. We never run out of things to talk about, and her voice never runs cold to me. She's put up with so much from me—the obsession I had to find Charlotte Reeves, my love for Peter and wanting to spend time with him. My staying late to work on a patient, my getting up early to sit at my desk and pour over medical journals until I found the answer I was looking for. She's never been first in my life, but she's been the foundation that held me up. Even if she doesn't realize it, I couldn't get through a day without her. She's phenomenal about being one step ahead of me and you can't imagine how much time that saves me both in my life and in my practice. Her needs are small, but they are huge to her. When she needs me, I know to drop everything including my stethoscope and run. She's been in my life a long time; I think I started to breathe the day I met her. And I'm having the joy of growing old with the young girl I fell in love with so long ago. Even though the wind has lifted away our youth and we are wearing the baggage of old age, we're clinging to the minutes now instead of thinking so far down the road. We're approaching the winter of our lives with expectation and wonderment. I know just as I sure as I see the sun coming up every morning that one day I'll lay down my stethoscope and walk out of my office and never go back again. But I'm just not there yet. Not quite. There are a few more people out there that may need me and I don't want to miss that call. All the knowledge I've gained over the years is culminating in a place within me and when I need to call it up to the forefront of my mind, it comes in all its glory and I'm able to tap into it and help heal the person in front of me. I know that's a gift and I don't claim to own it. I think it came in the womb by the hand of the One who put me there. It's the same hand that guided Peter through that life he was left to live out. And it made him into a man that others look up to, and aspire to be like.

Two more days and we drive out of Crosgrove for a respite. I can leave without one drop of confusion or stress, because Charlotte Reeves has finally found her way back home. I've been through a lot and I've seen a lot in my life, but finding that young woman and restoring her to her mother is enough to walk me into eternity and never look back.

I'm headed to Peter's now to let him know that we're leaving for a few days. I can do that comfortably because I know Charlotte will watch over him while I'm away. He's starting to drift a little and I can't predict how long he'll last now. I've decided when I return that I'll sit with him in the afternoons until he decides he's ready to be buried near that old oak tree where my Anna went to sleep. I'm being honest when I say that I'm not quite ready to live without him. He's been quite an influence on us all.

CHAPTER 43

It was a cold morning and there was a smell of snow in the air. My hands were sticking to the steering wheel as we pulled out of the driveway on our way to St. Martins. Gregory was in the back already dozing off with his head leaning against the window. His breath was making a haze on the back window. Jill was lost in her own thoughts as I pulled out onto the main highway. It would be a nice little drive; just long enough for us to let go of the stress we'd all been through and get our minds wrapped around a Christmas tree, presents, and a rich glass of wine shared together.

The roads weren't too busy and that made the drive more pleasant. Trees were blowing in the wind that had kicked up and the sky was a winter gray. I was about to start a conversation with Jill but when I looked over in her direction, she was leaning her head on a pillow and finishing a dream she must have had in the night. It was early yet 5:30 in the morning. No one in their right mind would choose to travel this early. I didn't know what the rush was, but Jill wanted to get up and get going. So they were both asleep and I was fighting yawns and trying to keep the windshield from fogging up. Semis were passing me like I was standing still, but I just waved and stayed in the right lane. We'll get there when we get there.

Out of the silence Gregory raised his bald head, smiled at me in the mirror and said in his deep voice, "Hey, bud. How's it goin' up there?"

"I'm good, son. Just enjoying the quiet of the morning. It feels so good to be away from it all. You?"

"I'm relaxed for the first time in a long time. This trip's going to be good for me—a wonderful way to spend my Christmas this year."

"Just wait until you meet Olivia, and taste her crème brûlée. It's dangerous, Greg. My mouth's watering just thinking about it!"

"I don't need any help when it comes to thinking about desserts. You know that's one of my weaknesses. So don't encourage her to fill me up with sweets, you hear? I've gained enough weight as it is, eating lunch out with you."

I laughed and Jill woke up. Her face had a few wrinkles ironed in from the lace on the pillow. I smiled at her and patted her leg. "Hey, honey. You dreaming over there? We don't have too long to go. Do you need me to stop and get you some coffee or a pastry?"

"That sounds nice. But I'm ready to get there and see my dear friend. She's so excited about us coming and now that I look outside, we may just get a snowy white Christmas!"

"I think we have a great chance of it snowing. Won't that be a hoot! Greg? You need me to stop?"

"Nope. Just keep on truckin'."

Three hours later we pulled into Olivia's driveway. I turned off the engine and looked at the two of them. "Okay, guys. Our Christmas vacation has begun! Let's go in and see Olivia and make her day! She doesn't know what she's gettin' into, does she? All three of us pouncing on her at one time! But it might feel good to her to have some noise in the house!"

Olivia heard the car pull up and was waiting at the door when we got out of the car. We waved and got our suitcases out of the trunk. I noticed that Gregory suddenly got energized and started hauling suitcases into the house.

"It's so good to see you! Hey, Jill! How was the trip?"

"It was wonderful and badly needed. It feels so good to get away for a long weekend and visit with my best friend! Did you meet Gregory? He's the man who just walked into your house!"

Gregory stuck his head out the front door and waved. "Hello, Olivia! Sorry I barged in. I feel like I already know you after this five hour trip with your best friends. What a lovely home you have here. Are we promised a white Christmas?"

Jill grinned and winked at Olivia. "Nothing like putting pressure on some-one the first second you meet them! Olivia, ignore him will you? He's a man. That should clear everything up!"

I walked over and hugged Olivia and we all carried the rest of the bags into the house. The energy was already building and I knew it was going to be a great weekend. We got settled into our rooms and walked back into the living room where Olivia was putting the last ornament on the tree and turned on the lights. It was breathtaking, but suddenly I was overwhelmed with sadness. I turned and saw Jill standing by the door of our room, and her face was contorted as she tried to hold back the tears. I thought we were done grieving, but this was our first Christmas without Anna.

"Jill, come here, honey. I'm feeling the same way. Just seeing that tree did it for me."

I reached for her and held her close. "We'll be okay. It's just going to be hard going through holidays and birthdays for a while. Olivia, what say we head out for lunch? Is everybody okay with that? It might do us some good to get a bite to eat and get caught up with each other."

Olivia took the cue and chimed in. "I think that's a great idea. Jill, let's get our coats and sit in the back seat. Let the men have the front, so we don't have to talk over them!"

That seemed to snatch us back from the depths of sorrow for the moment. I knew this was going to be tough on both of us, but having close friends around should help us get through this memorable time. We'd had so much on us that a change of scenery was called for. We made it to the restaurant without using up all the Kleenex in the car and got our table quickly. I put Gregory next to Olivia so they could get to know each other. Ten minutes into the lunch and they were talking like old friends. Jill winked at me and raised an eyebrow. I knew exactly what she was thinking. But I swear I wasn't playing Cupid in this thing.

◦◦◦

Charlotte climbed the steps to Peter's house for her daily visit. He was going downhill and she really wanted to be there for him. The bond between them was growing every day and because she'd thought about him for years she had a false sense of knowing him better than she actually did. But somehow that helped ease the awkwardness that's normally there in a new relationship. And Peter adored her, so the feelings were mutual. Today he seemed particularly weak, so Charlotte wanted to be sure he was eating enough.

"Peter, I'm worried about you. You look paler today. Talk to me. Tell me how you're feeling."

Peter turned his head towards her face. Her brown hair was shiny, her dark eyes were no longer filled with sadness. And her face was not drawn and guarded. She looked so different now than she did the first time he saw her after her rescue. She'd been eating healthier, and just the fact that she was with her mother again had healed much of the damage that had worked its way into her heart. She was amazing and he felt honored to have her by his side when he was dying. And that's exactly what was happening to him. They didn't say the word "dying" but it was in the air all the time.

"Angel, I'm fine. I feel weak but after all, I'm gettin' old. My body is wearin' out. So enough about me; talk to me about what ya did yesterday. And I heard from Michael that he and Jill and Gregory were headed out to St. Martins! That was a smart move on his part, because this is the first Christmas they're goin' to have without their daughter."

"I know it's going to be difficult. I went through so many Christmases without my mother and it was very lonely. I cherish every day now; we never know what tomorrow will bring." She straightened his covers and put her hand on his head. He felt a little warm. "I'll fix you some lunch. What sounds good to you? And don't tell me you aren't hungry; you have to eat something, Peter. You're dwindling to nothing but skin and bones."

She ran a tight ship for someone who'd been locked up for eighteen years. "I'll have somethin' with you, dear, in a moment. But I want to talk to you about Lucas. How are you feelin' about his death? We haven't talked much about it, and I was wonderin' if you're dealin' with all of this inside."

Charlotte turned her head and looked out the window close to Peter's bed. It was cold outside and the windows were fogged up. Peter kept it warm as toast in the house. When she looked at him again her eyes were filled with tears. "It's difficult to explain, Papa—" She blushed. "I'm sorry. I don't know what made me say that. I meant 'Peter'!'"

Peter wiped his face with his hands. He was taken aback by the slip up. Papa. *She called me "Papa."* "Why, Charlotte, I'd love for ya to call me Papa. I don't think that was a slip up at all. I never had children, but I would've loved to have had a granddaughter like you."

Charlotte put her hand on his and smiled. She leaned over and kissed his head. "I guess I sort of feel like you are my grandfather. I loved you even before I ever knew who you were. I always felt like you were going to save me from the hell I was in. And to discover this sweet relationship with you that has come so quickly, well, it's a bit overwhelming. You feel like family to me."

"Child, I don't know how ya made it so long alone in that cellar. If I gave ya one second of hope as I walked passed your window, then my life was worth somethin' after all."

She grabbed a tissue by the bed and wiped her eyes. "I do love you, Papa. I never had a real grandfather and I just don't want you to leave me now that I've found you."

"Now, now. Let's talk about Lucas for a moment. Tell me how you are feelin' about his death. How it all happened."

"I really don't know how I feel about him right at the moment. At first I was so relieved to get out of the house I wasn't thinking about what would happen to *him*. But when I heard that the police came into the house and right at the moment he shot himself; well, it was too much for me to comprehend. I couldn't allow myself to picture Lucas sitting in his chair with a gun to his head. He had to be going through his own nightmare, trying to decide what to do. He always said he'd never let them take him to jail. He said he'd rather be dead than locked up like an animal. Ironically, that's exactly what he did to me."

Charlotte got up and walked over to the window, looking out at the gray hazy sky. Her eyes didn't focus on anything. She was seeing the cellar she'd lived in for most of her young life. In a sick way, that had been her home and all she'd had in her life was Lucas. "Even though he hurt me many times and forced me to do things that I could never tell anyone, I knew he loved me in his sick sort of way. And when a person is totally controlled by another person, they learn to cope and to accept their limited situation. I know now that was a coping skill for survival. I grew to care about him but also hated him at the same time. My counselor has helped me see so much."

Peter grimaced and turned his head. It was hard for him to hear how traumatized she was. If he'd been younger, he would've killed Lucas himself. Lucas dreaded going to jail and Peter would have gladly gone in order to free

Charlotte. Odd comparison. "Did he ever talk to ya about his life? Did ya ever feel like ya knew him at all?"

She thought a moment. "He did tell me accidently, in a fit of rage, that he'd shot his own father. That his father had abused his mother and nearly killed her. She never forgave Lucas, and I think that's what drove him to madness. He was insane, or close to it, because he wanted family so badly, and he thought he was saving his mother's life. Instead, she cut him off from her world and never forgave him. I don't think he ever meant to kill me; he loved me in his sick way. But over and over I heard him say that all he wanted was someone like family to live in his house."

Peter thought a moment. *So he saw his father abusing his mother for years and decided to get rid of the problem. He killed his own father. And the one person he loved more than anything turned on him and destroyed him. That would send anyone over the edge of insanity. I been there a few times myself and that edge is pretty slippery.*

"Do ya think you're dealing with these emotions pretty well? Can ya talk to your mother about it at all?"

"I can some but that's why I have this great counselor. I can dump it all on her and walk out of that room feeling lighter and stronger. I don't want Momma to ever really know what went on in that cellar. She couldn't take it. It would break her heart, which had already been broken by my being kidnapped. I don't know how she took the waiting; she must be made of some pretty strong stuff. And evidently I have her genes, because I was able to stand all those years of being alone. I'm sure I'm warped to some degree, but somehow I was meant to be free and I just kept hanging on to that hope."

Peter took her hand and squeezed it hard. "You're a very brave woman, Charlotte. I'm so proud of you and am amazed at your rapid recovery. I'm sure you have nightmares and will from time to time. Hell, it was years before I got over my parents dyin' and my brothers. I was so alone I made friends with the mice in my house. Bet you don't believe that, do ya?"

"Oh, I believe you. I talked to the walls. If I'd seen a mouse I would've made friends with him—Papa? Are you okay?"

Peter had turned his head away and was struggling to breathe. He coughed and coughed and finally cleared his lungs. "I'm not doin' too good today, Charlotte. I didn't want Michael to have to stay here because of me, but I'm goin' down fast. He's been the world to me and I've grown to love him like a son. I just knew this Christmas was goin' to be tough for both him and Jill, and didn't want to give him somethin' else to worry 'bout."

"Do you want me to give him a call? At least let him know you're getting weaker?"

"No. I'm not goin' to ruin his weekend. If I go, I go. I'll have you here to take care of me. But just know, Charlotte, when I die, you're taken care of. I set up a trust fund for ya that we haven't had time to discuss. I thought I'd wait until after Christmas, but just in case I don't make it that long, Michael knows all about it."

Charlotte was shocked. "What? You've set up a trust fund? I can't take any money from you! You don't owe me anything, and you know that."

"It isn't that I owe ya anything, child. I set this up before we even found you. I just knew I wanted to give ya some sense of security so that you could go on and finish college or buy a car; whatever ya needed to do to start your life over again."

"I'm overwhelmed. No one has ever done anything like that for me, and I certainly didn't expect that from you. What can I possibly say to let you know how much that means to me? I love you so much."

"Well, ya pretty much said it just then. I love you, too." Peter coughed again and wiped his face with his gnarly hands. "Guess I better rest now, Charlotte. Glad we had this talk today. It meant the world to me, and I hope you feel better 'bout your future now. Don't worry 'bout me, now. I want you t' go home and take care of your mother. I'll see ya tomorrow. Okay?"

Charlotte bent over and kissed his cheek. "I'll check on you later on tonight. I don't like the way you're talking right now. Like you aren't going to be here much longer. Let's not plan your funeral yet, Papa. You still have something to live for. Now that I've finally gotten to meet you and we have such a beautiful relationship, you want to go and die on me. I'm not having that, Papa. Not now."

Peter smiled and looked up at her. "You're so beautiful, Charlotte. It just wasn't your time to die in that cellar, but I think my time has come. They say ya know when you're gonna die, and I have that inner feelin'. It's not as scary as I once thought it would be. I just hope I have the strength to be a man about it and not wimp out. Just remember, child, that you've made my life by surviving what you went through, and by slipping up and calling me Papa. Nothin' in my whole life has affected me like that one word out of your mouth did."

She stood up and stepped away from the bed. The emotions she felt were so strong that she felt like running out the door. Years of pushing down feelings had made her a little hard inside. She felt the walls cracking and it was a little scary. But this was a moment in her life that she wished she could record, so that when things got rough she could watch and gain strength from. "I'll head home, then, but you promise me that you'll call if anything goes wrong?"

"I promise, honey. Tell your mother thank you for sharing her daughter with me."

Charlotte kissed him again and walked to the door. "'Night, Papa."

CHAPTER 44

I can't believe Gregory. He's been up the last three nights talking to Olivia, and of course I get the blame. Jill swears I set this all up but I had no idea they would hit it off like this. Well, that's not totally true. I've known Olivia for years and I figured Gregory would be her kind of man. But those things are so elusive, you can't count on feelings. Jill's angry with me because this is our first Christmas without Anne and Olivia's first without Case. I said, "What's wrong with a little laughter and good conversation?" She's not hearing it.

"Mike, I knew you had something up your sleeve. How do you know Olivia isn't just being polite to Gregory?"

"I have no idea what's going on, but I figure they're adults and they can figure it out. Are you afraid she might really like Gregory? Why does that bother you so much?"

That was the wrong thing to say. She burst out crying. "I—I—just wanted her to have time to heal, that's all. I'm missing Anna so much. You don't seem to be bothered at all. How can you be so flippant about it all?"

I looked at her, totally baffled. "Listen, Jill. I miss our daughter as much as you do. Maybe more. But this weekend was supposed to be light and enjoyable. We've mourned so much at home that it's time to take a short break. Anna wouldn't want us sitting around crying all weekend. And neither would Case. He'd kick my butt if I did that. You know that."

She wiped her eyes and nose. I thought I saw a small grin forming. "I'm sorry if I lost it, but it just seems weird that they just met each other and now they're staying up late talking. What do they have to talk about?"

"Well, I don't know. Why don't we sit in on one of their nightly conversations so we can tell?"

She burst out laughing. "Okay, I get your message. I'm used to seeing Olivia with Case and it feels weird for her to be talking to Gregory so much. But I know it must feel good to her to be laughing and having fun. So I'll take my pity party and go to bed. Forgive me, honey, for taking it out on you."

I shook my head and watched her walk toward our bedroom. I walked toward the front door and stepped out on the porch. It was very cold, almost bitter outside. I breathed in the air and it nearly froze my lungs but it felt good. I checked my watch; it was nine o'clock. I wondered if Peter was asleep yet. Might be good to check in on him once in a while. The phone rang and rang. No answer. That was weird. Maybe he didn't hear it, or maybe he was sound asleep. I took one more deep breath and walked back inside. With Peter on my mind I sat in on a conversation that Olivia and Gregory were having. I thought that might be a smart thing to do so I could relay what was going on to Jill.

"Hey, guys. What's going on? Olivia, what do you think of this guy?"

"I'm so glad you brought Gregory. He's very interesting and I'm learning all about his art collection and his interest in photography. Did you know he has won awards for his photography?"

I looked at Gregory and shrugged my shoulders. *What photography? This was the first I'd heard about any awards he'd won.* "So you're holding out on me, are you? I didn't even know you liked photography, buddy."

"I've taken hundreds of photos of nature and landscape. They've been used for calendars and I've gotten in some major magazines. Nothing like *National Geographic* or anything. I do it for myself, and if others gain pleasure from it, that's just an added plus."

"How come you've never told me about this before? I have to come to Olivia's to find out about your past? What's going on here?"

We all laughed. "I've tried to tell him what a fisherman you are!" She winked at me and smiled. "Case tried for years to get you to fly fish, and it never took hold in you like it did Case. I never could figure out why."

I scratched my head. "Case wasn't the only one who tried to teach me fly fishing. Peter Darby also attempted. And I was doing pretty darn good up until I got so caught up in finding Charlotte Reeves. Did Greg tell you about that, Olivia? Pretty cool thing that took place in Crosgrove! The whole town is excited about it."

"Yeah, we talked about that last night. I'm so proud of you, Mike. You really stretched yourself and took a huge risk to get that girl away from that demented kidnapper. I was curious as to how you knew he might be involved. He was your patient, right?"

"He was, Olivia. And I can't explain the strong feelings I had every single time he was in my office. It kept building until I finally had to find out for myself what was going on. I attempted earlier to go to his home to talk to him but he wouldn't answer the door. I knew he was there; I saw his truck in the driveway. After a little research I decided to go back to his house when I knew he was at the hospital. It was risky, and I dragged Gregory into it. But we loved every moment and it paid off big time. I had no idea I would find Charlotte in that house, but when I was standing at the cellar door and heard someone yelling down there, the hair stood up on my arm. What a moment, Olivia! This young woman was in that cellar for eighteen years! She's so happy being back with her mother and I think she and Peter have developed a great relationship. It's uncanny how they get along. Speaking of which, I tried to call Peter just now and there was no answer. It worries me a little. I guess he could be asleep."

Gregory shook his head. "Hey, buddy. Give it a rest, will ya? We're here to get away from everything and I don't want you worrying about Peter and Charlotte the whole time we're here. Just relax. Peter's a grown man and he can take care of himself for a few days."

I knew he was right but it smarted to hear it said back to me. I'd gotten too involved with Peter and it may have even encroached on my relationship with Jill. Gregory could stand up to me and tell me he was tired of hearing about it, but Jill wouldn't do that. I excused myself, winked at Olivia, and headed back to the bedroom. Jill was propped up in bed reading a book. She looked at me over her reading glasses and smiled. I turned and locked the door. I was ready to relax.

‿

Miles away, an old man was slipping away into eternity. He was alone, just like when he was a child, but he'd taken the time to write a letter to Michael. He stated again what he wanted done with his money and a few of his possessions, and sealed it and laid it underneath his hands, closed his eyes, and waited for the last breath to come. His life flashed before his eyes and he could remember so many things about his childhood. His brothers, his parents, and all the lonely nights he sat in that old worn out house, dreaming of where he would go in life. He had no fear about dying but he was sad that he didn't have the chance to tell Michael goodbye. Michael had become like a son to him and had been there so many times when he was in trouble. He'd never had anyone care for him like that. But Michael had no idea how those Sunday visits kept him going. If he could have heard his voice just once more. . . .A tear ran down his cheek as he breathed his last breath. He died on Christmas Eve, a happy man with many friends, in the quiet of his bedroom. Outside the snow was falling on Crosgrove, covering the footprints of a man who had lived all his life alone. But his quiet life had made more of an impact on the community than anyone who had ever lived in Crosgrove.

CHAPTER 45

Christmas Day was special. The presents were opened and everyone was sitting on the sofa in their pajamas sipping hot coffee and eating the rich pastries that Olivia had found at a wonderful new bakery in town. "You don't know what this meant to me to have you all here in my house at Christmas! I know this would've been a very tough time for me and you've made it memorable. Now I won't remember this time with sadness but with a new joy."

"Well, it was against my better judgment to bring Gregory here because I was worried you wouldn't be up to a stranger being in your home. We all have been through so much this year. But I must say this has turned out better than even Michael imagined for all of us." Jill looked over at Gregory and winked.

I stood up and with my coffee cup said a toast. "For all of us, I pray we have a better year ahead, full of laugher, joy, and good health. I'm so thankful for all of you in my life, and for the richness of having good friends."

Gregory stood up and said it was his turn. "I never dreamed I would have such a warm welcome here in your home, Olivia. I'll remember this Christmas for years to come. There's a lot to be said for spending a holiday with good friends, instead of alone, crying in your beer. I raise my cup to you, Michael. You have a lovely wife, a lovely friend in Olivia, and I cherish our relationship with all its drama!"

Everyone laughed and we drank to the toasts. I picked up all the loose wrapping paper and bows and threw them away. I was walking into the kitchen and found Olivia following me. She reached over and kissed my cheek and put her hand on my sleeve. "I just wanted to say thank you for bringing Gregory here on this trip. I was a little apprehensive about having him in the house but he's the perfect gentleman. You were right; it was just what I needed. I don't know what I would do without you in my life, Michael. You were Case's best friend and mine. I hope we can always stay close; I need you in my life."

I was moved by her honesty and love, and gave her a bear hug. "I love you, too, Olivia. I miss Case more than you know, and Gregory hasn't replaced him by any means. But I have immensely enjoyed his company and camaraderie and frankly don't know what I would've done without him. He came into my life at the perfect time, and maybe he has for you, too. I don't know where this will end up, but this weekend has been a breath of fresh air." I hugged her again and headed back into the living room. Jill and Gregory were sitting on the sofa talking so I grabbed my coat and walked out on the porch. The morning air was freezing and it was invigorating, but I knew I couldn't stay out there long.

I decided to ring Peter and wish him a Merry Christmas, so I dialed his number. Again, the phone rang and rang but he never picked up. That wasn't like him at all. I phoned Charlotte to wish her and her mother a Merry Christmas and they were laughing and having a ball. "Good morning! Are you two enjoying yourselves on Christmas morning? Charlotte, this is a first for you; I can only imagine how happy you are to be free and be with your mother today of all days!"

"I owe you my life, Michael. I've never been this happy. And guess who called me last night? You remember that guy named Jeff Windsor that I went to school with? Well, he called me! You and I haven't talked about this at yet, but when Jeff and I talked last night we remembered that the last time we saw each other was the day I was kidnapped! It all came back to me when I heard his voice. I was walking home from my girlfriend's house and saw him out washing his car. The reason I remembered it is because I had a silent crush on him; I always wanted him to ask me out. And now, eighteen years later, he finally got the nerve to do it. Can you believe it? It was so nice of him to call, and we're going to have coffee tomorrow and catch up with each other. He was so happy I was home again after all these years. I'm sure I won't even recognize him but it'll be fun to see him, anyway."

I scratched my head. Wonders never ceased. Jeff said he might have seen that pickup but he couldn't remember when. Now maybe he will remember after he talks with Charlotte. She was talking so fast it was hard to keep up with her. I could tell she was so excited to be going out with him. Who wouldn't be after being in a cage for half their life?

"Say, Charlotte, I was wondering if you'd talked with Peter today. I called his home and no one answered. I tried last night late and he didn't pick up then, either. That's not like him not to answer his phone; he knew I was going to call."

"I'll be going over there in a little while, Michael. Don't worry. He wasn't feeling that well last night when I was there, so he may be sleeping in today. I'll call you as soon as I get there to let you know he's okay."

I felt a little better after talking to her. But there was an uneasy feeling in my gut. "I'd sure appreciate it. I'll be waiting to hear from you. Merry Christmas!"

༃

Two hours later, Charlotte walked up the steps and used her key to get into Peter's house. "Papa! I'm just checking in on you. How are you feelin' today?"

The house was dead quiet. She walked back to his room and saw him lying still with his eyes closed and his hands folded on his chest. It gave her the creeps to look at him like that, like he was dead or something. "Papa! It's time for you to wake up. I know you're bound to be hungry and thirsty. Papa!"

He didn't move a muscle. Charlotte walked over to the bed slowly and leaned over. She didn't see him breathing and her heart started racing. She touched his shoulder and shook him. Nothing. She got no response at all. She called out to him again but he still didn't respond. *Oh my gosh. Is he dead? He can't be dead now. Please don't let him be dead, God. I waited so long to meet him . . .*"

Charlotte looked around the room and then focused on the envelope that was underneath Peter's hands. She slid it out gently and saw it had Michael's name on it. Her face went white. *He knew he was dying. He had to if he had the wherewithal to write a letter to Michael.* Her hands were shaking as she took her cell phone out of her purse and dialed Michael's cell number. She was in shock and felt faint. Peter was gone. She sat down in a chair next to the bed and put her face in her hands, waiting for Michael to answer his phone.

He finally picked up.

༃

"Dr. Lankford. Can I help you?" What I heard made my knees go weak.

In a muffled quiet voice, Charlotte spoke. "Michael. Oh, Michael! Peter's dead! Do you hear me? I just walked into his house and he's dead. I don't see any breathing and I can't get him to wake up. He's not moving at all. What do I do, Michael? What do I do?"

Her voice was a mere whisper. I could tell she was in shock. I was frozen for a moment and couldn't even think about what she was saying. *Peter's dead? How could he go down that quickly? It's impossible. I just saw him before I went on this trip. He was weak but not near death. What in the world happened? How could he be dead?* I rubbed my face and tried to respond in a calm manner, so she wouldn't over react. "Honey, tell me if you feel a pulse. Can you put your fingers on his neck just below his jawbone and see if you can feel a pulse?" I waited for her to respond.

"No! I don't feel anything. He's not moving at all, Michael."

"Okay. We need to call 911 and get an ambulance over there immediately. Tell the person who answers that this is an emergency and that you're in Peter's house and you believe he's dead. They'll contact the police for you. Can you handle this, Charlotte? Or do you want me to?"

"No, I can do it. I'll use his phone so you can stay on the line with me." She found Peter's phone and dialed 911 and told the operator that there had been a death. She answered all the questions and was told an ambulance was on its way.

"Michael, they're on their way. Now what do I do? I found a letter underneath his hands that has your name on it."

"Just put that in your purse and read it to me later. We are headed home in the morning so I'll see you then. I'm sick about this, Charlotte. I hate that you had to be the one who found him, but things don't always work out like we want them to. I really wanted a chance to talk to him before he died."

"I just saw him last night. I can't believe he's gone. I love him so much. . ."

Charlotte started crying and in the background I heard the doorbell ring. "The ambulance is here, Michael. I'll call you back."

I hung up the phone and wiped my eyes. *Old Peter was gone.* I walked into the living room where Jill, Gregory and Olivia were talking. "Hey, guys. Got some sad news to share. Charlotte just called me and Peter died sometime in the night last night. I'm sick that I wasn't there to help him or talk to him before he died."

Gregory came over and put his arm around my shoulder. "Buddy, I know that upsets you. You were so close to that man. I'm sorry it had to happen in this way, but at least he died peaceful. I hate even saying that because it sounds so cliché. But it looks like he didn't suffer much at all. He loved you, Michael. I bet you were like a son to him."

I nodded and sat down by Jill on the sofa. She kissed my cheek and kept quiet. She could tell I was overwhelmed by the sad news. Olivia walked over and kissed my forehead and whispered into my ear. "Michael, you were where you were supposed to be. With your family. I know it's tough because you spent so much time with him, but it's apropos that Charlotte found him. He was her saving grace while being caged for so long in that cellar. Things usually work out like they're supposed to in the end. Can you see that, honey?"

"Yep. It's just that I'm a doctor and I wanted to be there to make sure he was comfortable. He lived all his life alone, and now he had to die alone. That's pretty sad, Olivia. But maybe we all die alone in a way." I stood up and walked to the window. "All I can think about was how wonderful he was and how much I cherished those Sunday afternoons with him. You wouldn't know unless you'd been with him just how intelligent he was. Engaging. I've never met anyone like Peter in my entire life; the things he experienced as a young boy and somehow pulled himself through would take down even the strongest of men. Yet he found the strength to keep going and made such an impact on the youth of Crosgrove. He had something most of us don't have. A strong desire to overcome. He had big dreams. And I feel honored to have known such a man."

The room got pretty quiet and I could tell everyone was thinking about what I was saying. Peter would be missed. Gregory was sitting on the couch looking at me. He tapped his leg and smiled to himself. "Well, I tell you one thing for sure. The best thing I ever did was sign up to be on your team, Doc. I've enjoyed every moment we've shared together in that office and look forward to what we'll achieve together in the future. I hope we can have half the impact on Crosgrove that Peter had. You've put a good dent in your efforts to help the citizens of that town by finding Charlotte Reeves. I don't know if the town will ever get over that, my friend. It was an amazing effort on your part, combined with good ole intuition. I was nervous about going into Lucas's house, but in the end I was proud to be a part of that rescue."

"I couldn't have done it without you, Gregory. It was nerve wracking for us both, but well worth the risk. Charlotte has turned around pretty fast adjusting to her life again. I'm amazed. Hope Peter's death doesn't set her back. She was really enjoying her visits with him. Maybe her new relationship with Jeff will keep her busy."

"Olivia, we all hate to leave you tomorrow. You've been the perfect host and so patient to put up with all of us. I've loved seeing you again, and hope you'll come to see us soon. I miss our talks and going to lunch and shopping together." Jill got up and hugged Olivia.

Olivia smiled and kissed her cheek. "I'll always find time for you, Jill. We're family now."

Christmas was ending on a melancholy note, but with some warm memories of Case mixed in with the new friendships formed. I was eager to get home and discover what the note said that Peter had written. My heart ached as I lay down to sleep with Jill by my side. Her sleep came quickly; mine was fitful. I would miss the tapping of that cane and the opportunity to be a better fly fisherman.

CHAPTER 46

One of the most difficult things I've ever had to do was plan a funeral for Peter Darby. I chose a church in the center of town that was large enough to hold a crowd of people because I knew everyone in town would attend. The church set up chairs outside the sanctuary and put out speakers so that those who wouldn't fit in the church could hear the service. I had no problem finding volunteers to speak at the funeral, sharing their thoughts about Peter and his life. I did have a problem limiting the number of people who wanted to speak! I moved through the difficult day like a robot because my heart was frozen in time, remembering the last time I was with him. And the life in that dear man's eyes.

Charlotte, Jill, and I sat on the front row. I couldn't look to the left or the right because I was holding back a body of water that would overflow the church. Charlotte was doing her share of crying and I spent most of my time consoling her. Jill was kept busy passing the Kleenex and keeping me from falling apart. For some reason I couldn't get over the fact that I wasn't home when he died. I wanted that last conversation with him so badly and now it was too late. I'm a grown man and I'm totally aware of how death sneaks up on a person and takes them away without much notice. I've seen it with my own eyes. But it wasn't supposed to happen to Peter. Not on my watch. *We doctors have egos, and I'm angry at myself for not seeing this coming. Perhaps he hid a lot from me. His discomfort level was higher than he allowed me to see. I appreciate his wanting to protect me from that information, but when I see him in heaven I'll want a full explanation.* I learned again the hard way that it's intensely important to say all we have to say to the people we love because we may not be around at the exact moment they are snatched from this earth. In the twinkling of an eye.

Several people spoke about their love of Peter. How he had affected their lives. Charlotte was the last to step up to the podium. I was actually amazed that she had the wherewithal to pull it off. It was so quiet in the room you could hear a pin drop as she unfolded her notes and began to speak.

"This is one of the saddest days of my life so please forgive me if I have a difficult time speaking to you. As some of you know, I was kidnapped eighteen years ago and lived in a cellar down the street from Peter Darby. I used to hear the tapping of his cane as he made his daily walk down the street past the house I lived in. I had no one to talk to, nothing to believe in, and gave up hope years ago of ever escaping my kidnapper. Listening to the cane tapping on the sidewalk gave me hope for some reason. In my mind this person was going to save me at some point. I finally was able to look out of the cellar window one day and I got a glimpse of Peter as he passed by my window. After Dr. Lankford found me, I was able to meet Peter in person and a precious relationship formed between us. In the end, I called him 'Papa'. I knew I was in the presence of a rare individual and I cherished those long talks on the days I visited him.

"We had things in common, Peter and I. He grew up alone with no one to talk to or help him. I was alone for eighteen years. We both developed a way to survive and that something that was within us connected us in a place that we could not see. He was a listener and made it easy for me to pour my heart out to him, and I craved hearing about his life. I knew I had much to learn because I had been shut in for so many years. On the outside Peter may have looked like a bent over old man who was ignorant and knew nothing about life. But to those of us who were fortunate to have known him, we discovered quite the opposite. He was well-read, patient, kind, one of the best teachers Crosgrove has ever seen, and pretty wise for all his years. I will miss him terribly but am so thankful for the time we had together."

There wasn't a dry eye in the place. And on that note, it was my turn to get up and speak about my friend. I helped Charlotte get to her seat and gave her a reassuring hug, and then headed up to the platform. When I turned around I saw all the faces of the hundreds of people who had loved Peter Darby. It was overwhelming to see how many were out there. At my funeral only the first few pews would be used. I swallowed and then began a difficult speech that I owed him the honor of saying.

"I'm not going to say anything magically profound to you this afternoon. I look around the room and see many people I know and some I've not had the pleasure of meeting yet. Obviously, you know Peter Darby or you wouldn't be here today, so I imagine many of you are saddened by his death like I am. When I moved to Crosgrove, I was compelled to make that move to be near my daughter, and yet it was a tough decision to make. After I found a building for my practice and Jill and I located a house we could buy, I opened up my practice and put out my shingle, not knowing what it would be like in Crosgrove for us. I was nervous about the decision, and saddened by the fact that I had ended a partnership of many years with a good friend of mine, Case McPhail. Not long after I had settled into my new practice I received a phone call from Case that he was dying of lung cancer. I was overwhelmed with this news and after his death it took me a while before I felt like I could be myself again. My daughter and her husband lived in Crosgrove and announced to us that they were expecting twins. She had complications and lost the babies at five months. Unbeknownst to any of us, she fell into the claws of depression and took her life."

I paused and wiped my eyes. I needed to perk this speech up or I wasn't going to make it through it.

"One day Peter Darby walked into my office for help with his health issues and we became fast friends. I was intrigued by his wit and that twinkle in his eyes. I took it upon myself to get to know this dear gentleman and we got into a routine of visiting on Sunday afternoons at his house. Sometimes we would sit out on the porch if weather permitted, and other times we were in the house sipping tea and eating homemade cookies. Even in his ill health, he found a way to comfort me in my pain of losing a daughter and those two babies. But listening to how he came through such a difficult childhood and worked his way through school, college, and a successful teaching career caused me to see my world differently. He made me focus on what lies ahead and not what happened in the past. He pointed out that suffering is an ugly part of life that creates a beautiful character in us. That we all have to go through things that could tear us down if we let them, but we have a choice. I was amazed at his candor and the strong ability to move forward in spite of what the circumstances were. I'll cherish my time with Peter for the rest of my life, as I know you will, but I don't want to focus on his death and the loss I will feel in my own life. I want to allow what I gained from standing next to such a man to push me forward to become a better man. I challenge each of you to do the same in your own lives.

"Thank you for coming today and I pray we leave here with lighter hearts and an eagerness to face tomorrow."

I stepped down from the podium and Jill rushed to meet me. She wrapped her arms around me and we both wept silently. People from the back were coming up to shake my hand and to talk to Charlotte. I knew this would be a day none of us would soon forget. I thanked God silently that Jill was by my side, for my legs didn't seem to want to hold my body up. I was good in my office, one on one. But speaking to a crowd of people was not my cup of tea. However, for Peter Darby I would have been willing to do anything. We don't have many real friends in life and I was fortunate to have had two great friends. I never planned to bury both of them in the same year.

CHAPTER 47

It's early morning and as usual I'm sitting at my desk going over some new medical publications before I head in to work. Several years have passed since Peter's funeral, yet it seems like yesterday. Spring is here in full bloom as I look out my window at the front yard. My hand inadvertently touches the frame that holds the photo of Case and me and I smile, shaking my head. What a neat guy he was. I'm heading into sixty-five like a dog being dragged into the vet's office, with all fours pushing away from the door. I've enjoyed having my practice here in Crosgrove but Jill is talking more and more about wanting to travel, to take a cruise. I'm not sure I'm ready to quit yet, but gravity is pulling me in that direction and I don't seem to have much to say about it. I've enjoyed every single second of my life here even though we took on a lot of sorrow making this move. I suppose all of it would've happened even if we'd stayed in St. Martin, so there's no point in rehashing that decision now.

Gregory has been a real gem. I don't regret one moment taking him on as a partner in this practice. He's up for grabs every single morning when I come in, and has such a wit about him that keeps me from getting too bogged down. This ability I've acquired from a higher place has been tough to cope with at times, but I've enjoyed the looks of surprise on some of my patients' faces when I've been able to hit the nail on the head. My goal to help people in a new way has been reached in a way I'd never imagined, but I don't know what's yet ahead for me in that area.

My wandering thoughts bring me to look at the corner of my office where Peter's fishing pole laid to rest against the wall. I reach in my drawer and pull out his letter to me and reread it.

Dear Michael. I find it hard to write this down on paper. I was hoping I would have my last conversation with you in person. But nothing in life is guaranteed. I've come to know that only too well. It's odd how I know it's time to go; I'm letting you know now that I'm not sad at all. Only wishing I could see you one more time. You've been like a son to me, and I should have said it when I had you here. I kinda liked those Sundays we spent together and was afraid that one day you'd tire of giving up that precious spare time to me. It's not like you didn't have other things to do. I knew Jill sacrificed her time with you, and allowed me that gift. Thank her for me, will ya?

I'm leaving you my fly fishing rods; I expect you to practice and improve your technique! I would've loved to have gone fishing with you from time to time but we got side tracked in our efforts to save Charlotte. She's been a delight for me to have around and I thank you for sharing her with me. She'll never know how special those talks were, but I know you'll let her know in your gentle way. I want you to give her my cane, if you will. I think she's the only one that would want it. I've never known a man like you, driven to helping others in a way that isn't normal, you realize. I was happy to be a part of your world for a brief time and want you to know I'll remember you to the Man upstairs. If I get a choice, and He's agreeable to it, I'll pick a spot to live where there's a lake so we can fish together when you get there.

Take care of Jill, and Charlotte. And give yourself time to reflect. Life passes by like a speeding bullet and I'm more like the tortoise than the hare kind of guy. I just couldn't keep up with the technology of today which is obsolete tomorrow. I love you and wish you well in your life. I'll look for you by the lake. You'll know it's me; I'll be the one sitting next to an old oak tree, with a blade of grass in my mouth, and a fly fishing rod in my hand, waiting for you.

All my love, Peter

Reading it for the zillionth time, I still get a tear in my eye. I hope to live up to his expectations on that fly fishing. I kinda' doubt it, but I'll give it my best shot. I don't want to get there and not have improved at all. There's a smell of weddings in the air and I wouldn't be surprised if Jeff and Charlotte don't tie the knot by the end of the year. She is enraptured by him and I think they make a cute couple. I just hope she continues in her counseling for hidden inside are deep issues that she needs to face so that her life with Jeff will be whole.

Gregory, on the other hand, has swept Olivia off her proverbial feet. They don't see each other every week but the phone line that is stretched between the two of them doesn't get much rest. I'm thrilled for Olivia because I know Gregory's a wonderful man. He'll be good for her. I just hope Case isn't mad at me when I see him. I would think that he'd want her happy and that's all I'm thinking about.

I reach for my briefcase and walk towards the door, but I have a real desire to play hooky today from the office and on a whim I grab the fly fishing rod in the corner and head outside. Out of the corner of my eye I see Jill standing at the top of the stairs shaking her head with a sly smile on her face. She knows when to keep her mouth shut. For what I need today is a quiet morning in the woods, sitting next to an oak tree, with a blade of grass in my mouth and a fishing rod in my hand. When I get to the lake, there's a cool breeze blowing, the sun's sending shimmering lights across the water, and as I walk slowly into the water, I stand knee deep, letting my line sway to and fro. It feels so good to take a deep breath and allow the fresh air to swirl in my lungs. Peter had it right when he said that fly fishing could straighten out pretty much any kinda day. I might as well get to practicing this illusive skill because I just never know when I might see Peter again. . . .

EPILOGUE

On any given Sunday if you were to drive out to the lake outside of town in Crosgrove, you would've found a tall, handsome graying physician standing out in the water alone, swaying his line as graceful as any man had ever done, lost in the rhythm that had captured the minds of men for centuries. He wasn't an expert yet, but he was close. And if you were to have stayed for a while you would've seen him pull his fish out of the water and lay them in a bag attached to his cooler.

On this particular Sunday, when summer was at its best, and the June flies were buzzing around the fishing line, the hot breeze was just enough to cool the sweat on his brow. There were standing in the haze where the sun reaches the horizon two men with their hands in their pockets, watching their friend from afar; one of them leaning on a cane. It'd been years since they'd seen their friend, but today was a different kind of day. It was nearly time to bring him home.

Michael walked through the water to the lake's edge and stepped out on the grass. He was tired and it was almost too hot to be fishing. He pulled his hat forward to block the sun and sat down slowly against the great oak that he'd grown to love. Its branches stretched out across the lake making shadows in the noonday sun. He'd caught more fish than he'd ever thought possible but suddenly felt tired. His body was worn out and he just wanted to take a long nap. He stretched hard and laid his head against the tree. Closing his eyes he fell into a deep sleep and dreamed he was sitting with Case on an old log near a lake, talking about old times. He heard the tapping of a cane and looked up and saw Peter. The dream seemed so real. Only this one time, the dream lasted forever . . .

Other Books by Nancy Veldman

Coming Home
The Journey
Withered Leaves
Dream Catcher
The Fisherman

The Box of Words, A Novel
Edgar Graham, A Novel

Nancy Veldman, author, watercolor artist, and pianist, has a story that changes lives. In the middle of her life her father passed away and God reached down in His divine mercy and gave her the ability to hear music. She has heard over 100 songs and released nine piano CDs that move mountains, make the grouchy smile, change a rainy day into one of power and hope, and cause someone who is tone deaf to hum to her music. This music is played across America in hospitals, cancer centers, cardio centers, offices, schools, restaurants, homes, iPods, iPhones, computers, and cars. She also has written inspirational books and has received the Key to the City of Memphis for her humanitarian efforts for mankind. She has a non-profit ministry called Nancy Veldman Ministries wherein she helps cancer patients, autistic children, and families going through tough situations.

Nancy owns Magnolia House, a gift shop that carries fine gifts, jewelry and home accessories. People come from all over the world to Magnolia House and experience the words and music of Nancy Veldman. Her works can be purchased on Amazon.com and magnoliahouse.com.

Nancy lives in Sandestin, Florida with her husband Richard. She is currently working on a fourth novel. She welcomes your comments.

Made in the USA
Columbia, SC
06 February 2021